THE TRUTH
ABOUT
LEAVING

NATALIE BLITT

AMBERJACK
PUBLISHING

Idaho

Amberjack Publishing • Idaho
Amberjack Publishing
1472 E. Iron Eagle Drive
Eagle, ID 83616
http://amberjackpublishing.com

Poetry printed with permission from the Estate of Yehuda Amichai.

Library of Congress Cataloging-in-Publication Data

Names: Blitt, Natalie, author.
Title: The truth about leaving / by Natalie Blitt.
Description: New York ; Idaho : Amberjack Publishing, [2019] |
Summary: A break-up and her mother's absence threaten Lucy's plan for
a carefree senior year at Wilmette Academy, but her growing attraction
to Israeli transfer student Dov changes her perspective.
Identifiers: LCCN 2018036997 (print) | LCCN 2018043150 (ebook) |
ISBN 9781948705103 (ebook) | ISBN 9781948705097 (pbk. : alk. paper)
Subjects: | CYAC: High schools—Fiction. | Schools—Fiction. | Dating
(Social customs)—Fiction. | Single-parent families—Fiction. |
Brothers and sisters—Fiction. | Students, Foreign--Fiction. | Israelis—
United States—Fiction.
Classification: LCC PZ7.1.B634 (ebook) | LCC PZ7.1.B634
Tru 2019 (print) | DDC [Fic]—dc23
LC record available at https://lccn.loc.gov/2018036997

For Jessica Blitt, who read this story way too many times.
I'm really, really sorry it's not about Chess *anymore.*

"Life isn't about finding yourself. Life is about creating yourself."

—UNKNOWN

ONE

· · · · · · ·

The sun sets as I sit on the porch. When Scott rang the doorbell, there was no pink in the sky, no explosion of color. The sky was so pale, it wasn't even blue. And now it's like it's on fire.

It shouldn't be this pretty right now.

My phone chirps, and for a split second—damn you Scott—I think it's him. But I'm actually relieved when it turns out to be Maddie.

"Hey."

"Tell me the Scott thing is a joke." Her voice is hard, and if I hadn't known her since third grade, I might think she was mad at me.

But no. She's the perfect best friend, her ire completely focused on my now *ex*-boyfriend. I hope for his sake he's long gone because while Maddie is a pacifist, she doesn't put up with his bullshit.

"No joke."

"What a fu—"

"Preaching to the choir."

The wonderful thing about being best friends with someone since the third grade is that you barely have to speak in full sentences. It's like everything is in shorthand.

She lets out a sigh that sounds more like a growl. "I told you that you should have—"

"Not the time." Would it have made it easier if I'd broken up with him in the spring, like Maddie had suggested? Who knows. Do I feel stupid for thinking we were both committed to making it work while he was at college when he evidently decided not to bother? Definitely.

"I'm so glad you didn't sleep with him," Maddie grumbles, and I want to agree, but suddenly my throat is clogged.

God. I can't believe I'm going to have to go through all of that with another guy now. Another "Do I like him? Does he like me?" Another "Is this what I want?" Another "Does this feel good? Do I want this?" And then the painful "Am I ready?" "Am I saying yes because I don't want to upset him?" and "Is this the guy I want to remember as my first?" Not that I thought Scott was my forever . . .

At least, I hadn't thought that in a while.

Right now, he's probably on I-57, listening to the news. When he came by, his car was packed so high I was amazed he could see out the back window. At first I didn't get it. He still had a week before move-in day. We still had a week to spend together before we had to be long distance. Apparently he decided that the pre-orientation camping trip was worth doing, even though he'd originally mocked it. But the worst part is that he changed his mind a month ago but decided it would be *easier* if he didn't tell me.

Asshole.

"I know you think we can do the distance thing, but I just don't know if I can," he'd said, his voice so sincere I almost believed the whole thing pained him. "Especially since it's not like we'll be together next year. You'll be at Northwestern and I'll be downstate, and three more years of long distance . . ."

It's not that I don't get why it would be hard, and maybe even *too* hard. But I thought we both wanted it enough to try.

"Honey?" My dad's voice has an edge to it as it ping-pongs down the stairs.

"I need to go," I tell Maddie.

"Do you want me to come over?"

"I'm fine." I hear the chaos of my brothers upstairs, which reminds me that I'll need to tell them about Scott. "I should go."

"It's just," she says, her words slow as molasses, "maybe this is a good thing. It's our senior year, and maybe it isn't bad to look for something new . . ."

I close my eyes and take deep breaths. According to family lore, my mom signed me up for Wilmette Academy when I was still in utero. Some of my first memories are of eating Play-Doh in the infant school. Most of the fifty-four people in my graduating class also ate Play-Doh with me back then. There's nothing new to discover now.

Next year, I'll be at Northwestern. Next year, my real life will start.

"Between having to spend extra time with my brothers, now that Mom's out in California, and dealing with senior year, I don't think I'll have all that much time to find someone new." I rise from the bench and try to stretch out the stiffness in my back.

"You're not their mother," she says, and suddenly I'm so tired, I want to plop right back down.

Sore subject. Too soon, Maddie. Too soon.

"I'll see you tomorrow," I say with all the kindness I can muster.

"I'm sorry," she whispers.

"It's fine. It'll all be fine. We'll get through this year, and then we'll be in college with a million other people who don't know Scott or Wilmette Academy. It's just a matter of getting through this."

"Lucy? I need your help!" Dad's voice already harbors a hint of desperation. It's only been two days since Mom left.

Thank god school starts tomorrow.

"Talk to you later," I tell Maddie quickly and shove the phone in my back pocket. "I'm coming!" I yell back to Dad.

"Can I just send the boys outside to you? I have a call with a grad student in a few minutes."

When my mom's around, there's no bellowing from floor to floor, especially when the front door's open. But, by mutual agreement, the two of us now bellow to our hearts' content. Not that either of us has made mention of it, but it's one of those, *You don't like the neighbors to hear us yelling? Maybe you should have stuck around.*

Before I have a chance to say yes, Gabe and Sam come tumbling through the door. Luckily, being nine and seven, my brothers have bigger things to focus on than my tear streaks, especially while in the middle of a lightsaber fight.

"Take it to the lawn!" I say, picturing one of them flying off the porch railing. Sam, who's younger and more fearless than his brother, takes the stairs two by two to claim the lower ground.

"Steal yourself away, you landlubber!" Gabe calls, the serious look on his face belying the ridiculousness of his pirate talk. But before I can even laugh, he's tossing a lightsaber over his shoulder at me as he carefully makes his way down the stairs. Thankfully, with two younger brothers, I have quick reflexes even when exhausted. "It might look like a lightsaber, but it's really a sword," he yells.

"No, it's not. It's a lightsaber," Sam shouts to Gabe, buoyed by righteous indignation.

"We're playing Jedi versus Pirate, so mine's a sword," Gabe answers.

"Fine, but Lucy's on my team, so hers is also a lightsaber. And plus, it's dumb to play with a sword against a lightsaber because the lightsaber will just melt the metal sword."

"My sword is made of heat-resistant metal," Gabe taunts him.

If I let them go on, they will spend the entire battle arguing about the rules. "Why don't we say that we all have lightsabers," I say, staring Gabe down until he closes his mouth, "but they're for special use on pirate ships so they're disguised as swords?"

Sam and Gabe's lightsabers tilt down, and they wear identical expressions of "You've got to be kidding me."

When Mom got the job at the University of California at Berkeley, the only thing I cared about was not having to move out there for my senior year. I was willing to agree to almost anything to make it work. Even spending more time babysitting my brothers when Mom was out there.

But now . . . Is this how my whole year is going to be? Policing my brothers? Lightsaber battles?

Add that to being dumped by Scott and suddenly senior year is getting off to a truly epic start.

Screw Scott for not thinking we could make it through a year of long distance.

Screw Scott for not telling me that he was leaving early.

Screw Scott for walking away when I always gave him another shot.

I fill my lungs close to bursting, and then I work on letting go instead of shouting. "OK," I say slowly. "How about a water fight instead of a sword and lightsaber fight?"

Apparently, I can still do some things right.

TWO

· · · · · · ·

Wilmette Academy is perched at the top of a small hill a mile from Lake Michigan. Housed in a converted convent, it boasts gorgeous stained glass windows, more dark wood trim than you can shake a stick at, and a black-and-white tiled foyer that would warm the heart of any half-decent ballroom dancer.

Maddie and I step through the oversized front doors into the foyer, reveling in the privilege that comes from being a senior. After fifteen years of wearing a uniform every day, it feels almost decadent to no longer show up in a dark grey skirt, white top, and polished black shoes. Though I finally understand why there was an uproar from parents when the school decided to give seniors that privilege; it took me exponentially longer to dress this morning than it ever had before. Luckily, Sam and Gabe still need to wear a uniform, or we'd have to start waking up at the crack of dawn to make sure they were dressed in time for school. Though they definitely expressed their intense outrage when I'd shown up at breakfast wearing a pale green linen skirt, black T-shirt, and blue cowboy boots.

"That doesn't even go together," Gabe had said, and while he was probably right, I didn't care. Favorite skirt? Check. Favorite footwear? Check. Nothing else mattered.

I wonder what he'd say if he knew I was now standing in the front foyer, the formal entrance to the school that only adults are allowed to use. Students use the student entrance, grown-ups use the formal entrance. It's a ridiculous system. Perk of being a senior? We get to use the adult entrance.

"Scott was right. It does feel different to walk into the school this way."

Maddie and I are alone in the foyer. We should keep walking. We should find our way to the senior lounge. But there's something about the forbidden nature of the space that makes it hard to leave.

"Are you doing okay with the whole Scott thing?"

I know she had to ask, that if our places were reversed I would have asked too. But I wish I could just drop Scott's name and move on. I stare at the dark portraits of all the former headmasters. They moved on. When their term ended, they moved on.

My eyes briefly shut, and I nod. "I thought about putting *'Tis better to have loved and lost than never to have loved at all* on my wall of quotes, but then I opted for something less . . ."

"Clichéd?"

I chuckle.

My wall is a celebration of words. I began last summer when I took down the ballet posters and pictures that made my stomach hurt now that I was no longer dancing. My first piece was an Ingrid Michaelson song that described how I felt about Scott. Then there was Thomas Gray's statement that poetry is "thoughts that breathe, and words that burn." And then the line from T. S. Eliot that feels like me on a daily basis:

> And time yet for a hundred indecisions,
> And for a hundred visions and revisions,
> Before the taking of a toast and tea.

Eventually I printed them all out and surrounded my headboard with them. Then it expanded. Songs, poems, children's stories. Sometimes a full page, and other times a single line. It's so unlike me in its haphazardness, and I love it.

"So instead I found a quote that I'll have to tell you outside school walls because it includes words not appropriate for young children . . ."

Maddie laughs and I narrowly avoid being hit by her elbow. When Maddie laughs, her whole body moves. She's never been a delicate chuckler. It's one of the many, many things I love about her. One of the things I'll miss about her next year when we're in different places.

"What if your brothers see it?"

"I put it pretty high up. And wrote it in small print. But I know it's there."

I printed it last night, my pen practically etching the words through the pad of paper. I actually found it on one of those snarky greeting cards. It read: *It's better to have loved and lost than to be stuck with an asshole for the rest of your life.* Perspective is important. My new mantra: *my heart is my own.*

Maddie's lips curl into a grin. "OK. Let's start this year on a less morose tone. Shake off the dregs of Scott. Show me you're ready for senior year!" she says in a mock cheerleader tone.

The thing about Maddie is that she looks like the proper student, all nicely coiffed and appropriately dressed. She's never received a grade below a B+. But she has a hint of daring that I should know better than to listen to. Because while she keeps it well hidden most of the time, when it comes out? It's trouble.

"Yay!" I quietly cheer.

"C'mon, you can do better than that."

"Woop Woop?"

Maddie raises her perfectly sculpted left eyebrow and purses her lips. With her pale skin, black tight curls, and bright red lipstick, she looks like a china doll turned bad. "Do something bold to start off the year," she says. "Do something because *you* want to do it. Just for the fun of it."

We're still alone in the stately foyer. It's early in the day, so it's entirely possible that nobody is even in the administrative offices. And there's something about the formal nature of the space . . . how straight and narrow it all feels.

Not unlike my life.

Senior year was supposed to be about three things: getting into Northwestern, babysitting my brothers, and . . . Maybe there's only two things now that Scott is off the radar. Maybe a bit of hanging out with Maddie. School, brothers, school, brothers, school, school, Maddie, brothers, school, brothers, brothers, Maddie, school.

I walk into the middle of the room like it's the quiet stage before the music starts. That moment when everyone is waiting—when they may think they know what's about to happen, but really, they don't. Anything can happen.

I miss dancing. I miss how much you can feel and express, even in punishing costumes and tightly wrapped pointe shoes that do little to dull the pain. I miss the feeling of being able to let go when everything else is held in tight: all those muscles in line, toes pointed, smile painted on. How, in all that, you can fly.

If I'm honest with myself, really honest, that's what I want to do right now. If I'm to start my last year in this school in a bold way, I want to do pirouettes in the middle of the foyer. I want to remember what it feels like to fly.

And so, I begin to spin. Slowly at first, and then I gain momentum like a magical mashup of Cinderella in her ball gown and Maria von Trapp on the hills of Austria, pale green linen skirt fanned out, dark brown hair flowing freely, and blue cowboy boots pulling it all together.

It feels perfect. Even after an entire year and a half of not dancing, my body slips into the spin, muscles flexing and tightening, spine straight and aligned, despite the fact that I'm wearing cowboy boots instead of pointe shoes.

Until my boots begin to slide on the polished black-and-white tiles. And then there's nothing wild or happy or free about it. There's a mess of arms and legs moving in every direction and that awful feeling of being suspended midair when you know it won't last. And then the mortifying sensation of falling.

Which is nothing compared to hitting the ground and finding myself face-to-face with a guy whose curls are on the right side of slightly too long, and whose arms have somehow wrapped themselves around me. A guy with a faint scattering of scruff across his jaw and the darkest blue eyes I've ever seen, which I find myself staring into because, apparently, I'm lying on top of him.

And yet, not getting up.

Crap. Crap. Crap.

"Are you okay?"

Three tiny accented words.

"I'm so sorry," I whisper, head down, trying to yank my skirt down and slide off of him at the same time.

As I get up and grab my bag, I watch him stand and brush the dust off his pants. Then I stumble toward Maddie, my right knee stinging and reminding me of the ridiculousness of what I'd just done.

Why do I listen to her?

The irony is that I know better, I know that I can't just start turning and have it be magical. After years of working lines of pirouettes, I know that the key to twirling effortlessly is focus. "Eyes on the prize," my ballet teacher, Ginger, would call out when a distracted dancer messed up a straight line. Focus is what allows you to keep spinning in tight pirouettes forever. Focus is what gets you stellar grades and an all-but-guaranteed path to Northwestern. You don't look elsewhere, not for a second. Because if your focus strays, so will you. Everything turns out better when you follow the rules.

Well, except my relationship with Scott.

"Holy crap, are you okay?" Maddie hugs me hard and, as ridiculous as my wipe-out must have been, her laughter calms me.

"Tell me that wasn't as bad as I imagined it to be," I whisper. "Tell me I didn't scare some freshman to death."

I didn't recognize the guy whose path had accidentally intersected with mine. He must be a freshman because our school is small enough that I'd have recognized anyone else. I didn't get a close look at him, but he seemed too big to be fourteen . . .

"Um," Maddie whispers. "I don't think he's a freshman."

"Please let him not be a teacher," I beg.

Maddie bites her bottom lip and shakes her head quickly. "Maybe we should go back outside . . ."

The headmaster's door opens, and I turn toward the noise, the way you can't help but turn to see an accident on the highway. My breath hitches as my brain struggles to remind my body that—despite my ridiculous behavior—I'm allowed to be in the foyer. After years of only being here when accompanied by a parent or teacher, it's hard to remember that I'm not going to be in trouble. A quick look at Maddie and I know she's battling the same instinct for flight. But before we have a chance to either calm down or flee, a couple emerges from the office, led by Mrs. Schneider, my favorite teacher of all time, hands down.

She's talking quickly, hands flying in every direction as usual, while the parents who follow her appear vaguely shell-shocked by the whole experience. I swallow the giggle that threatens to erupt. She has that effect on people. Until you get to know her, and then you realize that you just need to ride the wave of her exuberance.

But instead of continuing out of the foyer, they stop where the guy I ran into is standing. Like they know him.

"Right," Maddie whispers. "That's the new kid."

"New kid? What year?" A feeling of dread fills my stomach.

"Senior."

Not possible.

"New senior?"

I can't remember the last time the school allowed a transfer during senior year. Officially, they say that because we're such a small school, by senior year we're a tight community and that it just wouldn't "work" to accept new kids. But I think it's some combination of wanting to discourage people from trying to move "problem kids" into the school to help buoy their college applications, and the academy not wanting to take a chance on a student that might mess up its college admission rate.

"That's what I forgot to tell you," Maddie says. "Apparently, someone pulled some strings, and we have a new classmate."

A new classmate who I body-checked to the ground. Whose shoulders hunch forward as though he's doing his best to disappear. And while scowly boys usually turn me off completely, there's something about him that makes it hard for me to look away. And it's not just because his eyes are the same color as my cowboy boots.

The last thing I need this year is to get involved with someone, I remind myself. *My heart is my own.* I only have one more year here. Boys are for college. I need to focus on securing my place at Northwestern, babysitting my brothers, getting to next year.

"He's cute," muses Maddie, her index finger now tapping her top lip. "Not my type but—"

I know exactly where she's going with this, where everything is headed. And I'm not going there. Eye on the prize, focus on getting to next year. College. New people.

"Let's get out of here before this gets more awkward," I say, but as I inch back, Mrs. Schneider turns, her smile genuine and warm. She motions me over, and I gulp. His hair. All those curls, messy and soft.

No. Boys.

"How about we meet for lunch in the stairwell?" Maddie whispers before I got too far. "You can update me on Dov."

"Dov?" The name feels foreign in my mouth, and everything is made more awkward by the fact that Mrs. Schneider and the couple appear to be waiting for me now. At least Cute Boy—I mean Dov—isn't paying any attention. I think.

Why isn't Mrs. Schneider calling Maddie over also?

"Lucy, it's great to see you," Mrs. Schneider says, one arm coming to envelop me in a loose hug. "Did you have a good summer?"

Cute Guy's gaze meets mine. For the briefest moment, there's a flicker of something. But just as quickly, it's gone.

I stammer a greeting as I wait for him to glance back up. But he doesn't.

"I'd like you to meet Mr. and Mrs. Meiri and their son Dov," Mrs. Schneider says. "They've just moved here from Israel, and Dov will be joining the senior class. Lucy, you started here in preschool, right?"

I nod, though given how carefully Dov is examining the floor tiles, I'm sure he has no idea I've answered at all.

"I'm very pleased to meet you," Dov's mother says, her words heavily accented. She's tall and very thin, with short hair cropped close to her head. When she extends her hand to me, I see her nails are polished in a dark maroon color. I'm almost embarrassed to put my slightly sweaty hand in hers, but I return her brief shake before she turns to the others. "I'm due at the office in an hour. Dov, you'll be okay?"

He nods.

"*B'hatzlacha*," she says to him.

"*Kol tuv*," he replies.

There's a long pause as his parents make their exit. Then Mrs. Schneider turns to us both.

"Lucy, Dov will be in a number of your classes, including my poetry seminar. I trust you'll make him feel welcome."

I swallow hard. "Of course."

"Great! First bell is about to ring. I'd love it if you'd show him where our class meets."

I nod, understanding why she'd pulled me over and not Maddie, who isn't in any of her classes. Mrs. Schneider smiles in a way that I'm sure means she can't remember where she put her notebook or she's already thinking about class. Or both. And then, before I have a chance to say anything, she walks away, leaving me with Dov.

Should I say something? Tell him about the school? It's not like this is the first time I'm helping out a new student but . . .

"I'm really sorry about before. I don't usually . . ."

"I'm fine." Only two words and yet they are worlds apart from the three words he'd said earlier.

Great. Now I'm counting words.

"Do you need help finding—" I try.

"No."

He swivels before I have a chance to react, and in three quick steps, he's gone.

Well, that went well.

THREE

· · · · · · · · ·

Mrs. Schneider's class is held on the third floor. It's another of the "perks" of senior year that we're given the attic classrooms, with sloping roofs and extra-large windows. Lowerclassmen have the bigger, more modern rooms on the ground and second floors. But by senior year, the academy transitions us to smaller and more specialized seminar-style workshops, like the class on Modern Poetry that Mrs. Schneider teaches.

The thing about going to school in a repurposed old convent? Very narrow hallways. Throngs of nuns apparently didn't need space to compare summer hookups and tan lines.

Despite having to dodge fellow students catching up from a long summer vacation, I still make it to the classroom early enough to get a good seat near the window.

Unlike Dov, who doesn't make it in until Mrs. Schneider is already passing around syllabi.

"Dov, why don't you take a seat over there?" Mrs. Schneider says after introducing him to the class. She points at the empty seat beside me as Dov drops his army green bag on the opposite side of the room, in front of the chair closest to the door.

"This is fine," he says, moving his chair back a few inches until it's almost outside the classroom door.

"I'd prefer you on the other side," she says firmly. "We're about to push all those empty chairs aside and make a circle."

Please don't sit next to me. Please.

Dov pauses, and even from across the room, I can tell he's clenching his jaw. With a small shake of his head, he straightens up and makes his way to the chair beside me. My cheeks flush. Cute or not, he's clearly a jerk with a giant chip on his shoulder.

I peek over at him during class as he sits, without even a notebook in front of him. He doesn't raise his hand, doesn't offer any comments. He doesn't crack a smile, not even when Tyler brings up dirty limericks as an example of cadence. It's almost like he's pretending not to be here at all.

Which makes me nervous when Mrs. Schneider tells us to turn to the person next to us for the last ten minutes of class. Marcus, to my right, has already glommed onto Katelyn, and Andrea, on Dov's left, has turned to Tyler. A quick scan around the room tells me that everyone is paired up and already chatting. Everyone but us.

Filling my lungs with air, I turn and put on my easiest smile. Next year I'll be in classes with hundreds of people I don't know, I reason. This is good training.

"So, we're supposed to discuss one poem that is particularly meaningful to us," I say, trying to keep up a friendly look. "Should I go first?"

No response.

I press my lips together. Nine minutes. I can talk about Yeats. "I have spread my dreams under your feet; / Tread softly because you tread on my dreams." Or maybe, "The Lady of Shalott" or—

"There's a poem by Yehuda Amichai," Dov starts, his quiet words stopping me in my tracks. He's staring down, like it doesn't matter if I'm paying attention. "In Hebrew it's called *Koter Ha'petsatsah*."

I force my lungs to expand and then deflate.

"How do you call the distance between two ends of a circle?" he asks, his hand forming a circle to demonstrate.

I'm so shocked by the fact that he's speaking that it takes a few seconds before I realize he's asked a question.

"Circumference?"

"Not that."

Geometry was years ago, and it's hard to remember basic concepts when Dov and I are almost maybe talking . . .

"Diameter?"

He nods. "'The Diameter of a Bomb' is what it's called. It's about how tiny a bomb is." He cups his hands into a small circle, the size of a plate. "But when it detonates, it can reach so much further. From here to the other end of the classroom, or maybe into the next classroom. Technically the explosion is limited, but the effect of the bomb is much greater. It extends into the lives of the people who have to deal with the wreckage, the people in the hospitals and cemeteries. And then there's the people who are affected by the bomb, the people who knew those who were caught in it, the people who loved them. The effect of the bomb is not limited to the number of meters it can reach. It seeps into other cities, into other countries even. He writes about how that grief extends out large enough to circle the whole world. And maybe even beyond that to the heavens."

His voice is so quiet, it's as though we're the only two people in the room. For the first time, I wish I'd paid attention in Hebrew school; I wish I knew I could hear the poem and understand it, not have Dov explain it to me. It feels like there's more meaning buried there, more I should be understanding. His voice is wistful, calm, as if the poet wrote the words, but every one is true to his experience. I want to ask him about it, ask him why he chose to share that poem, why it's meaningful for him. Did he lose someone?

In the distance, I hear Mrs. Schneider clap her hands and tell the class that if we haven't both had a turn to share, it's okay, there will be time tomorrow. And then, before I can say a word, Dov gets up, with no acknowledgment of what I thought had happened between us, turns away and walks out of the room.

I sit there for a long while, the lilting sound of his voice and the memory of his words still filling my head.

"Lucy, are you all right?" Mrs. Schneider asks. "Did you want to speak with me about something?"

For a moment, I wonder if she's talking about the poem. I wonder if I should tell her that Dov talked about the effect of a bomb detonating, but it didn't feel like a threat. If anything, his voice sounded sad, like he'd told me something intensely personal.

Should I be worried about him?

"Lucy?" Mrs. Schneider repeats.

I shake myself out of my daze. We're the last two people in the room.

"Uh, yeah," I stutter. The truth is, I do need to speak with her.

She leans back against her doorframe.

I try to regain my focus as I make my way toward her. "Just about college applications," I say, glancing at her gauzy Indian print skirt.

She nods without smiling. "Remind me what you're thinking about?"

I frown. We'd talked about it last year at least half a dozen times. It was all I ever talked about. It had been my dream since I was a little kid, sitting beside my dad during office hours, attending Dillo Day concerts at the lakefill. Even when Scott decided to attend U of I.

Freaking Scott.

"Northwestern. Early Decision," I say, feeling like I'm somehow disappointing her with my answer.

She pauses. Her face is unreadable.

"OK," she finally says. "Are you sure Northwestern is your top choice?" She doesn't put emphasis on the word *your*, but I feel it there.

My brain is still cloudy from the memory of the poem, and now I'm trying to figure out why my faculty advisor is discouraging me from applying to the only school I was seriously considering.

"It's a good school . . ." I hear the defensiveness in my voice, and I cringe.

"Well, you'll let me know what you need from me."

"Do you think I shouldn't—"

"No, no," she says, silver and turquoise earrings tinkling as she shakes her head. "Northwestern is a very good school. If that's what you want."

Again, the emphasis feels like it's on the *you*. I nod as though I understand what she's saying.

"Just remember that college isn't only about preparing for a future career. It's also about the experience: living on your own, making choices. All things that are hard to do when you're still living in the same city as your family."

I suck in my breath. "I can do all of that," I say. "I already told my parents that I won't be around when I'm at school. I won't go home to do laundry—"

"Oh, I know." Mrs. Schneider puts her hand on my shoulder. "But it's not the same as going away. If you can do it, it's really worth it. And you can always come back when you've finished school."

"I'm not sure," I mumble.

"Something to think about," Mrs. Schneider says. "Ordinarily, I'd bring this up later when we're examining all your acceptances. But given that Early Decision at Northwestern is binding, I wanted to bring it up now. My suggestion would be: don't lock yourself in. Even if you're pretty sure it's what you want, it might not be a bad idea to apply general admission, especially given your family situation. You never know where you might want to be in a year. You could decide to join your mom on the west coast."

I have to focus on not shaking my head so hard I'll give myself whiplash. But if Mrs. Schneider noticed the change in my expression, she doesn't let on.

"Your grades and extracurricular activities are strong enough to give you a really good shot without needing to commit now. That way you can apply to a bunch of places and make your decision in May. And it even gives you an opportunity to think about taking a year off and doing a gap year if that's an option."

"Not go to college?" Since when was that even a possibility? We're probably the only school that buys graduating seniors swag from the colleges they'll be attending, just so they have plenty of photos that showcase our college choices in the weekly school email. And then the end of the year class photo where we're all decked out in our college sweatshirts. What would I do? It was a ridiculous thought.

A wave of irritation courses through me. I don't want to go back to deciding. I have a plan. A good plan. Applying Early Decision to Northwestern means I'll hear back before the rest of the applications are due, which means with any luck, I'll be done with college applications before I have to apply elsewhere.

"I'll think about it," I lie.

"Why don't we discuss this again in a few weeks?" Mrs. Schneider picks up a Post-it note that was stuck to the cover of her notebook.

"Sure," I whisper, grabbing my bag. "Thanks for your help."

Maddie and I are finished eating on the second-floor stairwell landing by the time I've recounted my conversation with Mrs. Schneider to her. Most seniors go off campus for lunch or sit in the senior room. But we prefer the stairwell; it gets an amazing amount of sunlight from the glass bricks that make up the sidewall, and I'm a sucker for natural light.

Maddie isn't as freaked out by the meeting as I am. "You should totally think about coming to New York with me!"

"Maddie, I get what Mrs. Schneider is trying to say, but I'm not moving across the country just because you've always dreamed of attending NYU."

"Oh, because deciding on college based on where your parents want you to be is better?" Maddie's eyebrows lift.

Ouch.

"It's not the same thing. Especially since they're paying for it," I mutter.

"And yet, they've said you can look at other schools."

Maddie should seriously consider a future in criminal law.

"Yes, they've said I can go wherever I want. But, why not go here? My brothers are here, and especially now that my mom is commuting back and forth to Berkeley . . ."

Maddie raises her eyebrows at the mention of my brothers but doesn't say anything. I'd stayed at her house during the week I refused to talk to my mom after she announced she'd put in an application for a job at UC Berkeley. Maddie was the one who held me as I cried when my mom suggested it wouldn't be a big deal to do senior year in California.

Until last year, my house, school, the dance studio, and my parents' jobs at Northwestern were never more than five miles away. So even when my mom stayed late for committee meetings and faculty events, she came home. But when Berkeley offered her tenure and the opportunity to develop a new program—something she'd been requesting from Northwestern's Bioethics Department for years—she couldn't say no. It prompted an unprecedented number of closed-door arguments with my father. In the end, she took the job with the understanding that she'd be commuting back and forth until my brothers finished elementary school. Which meant she'd only be home on weekends and during the summer.

I was just grateful we didn't have to move. Which makes it even more important for me to stay local.

There's a long pause as a group of giggling freshman girls walk past us on the stairwell. I want to mock them, but I'm quite sure I'd sounded exactly the same when I was their age.

"All I'm saying is, would it hurt if you seriously thought about where *you* want to go? What does Lucy want, as opposed to what decision will make her parents or her brothers happy? What do *you* want when you remember that all of those other people will still love you no matter what you decide?"

"I'll think about it," I say, this time a little more truthfully.

Her smile is full and wide. "That's all I'm asking. That, and that you consider New York."

Now it's my turn to roll my eyes. "Fine."

"So, I hear you have the scoop on the guy you 'ran into' this morning," Maddie laughs. "Word on the street is that Mrs. Schneider made you two sit together and discuss poetry. Samantha said she looked over and you looked dazed."

Going to a college with thousands of students is going to have distinct advantages.

"Seriously?"

Maddie laughs. "I know, she's totally unreliable. I'm just teasing. He's cute in an old James Dean kind of way."

I think back to the sad look in his eyes. "Hmm," is all I have a chance to say before the bell rings.

FOUR

· · · · · · · ·

The senior lounge is in full swing by the time I make it there at the end of the day. At least three phones are blaring music, though I don't have a clue what they're playing. All I know is that they're giving me a headache.

I wish I was already home so I could slip off my First Day of School clothes, pull on my summer uniform of cutoffs and a tank top, and help Sam soak Gabe in another epic water fight. The easy smile I'd forced myself to wear when interacting with my classmates who were "*so* devastated to hear about you and Scott breaking up" was making my facial muscles twitch. I just want to go home.

Maddie is already in full-on student mode, the pile of textbooks in front of her locker almost reaching her knees.

"Every year, I have this ridiculous hope that the academy will finally get with the program and go digital," she mutters, dropping her calculus textbook to the floor with a thud. "I mean seriously, all those trees sacrificed because of some dumb math requirement that I'll likely flunk anyway."

I snort, uncertain which is more unlikely: Wilmette Academy getting with the times or Maddie flunking anything. The school still insists on teaching cursive with a fountain pen, which leaves everyone with dark ink splotches all over their fingers and clothing. Everyone except for Maddie, who received an A+ in penmanship, even then.

It was my first C.

Dov stands in the opposite corner, seemingly oblivious to the chaos. I debate walking over to him when he slams his locker shut, flips his backpack over his shoulder, and starts to make his way down the hallway.

It's only then I realize how much I don't want him to leave without saying something, especially after what he'd shared in class.

I run to catch up, my backpack bouncing up and down, smacking me squarely in my lower back. He keeps walking, oblivious or ignoring me, I can't be sure which.

When I'm finally a step away, I reach forward to touch his arm but between the momentum pushing me forward and his quick turnaround, I teeter on the verge of falling down. Again.

Thankfully, he grabs my arm, his grip at once strong and gentle.

"I seriously don't usually do this," I whisper, which is when it appears we both realize that we're still holding on to one another.

Please let no one have seen that.

"You okay?" Two words this time, and it's definitely not Dov's voice. Maddie holds out her hand, and mortification heats my face. I take her hand, if only to speed up my escape.

"And you call yourself a dancer," she says, adding insult to injury.

"I don't call myself a dancer." I know this isn't the time, but I can't help myself. I feel about as mature as seven-year-old Sam.

"Well, I'd call you a dancer. And I think this just shows you need to go back to the studio."

I smile, my mortification complete, until I see her slight wink. I have no idea what she's playing at, but now I'm going to really kill her.

"I'm really, really sorry," I say to Dov when I'm certain she's gone.

"'*Eyn ba'aya,* Lucy," he says, grabbing his bag from the ground. "No problem."

Crap. He's going to leave. "I just wanted to make sure you were doing okay," I say before he can hitch the bag on his shoulder.

"I appreciate that this time you didn't tackle me to the ground."

I blush and look down. Even his chuckle does little to make me feel better.

"I . . . I just wanted to ask you if there was anything I could do to help—with school and stuff. I've been here forever." My words trip over one another. Clearly, he doesn't want or need my help. I turn to leave.

"Lucy."

Dov is still standing in the same place, and for a moment I assume I've misheard him.

"They do a lot of talking in classes here," he finally says, his fingers pulling through his curls. "At my old school, there were more than thirty kids in a class, so we didn't have the same," he pauses, "class discussions."

He's looking at me.

Deep breath in. Deep breath out.

"Yes, we're all about class discussions here."

Dov chuckles silently, the curl of his lips and the movement in his chest the only indication he's laughing at all.

I smile, the sight of his laughter relaxing my whole body. "Your English is great," I say.

His smile disappears, and he stiffens. "People in Israel speak English."

And I've offended him. "That's not what I meant." I swallow and will my cheeks to return to a normal shade. "What I meant to say is that you don't have much of an accent."

He softens. It's mesmerizing to watch, to see the muscles in his face relax, his jaw unclench.

"We lived in Boston when I was a kid, while my dad was doing a post-doc. And then it was really important to my parents that we didn't lose the English, so that's all we spoke at home. Between that, after-school English classes, and summer camp in America, I can now communicate effectively."

Communicate effectively? What does that even mean?

Dov pushes his fists into his pockets.

Then he glances to the end of the corridor, and I know he's halfway out the door.

"Listen," I say quickly, pulling out the only thing I can think of before I lose him. "I've never met anyone my age from Israel. I'd love to know more about what it's like to live in such a conflicted region."

By the time I glance back up and see that his face has hardened again, it's too late. I take a small step back.

Apparently as soon as I open my mouth, offensive comments come out.

"I'm not a social studies experiment," he says gruffly.

My stomach drops because, unlike the other times, I can see the shadow of hurt in his eyes.

"Wait," I say. I can tell he's about to swivel around and charge out. "I'm sorry, I didn't mean to offend you."

He doesn't leave but his face doesn't change either. "If you're interested in the conflict, read the newspaper. People who live there, *live there*. They go to school and the movies, hang out at the mall; they do all the same things you do."

"Okay. You're right. I'm sorry. I guess the way people describe it, I pictured a war zone. And lots of sand. Weren't you afraid?"

That sounded way less ridiculous in my head.

He looks like he's trying to decide between yelling at me and walking away, and I'm not sure which I'm hoping for. "*We're* afraid of a lot of things, and most of them are no different than the things that frighten you."

I step forward.

But he continues. "Israel is a country of millions of people," he says, "We have major cities and fast food restaurants and bars. And sure, there's sand, but there are also busy highways crisscrossing the country and traffic problems and pickpockets. And while there have been terrorist attacks and wars, it's not our daily life. Just like when I watched the news, I thought Chicago was a city of crime and gang violence, but I've been here for more than a month and I've yet to be attacked by a street thug with a gun."

I don't even know how many times I've struck out in this conversation, but the fact that he's still standing here is basically a miracle.

I'm about to ask him why he chose the poem, why it sounded so personal to him. But then I decide I should just keep my mouth shut. He pulls one hand out of his pocket and glances at his watch. "I have to go. My mom's picking me up in two minutes. You don't need to worry about being nice to the new kid. I'm not sure how long I'll be here."

Maybe that's why the academy has a policy not to let seniors transfer in.

Before I have a chance to apologize again, he disappears around the corner, and I'm alone in the hallway. Feeling stupid.

Luckily, a quick glance at my phone tells me that I don't have time to worry about it anymore; I need to be home for my brothers.

FIVE

· · · · · · ·

"So, how was everyone's day?" Mom stares out at the boys and me from the computer screen in the study, but nobody has much to say.

Gabe keeps glancing down at his lap where he's trying to solve a Rubik's Cube, while I try to surreptitiously take it away from him. "Talk to Mom," I whisper, and he just shrugs.

"Good!" I pipe up. "There's a new guy in our grade."

I try to appear blasé, but my mom raises her eyebrows. "Does this mean that Scott has competition?" she asks.

Crap. I didn't tell her. In my defense, I was with the boys all evening after Scott left and . . . she wasn't here.

Sam turns a concerned look at me. "Is Scott coming for dinner tonight? Can he bring Sally?" To my brothers, Scott's like the young uncle on TV shows: fun, rambunctious, and with a limited attention span. Not unlike his dog Sally.

Shit. This isn't the way I wanted to tell everyone. Can I kick a cable under the table and turn the computer off?

"Oh, how nice that he's coming by to celebrate your first day of school. Is Dad making a special dinner?"

I can't tell if she's hoping I say yes because that's what she thinks we should be doing or say no because it'll prove that life isn't the same without her here. Not that I can remember her ever planning any special First Day of School dinners.

"I actually have to help Dad get dinner ready," I lie, figuring that's better than faking a heart attack. "Why don't the three of you guys chat, and I'll call you later?"

For a brief moment, there's a hurt look on her face, but just as quickly, her smile is back again. Just as I'm about to slide Sam off my lap, I realize that I don't even know where my mom is video chatting with us from. I can see books in the background, but this could be her home office or her work office. Or really anywhere.

How did we all get to this point?

"I love you, Mom," I say. I still need to tell her about my bizarre conversation with Mrs. Schneider. "Call you later?"

She wrinkles her nose and glances over to something on the desk. "I have a faculty meeting and then dinner until nine."

"That's eleven our time," I say.

"Tomorrow?"

I nod. It's not like when she was at Northwestern she was always home to chat when I needed it anyway. I turn to my brothers, who've been following this conversation. Shoot. "You guys are going to talk to Mom until dinner is ready, okay?"

Sam and Gabe give me identical *save me* looks, but right now I can't. They need to get used to talking to Mom this way.

God, today sucks, I think as I escape the study. Mom is talking about her new house or something, and I'm not sure she can tell that the boys are desperate to get out of there. Not my problem, I remind myself, and yet, it doesn't ring true at all.

"I'm surprised that you and Scott aren't off enjoying your last days before he leaves for school," Dad says when we're all seated at the table.

The boys turn to face me, like sharks sensing blood in the water. At this point, I am out of energy. "He actually left for school yesterday," I say, trying to tell my dad with my eyes to drop it.

"But I thought he wasn't leaving until next week?" he asks.

Apparently, we need to practice this signal reading thing.

I shake my head and focus on chewing the lightly charred potatoes he's prepared. Luckily, his barbecue chicken makes up for the potatoes.

Except everyone is staring at me.

"Scott had to go earlier than expected. We also decided that instead of doing long distance this year, it was probably a good idea if we broke up."

There's silence at the table.

Crap.

"What does 'breakup' mean?" Sam asks, and I glance at my dad.

Your turn, I say with my eyes, and miracle of miracles, he actually gets it.

"It means that Scott won't be around as often," he says, struggling to find the words. "It doesn't mean that he doesn't like you guys anymore. It just means that he's going to be busy with . . . other things."

If the earth could swallow me whole, that would be a good thing. Part of me hates my mom for not being here to defuse this. And part of me hates Scott for blindsiding me with this breakup. And yet another part of me hates my dad right now for making it seem like we're getting a divorce.

Instead, I focus on not letting out the tears that are accumulating behind my eyes. The fact is, I should have been better prepared for this.

Being with Scott was like everything finally fit together. Our parents were friends; even our grandparents had been going to the same synagogue since long before we were born. More importantly, I had someone to hold hands with as I walked through the hallways; someone to make plans with on the weekends; someone to make me feel like I was part of something bigger, something important. He was the fulfillment of every daydream I'd ever had about a boyfriend.

Until he graduated.

Something changed when he formally finished being a student at the academy, which is why I shouldn't have been surprised that he'd changed his mind about us trying to make it work. Suddenly he was hanging out with people that neither of us had ever liked.

Sometimes I would still be able to see the boy I'd been friends with since preschool. The boy who bought me children's books as anniversary gifts and read them to me softly late at night over the phone.

But despite what I told others, that boy started to get harder to find every day.

Later, I distract myself by looking up Yehuda Amichai's "The Diameter of a Bomb." I read it over and over again. It feels important.

I listen to a recording of Amichai read it in Hebrew, the words a mixture of sounds and silences. And then I carefully copy down the words in translation and tape them to my wall.

I try to read, try to listen to music, try to think about which poem I will tell Dov about in class. And finally, I pull out the only surefire way to calm myself down—running through *adagio* choreographies from the studio. I close my eyes in the darkness and mark the movement with my hands.

Développé croisé devant. My body relaxes. *Retiré en face, developpé devant*, I can breathe deeper, *cou-de-pied en fondu*. My body misses this so much. *Pas de bourrée* to the right, finish in fifth. Repeat to the left.

The dances I no longer dance.

And I can't help it. I curl into a ball and try to cry quietly so that nobody will hear me.

The next morning, when I wake from dreams of *glissades* that land me flat on the ground, it's Mrs. Schneider's class that gets me out of bed.

But Dov is back to being a statue.

And when it's my turn to share, he says nothing.

Nothing.

I choose the Yeats poem and try to describe how sometimes our dreams are as valuable as the richest of fabrics, about the anxiety of being judged for our dreams—

Not a word.

SIX

· · · · · ·

For the next few days, the only time I hear Dov's voice is in my head.

Mrs. Schneider's class returns to its regular seminar setting, and debates break out about line breaks and spaces, half beats and rhymes.

And the whole time, Dov sits quietly. I catch Mrs. Schneider glancing at him on occasion, but she doesn't push him. I want to forget about him, forget the sound of his voice, his quiet intensity. I focus on enjoying my last year at the academy with Maddie. I spend extra time playing with my brothers. And yet, I can't help trying to catch Dov's eye. But I always seem to look at him just as he's walking away.

Which makes the sight of him sitting on the steps of Temple Beth Emet as I drop my brothers off at Sunday school a little startling. I almost don't recognize him. He's wearing a blue button-down shirt over pressed khakis, as opposed to a concert-T and jeans. Not that I'm keeping track of his wardrobe.

"I'm starting to think you're following me around," I tease as I usher the boys to the front door.

"I was here first," Dov says as he stands and starts to walk toward the intersection. "And I'm leaving."

Crap.

I quickly ask Gabe to walk Sam to his classroom and then jog over to Dov. "Wait a second," I call out. "What are you doing here?"

Dov hooks his right hand behind his head and rubs it across the back of his neck. "Long story," he says. "Suffice it to say, nothing worked out as planned." He shakes his head and continues on his way.

"Do you need a ride somewhere?" The only response I get is the back and forth movement of his head. I peer up at the darkening sky. "It's supposed to rain," I try again. This is the last time, I promise myself.

His back is still turned. He shakes his head again.

climb into my car, surprised by how annoyed I am. Plans change. Deal with it. I thought I'd go for a run this morning, but it looks like it's going to rain. It's not like I'm sulking about it. I turn out of the parking lot and call my favorite person.

"Sweets," my grandmother says, "you know I'm always happy to hear from you. But we're supposed to be at the museum at eleven o'clock, and Megan and I decided that the first one dressed and ready to go gets to take the Greek and Roman room. And you know how I like to lead those tours. I'm already at a disadvantage since she puts so little time into her makeup."

I snort. My grandmother frequently has that effect on me.

"Hi Amy! I dropped the boys off at Hebrew School and thought I'd try you. But go if you have to."

"You sure, hon?" she whispers conspiratorially. "Because I can lie to Megan and tell her she has bags under her eyes that really need covering up if you need to talk."

My grandmother, all five foot nothing of her, is not like other grandmothers. And not just because she insists I call her Amy.

"How's my favorite other grandmother?"

"Oh, good," she giggles. "She says to say hi."

From a distance, I hear Megan's voice. "Tell her we'll take her out for lunch."

"Well, of course we'll take her to lunch," Amy tells Megan. "That is if she wants to hang out with two old ladies."

I roll my eyes. She knows how much I love hanging out with them.

"OK Ames . . ." I put her on speakerphone as I start driving east on Dempster, quickly passing Dov who's walking with his head down. "Have a great time at the museum. Can you call me later? I miss you, and Mom's out of town . . ."

I can't believe I have to guilt my grandmother into calling me.

"I'll try sweets. But Megan and I have date night tonight, and then I'm playing cards with the ladies and . . ."

There's a huge clap of thunder, and I glance in my rearview mirror in time to see Dov pause.

"Hold on a second." I interrupt my grandmother as she starts telling me her very complicated schedule. Pissed off or not, I'm not going to leave Dov walking in a thunderstorm.

I make a quick U-turn and reach him as the rain starts, dark patches staining his shirt. "Get in," I shout, opening the passenger door.

"What, honey? Where do you need me to go?" My grandmother asks.

Dov looks at me like I'm crazy.

"Amy, wait. Dov, get in."

My grandmother, mercifully, goes silent.

"I'm fine," he mutters, his body still.

"Don't be ridiculous. You're going to get drenched." Just then there's another thunderclap. Dov looks up uncertainly as the car behind me honks. "Please don't make me beg."

"You shouldn't dear, she embarrasses easily," comes a voice from the front seat console.

This isn't happening.

I swear Dov gives me a half smile even though his head is still down. But he finally climbs in as the rain comes down in earnest.

"Thanks," he says, staring at his hands. "You didn't need to do that."

I resist the urge to grin. The fact that he's talking to me feels like an epic victory.

"Can I speak now?"

Crap.

"Uh, Amy, sorry about that. OK, you go to the museum and call me when you can."

"I don't have to go so quickly, dear. Introduce me to your friend."

I focus intently on the road in front of me instead of allowing myself to glance over at Dov. Thank god she didn't hear a male voice and assume it was Scott.

"Amy, this is Dov. He's new at the academy this year, and he's in my poetry seminar. Dov, this is my grandmother, Amy."

"Nice to meet you, dear," Amy says. "Where are you from?"

Dov clears his throat.

This is mortifying.

"I'm from Israel."

I pull over. Clearly we'll be talking for a while.

"Well, I figured that from your name and your accent, but where in Israel?"

I shoot a glance over at Dov, who appears to be just as confused as me.

"Jerusalem."

"Beautiful city. I haven't been there in decades, but a close friend of mine sent me a bunch of pictures from her most recent trip. I'd love to go back."

"It is beautiful." Dov doesn't sound annoyed as much as wistful.

"When did you go to Israel, Amy?" I ask. How did I not know this?

"Oh, long before you were born. I'll tell you about it someday. It was in the late seventies."

My eyes dart to Dov's, and his raised eyebrows match my own.

"So what brings you to Evanston?" Amy continues. She's clearly perfectly happy to miss out on the Greek and Roman room when it comes to speaking to strange boys in my car.

"My mother got transferred here."

There's a pause that goes on for a few beats too long.

"Amy, did we lose you?" I try not to make my voice sound hopeful.

"No dear, I wasn't sure if there was more to what Dov was going to say."

Dov shakes his head.

"We should go. It's raining, and I shouldn't be on my phone while I drive."

"But you pulled over. I know you too well."

I shake my head. How this woman gave birth to my mother is a mystery.

"So where are you kids off to right now?"

"Uh—" I look over at Dov, and he raises his shoulders.

"We're not really going anywhere. I just picked Dov up because I didn't want him to walk in the rain."

"That's sweet of you dear. Where were you headed, Dov?"

It's like she's in the car with us, sitting in the backseat, her head stuck between our shoulders.

"Uh . . ." Dov mumbles something I can't quite make out.

Apparently neither can my grandmother.

"Speak up, dear. I'm old."

I shake my head. Bad to worse.

"I don't know," he says, this time more clearly. He looks out the window at the driving rain. "I was trying to get to a synagogue today. But the place I found doesn't do services."

"Yes, Beth Emet only has regular services on Saturday mornings."

It's like I'm not even here.

Dov opens his mouth and then closes it again, shaking his head.

"Are you Orthodox?" she asks.

"No!" He sounds shocked, as though Amy should know better.

"I wasn't trying to offend you, dear," she says. "Given that you're looking for a daily service, I thought I'd check. I know this area well; I just wanted to give you the right options."

She's not in the car with us, I repeat to myself. She knows where we are because I told her I just left Beth Emet. Either way, I need to end this before she ensures Dov never speaks to me again.

"Amy—"

"No, I'm sorry," he says, his tone contrite. "You didn't know. It's just a bit of a sore subject. Synagogues are not my thing, but I needed to go today."

There's another long pause, and I can tell my grandmother is gearing up by the length of the silence, like the eerie calm before a storm.

I'm about to say goodbye, accidentally shut off the phone, and throw myself on top of it, but I'm not fast enough.

"Why are you trying to find a synagogue today?"

I stare at the numbers on the dashboard: 92,761 miles driven, the gas gauge (almost full), the familiar tire pressure light on (a faulty sensor that was ridiculously expensive to replace).

I don't look at Dov.

But from the corner of my eye, I watch as he interlaces his fingers in his lap and twists them hard.

"It's the anniversary of my brother's death," he says softly, his voice barely discernible over the sound of the rain.

Oh shit.

So help me god: if my grandmother didn't hear that, I'll throw the phone out the window before he's forced to repeat it.

"I'm so sorry," I whisper, not quite to Dov—more to myself.

Dov shakes his head and looks out the window. "My parents didn't want to do anything to mark the day. I mean, we can't go to the cemetery since we're here and he's . . . over there. But, while I'm totally not religious, it seemed wrong not to say *kaddish*." He gives a sad chuckle. "I lit a *yarzheit* candle for him last night, and they didn't say a word."

He pauses, and I search for something to say, but I can't think of anything. I remember the couple who'd stood with him in the middle of the foyer at school: the way their hands were clasped and how he'd stood at a distance.

"It's not that they don't care. They don't know what to do anymore. It's all a mess." He glances over at me. "Sorry, I don't know why I'm telling you this."

His words hang in the air.

I can't imagine not having my parents to turn to, however frustrating it is that my mom is halfway across the country. I can't imagine facing that level of despair. Alone. Far away from everyone I know and love.

For once, I'm content to let Amy speak.

"I'm so sorry for your loss," she says quietly, her voice soft and grandmotherly. "I can't imagine losing a sibling, especially one so young. And I don't presume to understand what your parents are thinking, except that they are clearly still lost in their own grief. But in terms of finding a synagogue, given the late hour, I'd suggest the Hillel on campus. They have a lovely rabbi there, a woman with two young children. Very smart."

Dov looks at me oddly, and I shrug.

"I've taken classes with her. I'm sure they won't be starting too early since their primary attendees are students. Lucy, why don't you drive him over?"

"Don't you have somewhere to be?" Dov asks me.

"No," I shake my head. "I was planning to go running, but someone forgot to tell the rain."

"You run?" He snickers.

"Yes, I run." I punch his arm and then take it back quickly when his eyes lift at the contact.

His mouth widens into a smile.

I feel a surprising rush of happiness when the tension clears from his face, even if it's only for a moment.

"Good to know."

He's teasing me. I feel almost giddy.

"Well, I'm going to leave you guys. Nice to meet you, Dov."

"*Na'im me'od,* Amy."

"I hope to meet you in person one day."

I'm close to being home free. But Dov surprises me. "Me too, Amy. Thanks for your help."

Without Amy's presence between us, the car returns to the uncomfortable silence we shared before.

I drive the last few blocks carefully, signaling at every turn, until I finally come to stop in front of the Hillel Jewish student center.

"Thank you," he says, and this time his eyes find mine. "I really appreciate it. And your grandmother is interesting."

I laugh. "Thank you for putting up with her. She can be a lot."

Dov shakes his head, the corners of his mouth turned down. "She sounds pretty amazing."

I realize I was mistaken when I first saw him; his eyes aren't quite the color of my cowboy boots. They're a far more complicated mixture of blues and greens than I'd originally observed.

"Do you want an umbrella or something?" I ask, feeling ridiculous and trying not to make it obvious that I'm staring at his eyes. Also, I don't want him to leave.

"I'm fine." He smiles. "I actually live nearby. Funny, I walked all the way out to that synagogue when I could have slept in and walked the few blocks here." He opens the door and stares up at the building. His face looks uncertain, scared even.

He slowly makes his way to the front of the building, and I hold my breath, hoping against hope that maybe services have been canceled, or he's missed them. When he gets to the door, he turns and waves slightly. Then he enters the building.

SEVEN

. . . .

The car is uncomfortably empty without him. After he disappears from view, I spend a few minutes trying to find the right music to listen to, maybe something upbeat that will dispel the sadness he left behind, but then that feels all wrong. So I swipe through quieter songs, more melancholy.

Part of me wants to drive at breakneck speed back to Beth Emet, pull my brothers out of Sunday school, and make sure they know that I can't picture my world without them. Or call my dad and offer to pick them up at the end of the morning, take them out for a special lunch, spend the day not griping about babysitting them but recognizing that I'd lose my mind if anything happened to either of them.

And then my thoughts switch to Dov intoning the memorial poem for the dead in a room full of strangers. The ache slips around me like a tight rope, making it hard to breathe, hard to imagine putting the car in drive and paying attention to the roads.

I don't know how long I sit there before the doors to the Jewish Center open and a dozen or so college students file out. They're chatting, laughing, and even through my closed window, I catch plans for coffee and breakfast, study dates in the library.

Is this what Scott is doing at Illinois? Not that I can picture him attending services; he'd only tolerated them for his parents. But the breakfast plans, the laughter about last night's parties . . . It's only been a couple of weeks, but it's amazing how little it hurts to think of him hanging out with other people. Even dating.

How could I have thought he was worth staying committed to if it doesn't even hurt now that we're apart?

I startle when a knock on my window interrupts my reverie. Dov is looking at me curiously. He looks exhausted.

"You okay?" I ask when I roll down the window.

He nods. "What are you—"

"I got distracted," I say. "I got a call, and I didn't want to drive and talk, and then . . ." The lies pile up, and my face flushes uncomfortably. I'm a terrible liar.

"Okay," he says, tapping the window frame a couple of times distractedly. He gazes down the street and takes a deep breath. "Thanks again for bringing me here."

"Was it what you expected?" I ask. I don't know what to ask really. He'd reacted with such offense when Amy had asked him if he was religious, and I don't know how to ask him about the service without angering him.

"It was a traditional service."

"I should try it one day, I guess. I grew up at Beth Emet, the synagogue where I saw you. It's where I had my bat mitzvah, where I went to Hebrew school for ten years."

"*'At medaberet 'ivrit?*" he asks.

"Well, no, I don't speak Hebrew," I admit with a nervous laugh. "Hebrew school isn't just for learning Hebrew. Or even mostly for learning Hebrew. It's more about Jewish life and prayer stuff."

Most kids I knew hated it, but the truth is, I loved it. I still remember a time I loved going to synagogue at Beth Emet, loved the cadence of the rabbi's voice when she'd speak, loved the way the cantor and his guitar would fill the sanctuary. For a while, I'd pushed my parents to attend on Saturday mornings, back when there were only three of us. I'd sit between them, a prayer book on my lap, and I'd just listen, waiting for the moment the people on the *bima* would open the ark and I'd finally see all the Torahs lined up in rows, cloaked in velvet, silver, and gold, the moment when they'd take them out, the faint sound of the bells on the Torah crowns singing.

But that was a long time ago. A whole different lifetime ago, when Mom would read me books at night and stay with me until I fell asleep, often falling asleep herself. Back when I was young enough to insist upon it.

I take a deep breath of the slightly cool air, the early smells of fall that follow a rainstorm. For the first time in years, I feel a longing for those moments of sitting in synagogue, one hand in each of my parents', legs crossed in my seat. Back when things were so much simpler.

"I've never been a *shul* person," Dov says softly. "The only time I ever really went was with my *saba*. I used to go with him when we visited Haifa, sit by him in *shul*. I loved the moment when he'd take out his *tallit*, his prayer shawl. He'd unfurl it like a cape, lowering it over his head, and then taking the ends, he'd flip them over his left shoulder—almost like a *keffiyah*, like the scarves Arabs wear—and he'd pause like that just for a moment. I loved the action of it, the drama, wondering what he said in that moment, the *tallit* covering his face, shrouded almost. And then he'd reposition it around his shoulder and sit down, and he'd say, *Bo' tatele*, come here, little guy, the mixture of Hebrew and Yiddish, two worlds in those two words."

We both stare forward in the same direction, the familiar Northwestern Campus only a half block away.

I don't want to go meet Maddie to study or talk about college essays. I don't want him to go back to a house with parents who are ignoring today's significance.

"Do you need to go home? Because I have some time if . . . I don't know. Forget it. You've probably got other things . . ."

"No, I don't." His words come out in a rush.

I purse my lips together. Maybe. Maybe we could—but then, maybe if I say something stupid again his shield will come back down. Maybe he'll say no. Tell me he doesn't need help. That he wants to be alone. Why am I still here?

"It looks like the rain has cleared," I say cautiously, feigning nonchalance. "Do you want to walk a bit? I've spent a lot of time on this campus—"

"Do you tackle people to the ground here too?" He laughs.

I want to high-five the universe for that laugh. But instead, I focus on swallowing the smile that threatens to engulf my face.

"No." I smirk. "I very rarely tackle people to the ground."

"So was that just for me?"

His words are buried in his laughter, so at first I'm not even sure I've heard them properly. My breath quickens. Is he flirting with me?

And then his smile falters, and for a moment it seems like he's about to say something, but instead he nods. "I'd love to take a walk," he says.

I check to make sure my car is legally parked and grab my bag.

We make our way through the empty campus, and for the first time, the silence doesn't feel oppressive. When he approaches the lakefill, I make sure he knows not to get too close to the giant fish.

He stares at me like I'm crazy, but that's just because he didn't grow up in Evanston. Everyone from Evanston knows you don't mess with the creepy fish who have clearly mutated due to their diet of college student castaways like Doritos and pizza.

We head up a small incline toward the rocky shores of Lake Michigan.

"Thank you for helping me, before."

I try to keep my heart from racing. "My pleasure."

"*B'kef*," he says.

I glance over at him, puzzled.

"It's how you say 'my pleasure' in Hebrew."

"*B'kef*," I repeat. The word feels surprisingly comfortable in my mouth.

"Perfect."

I grin.

B'kef.

"I feel like a bad Jew saying I don't speak any Hebrew. I mean, I know some prayers in Hebrew, but nothing—"

"Nothing a person would say on the street?"

I laugh. "Not unless people in Israel walk around saying things like 'Praised are You Our God, King of the Universe . . .'"

"Not often," he chuckles.

The silence returns as we both stare at the waves crashing on the colorful rocks below. Many of them are graffitied with expressions of love. *Mike + Doni = 4ever. April 6th, 2015.* I wonder what it's like for those people now, whether they're still together, whether they come back to this spot.

I used to come here all the time when I was a kid. The clearing behind us is where I'd first learned to ride a bike, fly a kite. What would it be like to go to college among these childhood memories? To have someone paint our love across from where we used to picnic before my brothers were born, where I used to turn cartwheels? What would it be like to leave this place?

"So, what do you like to do when you aren't rescuing people from unexpected rainstorms?"

At first, I'm too distracted by the fact Dov is making conversation to reply. But the question lingers, and I'm forced to think about it. I shrug, vaguely embarrassed that I don't have a good answer. "Study mostly. And try to make time to hang out with Maddie. I spend a lot of time with my brothers. My mom is . . ." I pause trying to think of how I want to spin it. "She's away a lot. So I like to make sure I'm around as much as possible, not just to babysit."

"How old are they?" Dov asks, his voice quiet.

"Seven and nine."

He smiles sadly. "Your friend said you're a dancer?"

I stare at him blankly until I remember Maddie's comment from when I fell into Dov in the hallway. I'm going to kill her. "Right. Maddie. Well, I used to dance," I say. "Until last spring, I took a couple of classes a night, usually five or six days a week. It was everything to me, all I thought about, all I cared about."

"Why did you stop?"

I shrug, as if it doesn't matter much, as if I don't have to stop myself from lifting up to a *demi-pointe* when I'm standing at the kitchen counter and sinking into a *plié* when my legs are stiff. I struggle to find an answer that will feel big enough to warrant the decision I made. "I was going to have to stop eventually," I finally say. "It's not like I was going to become a professional dancer. It didn't really make sense to keep investing the time into it if it wouldn't lead anywhere."

"Huh," he says, as though he knows I'm lying but he's not going to call me on it.

"What about you?" I ask. "What do you do when you're not . . ." Looking for services to honor your dead brother? God, I feel like an idiot.

He chuckles as though he went through the same thought process. "I'm not really sure. I only just got here a little while ago. But so far, a lot of working out, making sure I'm in the best shape possible for next year."

"What's next year?" I ask after a moment when I can't figure out what he's talking about.

"The army," he says, and my stomach flips. "Israel has mandatory army service for eighteen-year-olds. Well, mandatory for most."

I fill my lungs with air and then slowly let it out. I feel like there's a whole story there I'm just not ready to hear, as badly as I want to.

So instead, we walk quietly through the empty campus. As we pass the lacrosse fields, I notice Dov is holding something attached to a chain around his neck. He's pulling on it so hard that the silver chain is creating an angry red line on his skin.

"What's that?"

He startles and drops what he'd been holding. It's a disk: plain metal, though it looks perforated, engraved with small symbols. Dov grabs it and closes it in his fist. His words come out like a whisper. "It's my brother's dog tag," he says finally. "From the army."

The army.

"Your brother was also in the army?"

His head bobs gently. "Everyone goes."

Suddenly all my wondering about whether to apply to Northwestern, binding decisions, dance lessons, complaining about my brothers— it all feels juvenile.

"Did he die in combat?" I ask. Dov chuckles, a choked sound, and shakes his head. He rubs his eyes with his free hand and pinches the top of his nose.

And then I remember the poem. The bomb. Dov's hands cupped together. The impact of the bomb. "Was it a terrorist attack?"

"No," he says, his voice strained and forceful. "He was killed in a perfectly normal way, in a car accident."

"I'm sorry," I whisper.

"Don't be," he says quickly. He takes a deep breath, and I steel myself for the probability that he'll make his escape, decide that this has already gone on long enough.

"He was coming home on leave from the army," he surprises me by saying. "My mom had been cooking up a storm, all his favorite foods. Since his visits were so rare, each time he'd come, it'd be like a state visit, everything had to be perfect.

"Anat, his girlfriend, had already arrived. She and my mom were discussing the weekend: who was coming for dinner, how many we'd be. I was . . ." He laughs, that awful choking sound again.

"I was feeling resentful." He spits the words out. "I was thinking to myself, *Perfect Yuval is coming, and I'm going to go back to being nothing.* Yuval was the golden child—the easy son. He was the one who could always get my dad to come to the dinner table. He was the one who'd talk to my *safta* on the phone when she was missing my *saba* after he died. He was the one in the elite unit, selected as a result of his stellar test scores and interviews." Dov's voice is tinged with a hard edge.

I concentrate on putting one foot in front of the other, my hands so tightly clenched into fists that my fingers ache.

"I was thinking of skipping out early on dinner and going over to my friend Tomer's house to get stoned. And then the police were at the door, and we all knew something was wrong but, truthfully, nobody thought . . ." He takes a deep breath. "Nobody thought it was Yuval. They thought it was me, that I'd been in the accident. Even though I was sitting right there, shelling peas in the kitchen."

He takes another deep breath. "At first my mother didn't believe the policeman. Even when he showed her the dog tag . . . I don't think she really believed him until he told her Yuval had been killed changing a tire. Apparently he'd seen a stalled car, a pregnant woman with a small child on the side of the road, and he stopped to help. Somebody wasn't paying attention, or maybe Yuval was entertaining the kid as he changed the tire, and a car barreled into him. He was killed instantly."

His words hang between us, and I wish I knew how to push them out of the air we're breathing. I wish I knew what to say, something comforting. "I'm sorry" feels trite, as does every other phrase. So instead, I remain silent, hoping it conveys that there's nothing I can say, that this is bigger than anything I can imagine.

I direct us down a path past Annenberg, and then the Dearborn Observatory with its magnificent slate dome. I want to tell Dov about the nights my mom would take me to look through the big telescope, the thrill of staying up late, the two of us walking through campus with our hands clasped. I want to distract him from the grief that sits on his shoulders, sinking them. I want him to let go of the dog tag he's still clasping in his right hand.

But I stay silent, hands gripping my backpack straps because I'm afraid of what I'd do if one of my hands was free. Holding his hand is not an option.

At first we meander, following the empty paths around the ivy-covered buildings. But when we pass the opening to the Shakespeare Gardens for the second time, I detour inside. Dov follows without question. Taking a seat on one of the rustic wooden benches, I'm grateful the gardens are empty. He doesn't question our change of pace, doesn't even react to being seated now instead of standing.

He doesn't even ask me about the secret garden we're sitting in. And so I busy myself searching through my backpack for the packages of animal crackers I keep in case the boys get hungry at soccer practice and the juice boxes they usually reject because the other kids drink Vitamin Water and apple juice is "lame."

"Help yourself," I say, setting the food between us and opening an animal cracker bag.

He moves slowly, like he's still halfway between there and here.

He puts the dog tag back in his shirt and reaches for a bag of cookies.

We sit on the bench eating childish snacks. It's only when a group on a guided tour invades our quiet space that we make our way back to the car.

When we reach Dov's house, he puts his hand on the door handle but doesn't open it. "Listen," he says, "I really appreciate everything you've done today. I know it's not what you would normally have done with your free time."

I shake my head. "It was a pleasure. *B'kef*," I say and laugh as he rolls his eyes. "No, seriously. I got to know you a bit better."

He opens his mouth and closes it again. "I'm not sure I'll ever be able to tell you what a big difference you made today, Lucy. I hope you'll let me know one day if I can repay that favor."

And before I have a chance to react, he opens the door. "See you tomorrow?"

I nod, and he smiles. A real smile.

As he goes inside, I wonder if the candle he lit for Yuval was still burning. The house appears deserted. I wonder what Dov will do for the rest of the day, whether his parents will come home, whether they'll comfort him.

EIGHT

· · · · · · · ·

Dov's eyes are guarded when I slip into my seat in Mrs. Schneider's class the next morning.

His silence hardens the spaces between my ribs until it becomes hard to breathe. I want to joke about animal crackers and apple juice, ask him how the rest of his night went. I want us to go back to the ease we had around each other yesterday.

It isn't until he turns to me, chair legs scraping the floor, that I notice we've been directed back into partners.

"I—" I try to get an indication from the sounds around us as to what we're supposed to be doing.

He pushes his book between us, which makes me realize I haven't opened mine.

"You okay?" he asks.

My mouth shifts into a smile. I want to tell him how I spent the evening having fun with my brothers. How I had them help me cook dinner, even when it meant that we were eating crêpes and ice cream. How I told my dad that it was all in honor of Yuval.

But I'm not sure what to say.

"Um, yes. Just a lot on my mind. How was yesterday when you got home?"

Dov opens his mouth, but right before the words come out, he bites down hard on his bottom lip. "It was fine," he says after a moment.

It was fine? A movie can be fine. A bowl of soup is often fine. Borrowing someone's pencil and then accidentally losing it is usually fine. The anniversary of your brother's death? Whether his parents pretended it was happening or not, it couldn't possibly have been fine.

"Did your parents—"

"Listen, I really appreciate your help yesterday," he says, "but can we just go back to discussing poems?" His words slice through the air.

"Okay." The heat rises in my cheeks, making it difficult to do anything but stare at the edge of his book. "Sorry."

He takes a deep breath and shakes his head. "Did you hear the assignment?"

I search through my memory, but I can only recall thoughts about apple juice and animal crackers. "I think I spaced out."

"We're supposed to work in partners for half the period, having a *dialogue* back and forth in poetry." He says "dialogue" like it's a dirty word. "We trade off; one day you bring a poem and we discuss, the next time I bring a poem. But there needs to be a link between them."

"A link?"

The idea of poetry as conversation excites me, but the curve of his mouth makes it clear that Dov doesn't feel the same way.

"A connection," he says. "My poem needs to be in some way connected to yours, and then yours to mine after that. We keep a log of our poems and our thoughts."

"Okay," I say.

The bell rings, and as we pack our bags he says, "Can you choose the first one?"

And before I get a chance to respond, he gets up and walks away.

Two days later, I bring "In Exile" by Emma Lazarus. I present it like it's no big deal, like I'd put zero thought into what would be the poem to start off our conversation.

It's a lie.

I worked for hours finding the right one. A poem that would return us to the easy back-and-forth of Sunday. I examined dozens of poems, first on grief, then on dance, then on displacement. I read through Israeli poems I found online but ultimately rejected them for being far too obvious.

And finally, I settled on "In Exile," the image of birds in flight taking root in my mind:

The unimprisoned bird that finds the track
Through sun-bathed space, to where his fellows dwell.

When I finish reading it to Dov, I tell him about the feeling of doing a *grand jeté*: the easy few steps that start it off, like it's nothing, then the sensation of leaping, muscles pulled in, back straight, arms firm but appearing relaxed, toes pointed. The strength it requires to make the leap, keep it in check, all those muscles working together. And then that amazing moment in the midst of it all, the moment when everything is tight and strong, and you know what it feels like to be a bird in flight, soaring. And as I'm about to ask him his thoughts, the bell rings, and he gets up and walks away.

Friday, he brings "Last Night I Dreamed of Chickens" by Jack Prelutsky.

I stare at him in disbelief as he reads, haltingly, the poem about dreaming of chickens and waking up with eggs all over him. The boy who read me a poem about the impact of a bomb on the whole damn world brought a poem about chickens because chickens are birds. That's the connection.

"I'm sure Mrs. Schneider wouldn't mind if you choose an Israeli poem," I say after he explains his poetry choice by saying, "It's funny."

"I know," he says, and then the bell rings and he leaves. Game. On.

I bring "Hope is the thing with feathers," and he retaliates with "Colonel Fazackerley Butterworth-Toast," a poem about a British colonel who buys a castle with a ghost and then proceeds to scare him away.

I lift my eyebrows, and his lips curve into a smile. "What's the connection?" I ask, knowing I'm walking into a trap but enjoying the ride.

"Hope is like a ghost," he says, the words sure and practiced. "Lovely to believe in, but it doesn't exist."

I can't help it; I burst out laughing. And this time, when he smiles, it feels genuine.

But if my daily interactions with Dov keep school feeling buoyant, home is anything but.

"Mrs. Schneider mentioned that maybe I shouldn't apply to Northwestern Early Decision," I finally tell my mom when she's home one Sunday. "She thinks I have an excellent shot at general admission and—"

Mom bristles. "Why waste money applying elsewhere?" She frowns at the clock on her nightstand as she rummages under her bed for a cell phone charger. "I can't remember if I left my charger at home in California, or if I brought that one here. I should label them."

I'm offended by the equal treatment given to both places, but I attempt to keep the exasperation out of my voice. "If I apply early, it's binding."

"You can apply wherever you'd like," she says, peering over the bed, evidently not caring about keeping the exasperation out of *her* voice. "But I don't know when we'll find the time for college visits. And keep in mind that it'll be great to have you nearby. I'll have a heavier course load next year, and your dad will need the help. Northwestern is a win for everyone. But if you really need to talk about it more, let's do so next weekend when I'm back in town. Actually, maybe call me during the week because I might need to stay in California next weekend for a conference. Or just talk to your dad about it."

After four attempts to reach her that week, I try Dad.

"But I thought Northwestern was what you wanted?" he says.

"It is, I think. I mean, I thought. But maybe it isn't a bad idea to broaden my options. Just because Early Decision is binding and all."

We're at the kitchen table where I'm trying to get my head around "The Unknown Citizen," a W. H. Auden poem I'd chosen in response to Dov's last choice: "In Flanders

Fields," a World War I poem about fields of graves. We'd talked about it at length, even after the bell rang.

By this time, I've moved our "conversation" poems to a different wall of my bedroom, creating a line of call and response. A dialogue.

But his last poem haunts me. I try to find a poem about peace to respond to his nonchalant shrug at the awful cost of battle, but no poem holds the power of his. So I finally pull out "The Unknown Citizen," Auden's response to all the memorials to unknown soldiers after the war.

But I'd been staring at it for an hour, and I'm no closer to creating the basis for a discussion that will lead us away from war and death, despite how many times I reread Auden's words.

The poem is about a man who seems to have a good life because he did all the things he was supposed to do— worked hard, married, supported the appropriate government policies, bought a paper every day—a litany of all the markers of a good life at that time. The poet appears to be calling society out on the assumption that all of this naturally means one is happy.

Are there markers you can examine to understand a person? If I line up everything I know about Dov, will I know if he's "happy" or "free" as Auden wonders about the "Unknown Citizen"? Would he know something about me by knowing what music I listen to, the people in my family, the grades I receive?

Was Auden suggesting we are all unknown citizens, thinking happiness will come from doing what is expected of us?

"I wish I could help with your decision about where to go next year," Dad says, and while I understand his words,

I'm so lost in the poem I almost can't remember what conversation he's referring to. "When I was going to college it was expected that I would just live at home and go to Northwestern. They had a great engineering program, and I could save money, so I never thought about other programs. But if you want to apply more broadly, that's fine too. Even if you just don't want to make the commitment right now, that's fine too."

"Thanks, Dad," I say, finally lifting my eyes from the page when I notice he'd stopped talking. "I'm sure I'll wind up at Northwestern. But maybe it makes sense not to put all my eggs in one basket right now."

He takes my hand and squeezes it gently. "I get that. And I'll support whatever you choose."

The next afternoon, the poetry discussion with Dov grows heated. We argue about whether being an unknown citizen can even compare to the terror of being an unknown soldier.

"Are you suggesting," he says, "that to die alone, on a battle field, to be returned in a box with no one to identify your body, no one to claim you as—"

Without thinking, my eyes lower to the chain poking out from under his collar.

"I've got to go," he says. And before I can respond, before I can apologize, he's gone. I stare at the open doorway, not sure what to do. At Wilmette Academy you don't walk out of class. And where was he going to go? He wouldn't just walk out of the building, would he?

What did I do?

Mrs. Schneider appears unconcerned and has me work on my own to fill out our conversation log with my thoughts. I punt, unsure how to describe the back-and-forth we just had. Instead, I write about the Auden poem as a denunciation of the media and its practice of making evaluations about people based on a list of facts.

My head pounds as I scan for Dov's unruly hair the rest of the day.

I can't believe I fought with him about soldiers. I can't believe that I made him so angry, so upset that he walked out of class. That he might have walked out of school.

"Are you okay?" Maddie asks after I've ignored her repeated calls from across the hallway.

No.

"Just stressed about this Northwestern situation," I lie. I don't know how to tell Maddie about the conversation without explaining about his brother and the army and everything else he's told me over the last few weeks. I want to write it all down on a massive whiteboard, like on those crime shows where they log in all the facts. This is what I know about Dov, I'd write and then list out the facts. These are the questions I can't ask.

"Maybe you need some exercise to work it off—"

"Maddie, if this is about me going back to dance, save it. It's not that I don't want to. I do. So badly. But I can't. Ginger won't let me attend only one or two classes a week, and there's no way I can do more than that and still be there for the boys."

I almost feel badly about losing it, but I don't. I'm tired of feeling guilty about quitting ballet. I'm tired of the little comments.

If there was anyone who'd been pissed off when I quit last year, it was Maddie. My parents bought the excuse that it was too much effort for something that likely had no payoff and would take time away from helping with my brothers, but Maddie saw right through it and knew it was about Scott. Making room for Scott. Making time for Scott.

But now Scott and I are over, and Maddie stares at me like I've grown two heads. "I was only going to suggest you go for a run or see if your Dad can get you into the Northwestern gym."

Now I have more than one reason to scowl. Because apparently between Dov's walkout, my indecision about next year, and this consistent lack of exercise, I've lost it and alienated my best friend.

"I'm sorry," I whisper, pulling her into a hug.

"We're still going to the Coffee Lab after school to go over our history project, right?"

"Of course."

"Great, why don't we talk about it in the car?"

But a text from my dad at the end of the day cancels that plan.

> Sorry to do this but can you be home this aft for the boys? Cindy's sick.

Out of the corner of my eye I see Dov approaching, and I inch forward so my locker door blocks him. I'm already feeling the beginnings of a headache. I'm not in the mood to be disappointed when he walks past me without a word.

Which he does.

Well, at least he didn't leave school because of my idiocy.

I toss my phone to the back of my locker, slamming the door shut. Dov glances at me quizzically then heads to his locker.

"What happened?" Maddie asks. She's made a pile of all our history books and source material in front of her locker, and now she's creating another one beside it with her chemistry books.

I bang my head against the locker door. "I have to go home," I groan. "I'm needed as the responsible sister."

"But what about finishing up our history assignment? We need to get moving on this or Mr. Seltzer will flunk us. Can't you just tell your dad you can't make it?"

Flunk us, my ass. Maddie is constitutionally unable to get anything less than an A-.

I keep my head pressed to the cool metal of the locker, letting it soothe my flushed skin as I try to take deep breaths. It must be nice to be an only child sometimes. What am I supposed to say? Cancel your class because Maddie and I want to study at a hip coffee shop?

"Could you come over to my house instead of us going to Coffee Lab? I'll put a video on for the boys, and they won't bother us." I turn to face her. She's already put the history pile back into her locker.

Maddie shakes her head. "I told my mom I'd meet her in downtown Evanston at five-thirty for dinner, so it'll be too tight. Let's just meet early tomorrow morning and work on it then?"

"I could drive you to wherever you're meeting her from my house. I'm sure the boys wouldn't mind a little car ride."

"I don't think it'll work," she says.

I sigh. There's no point in trying to reason with her. Maddie is who she is. "Fine. I guess we'll need to find another time."

Luckily I don't expect her to protest, so I'm not disappointed when she doesn't say anything.

"So, what are your plans for your birthday?"

My birthday. Crap, I hadn't even thought that far ahead. "No plans. I'll probably spend it going to soccer practice with the boys."

I can't believe I'm turning eighteen and have to spend the day with the U8 and U10 Evanston soccer teams.

"I wish I was going to be in town, but I'm visiting NYU with my parents. Is your mom at least coming home?"

"Nope. She has a conference in San Antonio that weekend."

"And?" Maddie's eyebrows lift.

"She was going to try to fly out early Sunday morning, spend a few hours with me, and then go back in the late afternoon to make some evening event. But I told her not to bother."

"Of course you did," Maddie mutters.

I pretend I don't hear her.

"Well, I have two weeks to figure it out."

Dov skirts around us as he heads to the exit. I must have let out a pent-up growl because Maddie turns to face me.

"I don't get you guys. I've never seen a casual friendship so fraught with anxiety and tension."

I scowl and pretend to look through my school bag. But I can't help myself, and I watch Dov through the window, walking across the grass toward the parking lot.

I push myself off my locker and open it to retrieve my phone. I shove it back into my pocket and make my way outside, jamming my earbuds in and blasting music. It isn't until I get to my car that I let my annoyance take hold. Why do I have to be responsible for the kids all the time? Why can't Maddie be a little more flexible?

I kick my tire. I glance over to where Maddie usually parks, but she's gone. I kick the tire again and wish I could just lie down on the pavement and have a tantrum. "Shit," I yell into the trees. "Shit, shit, shit."

When a hand lands on my shoulder, I spin around in fright.

Except it's Dov. Which is just great. "What?" I growl, the anger in my voice barely disguised. I yank the earbuds out of my ears.

Dov takes a step back, his hands up. "I just asked if you were okay, but you didn't hear me so I . . ." He mimics tapping my shoulder.

I lean back against the car and cover my face with my hands, the faint pressure of my fingertips on my eyelids begging the headache to go away.

I drop my hands. "My plans just got screwed up. I have to go home and take care of my brothers."

I cringe as I think of Dov's words the other day, and my stomach plunges. The difference is that he was complaining about his plans getting messed up on the anniversary of his brother's death, and I'm complaining because I actually have to spend time with my brothers.

I hope he doesn't also hear the echo.

"Oh, okay," he says and starts to move away.

Again.

I suck in a deep breath, trying to calm my heart. I should apologize for the poem, for the discussion that ensued. I should apologize for being irritated that I have to take care of my brothers when his brother is dead. I should . . .

I'm tired of apologizing. Maybe Scott had the right idea, going off to college without any commitments holding him back.

Maybe Mrs. Schneider is right. Maybe next year I need to be someplace completely different, someplace where I can just be Lucy Green.

I'm about to swing my car door open when Dov surprises me, turning around and staring at me intently.

"I'm sorry for the way I reacted in class," he says. "While I might be going through my own crap, I need . . ." He stares up at the sky, and I'm not sure if it's a language thing or something that's difficult for him to put into words. But I don't want to step in. "I need to be better."

"OK," I whisper, like I'm stuck in some sort of alternate universe.

Then Dov turns and strolls toward a bright green Volkswagen at the end of the row of cars.

NINE

· · · · · · ·

wake up slowly on my birthday. For mid-October in Chicago, it's unseasonably bright and beautiful. It's one of my favorite times of the year in the Midwest; all the trees are at the height of their glory. From downstairs comes the sounds of dishes clanging, the juicer running, Sam and Gabe yelping.

I stretch out on the bed, sighing happily at the dozens of pages taped to my pale green walls.

The latest is "A Man in His Life," an Israeli poem Dov brought to class the day after he'd walked out. He was calm and friendly that morning, and the fact that he'd brought an Israeli poem felt a little like an apology. The poem, a response to Ecclesiastes, suggested that in reality, there isn't time for separate seasons, that man does not in fact have seasons enough for every purpose. Dov recited quietly,

A man needs to love and to hate at the same moment
to laugh and cry with the same eyes,
with the same hands to throw stones and to gather them,

to make love in war and war in love.
And to hate and forgive and remember and forget,
to arrange and confuse, to eat and to digest
what history
takes years and years to do.
A man doesn't have time.

I stared at him in silence when he finished reading the poem, his eyes trained on the sheet of paper carefully folded in half.

"Can you read that to me in Hebrew?"

"*B'kef,*" he'd replied, as if he wasn't surprised at all by my request. He read it slowly, ignoring the bell that indicated the end of class.

Since then, our poetry choices have intensified. The next class I came back with an e. e. cummings poem about heartbreak, and he returned with another Amichai poem, this time about the air of Jerusalem being saturated with poems.

And suddenly, every day at school is reduced to those last ten minutes of Mrs. Schneider's class.

Lying in bed now, listening to the faint rustling of the pages when a hint of wind moves through the room, I want to add more. Maddie dropped off two books of poetry for my birthday before she left for New York: a Mary Oliver collection and a thin volume of a Canadian poet, Michael Ondaatje. I'm about to reach for the latter when I hear my name from downstairs.

"I don't think Lucy's awake yet," Gabe says.

"I heard her moving around," Sam says.

I grin. Even Sam with his amazing hearing couldn't have been able to tell that I reached for a book.

"You couldn't have heard her. I didn't hear anything," Gabe says.

"I did too!" Sam's voice is defensive, and I can hear the beginnings of an argument.

Which means as much as I want to stay in bed longer, it isn't worth it.

The smell reaches me before I hit the kitchen. I laugh when I see Dad in a chef's hat flipping pancakes onto four plates. After I get tackled in birthday hugs by both Gabe and Sam, they quickly return to arguing over the sports section at the table.

"Nice hat," I say when I finally reach Dad.

I grab a pancake off a plate, roll it up, and take a big bite.

"Happy birthday." He smiles and kisses the side of my head. "I bargained with your brothers. If they agreed to eat pancakes, I'd wear the crazy hat."

"You shouldn't have to bribe kids to eat pancakes."

He shrugs. "Well, they have eggs and milk so that's better than the dry cereal they usually eat. Maybe it'll get them through Sunday school."

I reach for the pancake he flipped onto my plate, narrowly missing the spatula that comes down after it.

"Eat at the table," he says, pointing the spatula to the breakfast nook. "Be a good influence on your brothers. They look up to you."

"Ha!" I take the plate and head over to the table. "Aren't I always a good influence?" I ask Sam as I nudge him over to make room.

"Ha!" he answers back. Point taken.

After pretending to let Sam pour his own syrup while simultaneously ensuring his pancakes don't drown, I scarf down the food on my plate, and then put my dish in the sink.

"Mom said she's sorry again that she missed seeing you today." Dad grabs the last pancake from the frying pan and eats it with his fingers, shrugging when he catches my smirk. "She called earlier, but I told her you were still sleeping. She'll try you later in the day, and she says we'll have another celebration next weekend when she comes into town."

I'll believe it when I see it, I want to say, because lately Mom's regular weekend trips home aren't as regular as she promised they would be. Just like her nightly phone calls are no longer all that nightly.

The truth is, the whole arrangement is pretty much falling apart. Technically, Mom is supposed to be home from Thursday night to Sunday night, but lately meetings and events are lengthening her time in California and encroaching on what is supposed to be our time.

But instead of saying something that would likely be overheard by the big ears sitting at the kitchen table, I focus on my brothers, their little bodies crowding around the newspaper. Gabe has his arm around Sam and is showing him the standings, which Sam insists he can read just fine. But instead of contradicting him, Gabe listens patiently as Sam sounds them out, often reading them by recognizing the team logos.

For a moment I can't help but think of Yuval and Dov, can't help wondering what moments like these they shared together, what memories Dov turns to now that Yuval is gone.

"Do you want me to clear the table?" I ask Dad, trying to swallow the lump in my throat.

"You're such a trouper," he teases, pulling me into a hug and rubbing my hair. "So lucky to have a fabulous daughter, I am," he adds in his Yoda voice.

I snicker, hiding my smile in his worn flannel shirt. "Daaad, stop with the Yoda voice, you aren't good at it."

"Yes you are," Gabe yells, running up to the counter. "Talk to me in a Yoda voice. Please!"

"So grateful I would be when the young Jedi to the sink his plate he brings," Dad says, winking at me. Gabe rushes back to the table, grabs his plate, and runs to the counter.

"Now me," Sam says, jumping up from the table. "My turn! My turn!"

By the time the kids are ready to leave for Sunday school, I've amassed a great stash of gifts, including a still-wet, homemade paper house, hand-cut and glued by Sam; a Popsicle-stick picture frame from Gabe (it left red marker stains on my hands, but he didn't notice); a gift card from my grandmother; and a silver necklace and dark blue cashmere sweater from my parents.

Best of all, I'd won three back-to-back games of baseball card Guess Who—a game I'd created out of desperation earlier in the year when Gabe wanted to play with his baseball cards and Sam wanted to play Guess Who. We use fifteen of the cards both kids have in their collection, and it's become an almost daily event. Given that I'm way behind on the ongoing tally, three wins definitely fed my competitive spirit.

"Do you know what you're doing today?" Dad asks as he gets the kids into the car.

"I'm not sure. I think I'll just walk around Evanston, maybe catch a movie. Hit Bookman's Alley."

"You're sounding so grown up already. Are you sure I don't need to plan a birthday party for you where you'll eat too much cake and wind up crying at the end?"

I scowl.

"Just be home by six for dinner, OK? We'll order out whatever you like."

"No problem," I promise as Sam yells out the window: "Don't touch the paper house too much because the bricks might fall off." I wave wildly as they leave the driveway, excited for the empty house and the possibility of a beautiful day.

By ten, I'm bored. I squeeze oranges for a glass of juice, try to relax on the porch with some magazines, but everything feels like it's the appetizer for the main event. Except, I have no main event planned.

I check my phone, scroll through the birthday messages on social media, still feeling restless. Until I spot one of the early messages.

> DOV: Happy birthday. Hope you're having a great day.
> I have a quick question for you. Call me when you
> wake up.

My stomach hollows out as I stare at his phone number in my inbox. It's probably about the poetry assignment. Or—

My hands are clammy as I click on the phone number he left. As the phone rings, I find myself holding my breath, half of me hoping that he doesn't pick up, the other desperate to figure out what he wants. I'm about to hang up when I hear his voice, groggy and thick with sleep.

"It's Lucy," I say hurriedly. "I'm sorry I woke you. I'm an idiot. I'll talk to you later."

"*'Eyn ba'aya*, Lucy," he says, clearing his throat. "It's not a problem. I wasn't asleep. I just haven't spoken to anyone yet today."

I glance at my phone: it's almost eleven. I can't imagine making it through that much of the day with no one to speak with.

"Happy birthday," he says to the pause I'd left open.

"Thanks," I stammer.

"Um, so I guess you saw my message," he says, his voice still craggy and awkward. I wonder if there's something about talking on the phone that's different from a language standpoint than talking in person. "I just . . . I mean, this is probably really dumb. But I overheard you and Maddie talking a couple of weeks ago about your birthday. And I'm sure that you now have plans. But I thought, if you didn't, that maybe you'd want to come with me on a little road trip. I mean, you probably have a lot you're doing today with your grandmother and your—"

"I don't." My words are calm compared with his words which seem to be tripping over each other to get out. And yet, based on how my body is humming with misplaced energy, I'm quite sure we're in the same place. My cheeks flush, and I don't know what to say. Does he want me to let him off the hook? But then why would he ask?

"Great," he says slowly. "I can be ready in about fifteen minutes? Would that work for you?"

"Perfectly." I grin widely enough I'm sure he can hear it in my voice.

And then I start panicking. Because what if I'm messing with the quiet rapport we'd finally gotten back to? What if he feels obligated because I helped him all those Sundays ago? What if the Dov who picks me up is sullen Dov and not the teasing Dov?

But fifteen minutes later, on the dot, Dov pulls up in the beat-up bright green Volkswagen Golf I'd spotted in the parking lot. He leans over and opens the door. Like me, he's wearing jeans, but he's paired it with a white T-shirt covered by a dark green checkered shirt, while I'm in a long-sleeve grey Henley with a cream fisherman's sweater around my waist. I hand him the coffee I'd made, and he grins.

It's friendly Dov.

"You didn't need to," he protests, taking a sip and then closing his eyes to revel in it.

"*B'kef*," I respond, and his grin turns wider.

"Nice," he says. I raise my eyebrows and settle into the car.

I could get use to that smile.

But then I shut the thought down.

Driving with Dov is an experience. His car is stick-shift, and I watch in awe as he takes the curves up Sheridan Road, downshifting instead of putting on the breaks, his movements fluid and exact. It's as if the car is an extension of his body.

And he's driving my favorite route.

"Where are we going?" I ask after about ten minutes of heading north. The weeks since the last time we'd been alone vanish as he drives.

"How much time do you have?"

I glance at my phone. "Six hours, or so," I say, but then frown. He hadn't signed up to entertain me all day. I'm about to amend my statement when he speaks.

"Perfect. There's a place I like to go but it's a ways away. I think you'll like it," he says. "Is that okay with you? Are you in the mood for a bit of a hike?"

A place he likes to go? That doesn't give me much to go on, but everything is already totally outside the realm of what I expected. "I'm up for anything."

I blush when I realize what that sounded like, but Dov doesn't seem to notice. Screw it. I lean back, bringing my knees up to my chest and stare out the window at the flashing red, yellow, brown, and orange leaves that decorate the trees. Through the open window, I smell dirt and mulch, the leaves on the ground now wet with last night's rain, a thick scent that makes me think of fireplaces and hiking, my favorite parts of fall.

For a while I don't pay attention to the throbbing music, letting the waves of the unfamiliar sounds pour over me. It's unlike anything I've heard before. At first the words sound Arabic, but then gradually more guttural and then something else entirely. I glance over at Dov in confusion, but he's looking out the windshield, his long fingers tapping out the beat on his knee. Just then another voice joins in, this time in what sounds much more like Hebrew. My lack of Hebrew means most of the time I can barely tell what's Hebrew and what's something else, and part of me is afraid to confess my ignorance by asking. As we follow Sheridan Road's twists and turns, I can feel the effect of the music on my body, feel myself loosening, the different voices and unfamiliar languages oddly intoxicating. For once, it's nice not to be trying to decode lyrics.

After a few songs, Dov reaches over and pauses the music. I miss the sound immediately.

"Why did you turn it off?" I ask.

Dov shrugs, eyes still on the road. "I felt bad. It's probably not what you're used to listening to."

I laugh. "True. I listen to folk mostly. My dad teases me that they're all depressing songs about breakups and lost loves, but I think he's secretly glad that it doesn't hurt his ears." I stare off for a moment, silent strains of my favorite songs filling my head. "But I like songs with powerful lyrics, words that startle you."

"I see that," he says. "You get really excited when you talk about the poems in class."

Wait, what? The tinge of embarrassment I felt before has now been transformed into full-blown mortification.

"Not in a bad way," Dov says quickly. "You seem to care about the poems a lot, to think about them. You work hard to find the right one. And when you comment in class, I can tell you don't just say something so that Mrs. Schneider will be impressed. It's important to you."

I can't look at him so I stare intently at the road. "I like words," I say, avoiding the topic of why I'm trying so hard to always find the right words, the right poems.

"Sometimes I think I understand things about myself more when I hear other people's words. I'll hear a song, or a poem, or read a story and it will help me understand something in a way I couldn't have before."

And then, before I know it, I'm describing my bedroom walls, the poems and quotes I've placed around my bed, the wall I've designated for our back and forth poetry conversations. "Now you must think I'm crazy."

"No," Dov says. "I don't. Do you think you want to study literature in university?"

I pause as I let the question settle. While I'd finally informed my mom that I wasn't going to apply early to

Northwestern, the fact that I now had hundreds of potential colleges to choose from, in addition to dozens of potential programs, was so overwhelming that I'd pushed it from my thoughts for a bit.

"I'm not sure. I love the class, but I don't have any idea what I want to study. My mom wants me to study bioethics, like her. She thinks that the fact that I'm good at sciences and humanities means that it would be a good combination for me."

"Is that what *you* want?"

I've known most of the other fifty-four people in my graduating class for more than a dozen years, and apart from Maddie, I've never talked to any of them about this. I never talked to Scott about it. What was making me suddenly open up to this boy I'd only known a few weeks?

"I like studying ethics," I say, trying to make sure that as the words come out, they're true. "But I'm not sure it's what I want to study. And I have to fill out all these college essays, bare my soul to them in hopes they'll want me, and . . . I'm not sure I know what I want."

Is it poetry? Or is something else entirely?

The car is quiet, and I wonder how the hell I'm going to figure that out.

"What were we listening to just now? Was it Hebrew?" I distract myself from the faint panic that pulses through me at the thought of all those possibilities.

"Hebrew and Amharic, the language of Ethiopia. Idan Raichel's music is unusual but very powerful."

"It felt like a mixture of different cultures and languages. Like they're all coming together."

Dov nods. "It does, doesn't it?"

"Can we listen to it again?" I ask, and he flips them back on. I want to close my eyes, but that feels too intimate, so I stare at what's likely to be one of the last weekends the trees will remain this colorful before the leaves fall. Dov turns the music louder, and the strange sounds fill the car.

"What's he saying?"

Dov doesn't answer for a long moment. "How about I tell you another time?"

I turn to him and he smiles wryly. I think about protesting, but then I realize what he'd said. There'd be another time.

"Deal."

TEN

. . . . . .

Apart from a quick stop at a roadside stand for fresh doughnuts and apple cider (we both agree it's likely to be far superior to animal crackers and apple juice), we drive straight out of Chicago toward Wisconsin. After another hour, Dov pulls off the road into a deserted parking lot that abuts what appears to be a small forest. There are a few picnic tables along the side of the parking lot but no sign of other people.

"Ominous," I mutter as he turns off the car. "Usually in movies, this is the place where the young couple discovers the dead body." I grimace.

Did I really say "young couple"?

Dov grins and pulls out the grease-stained doughnut bag and the jug of cider. "Picnic table or grass?"

"Grass," I say immediately, and he nods, walking toward the tree line. "You sure you know where we're going?"

He doesn't answer.

Five minutes later, we're in a little clearing, protected on all sides by thick trees. Even though we're right up against the highway, the trees cushion the noise, and it's silent but for the sound of the leaves in the wind and a few birds tweeting.

For half a second, I debate the wisdom of going off into the middle of a deserted forest clearing with a boy I barely know. But I don't feel scared. There's something about Dov's presence, the way he holds himself, that makes me feel safe.

But that momentary feeling of happiness is replaced by the reminder that if Scott were here, I wouldn't have felt comfortable at all. I'd have been wary. I'd be worrying about the message I was sending by going to a deserted place with him. I can totally picture him grabbing a blanket and assuring me that this was a perfect "private" location.

The pit in my stomach grows. I can't believe I thought I was in love with a guy who made me feel like I needed to rationalize why I didn't want to sleep with him.

I can't believe how many times I lied about having my period. How many times I decided it was just easier to let him—

"Lucy?" Dov sits in the center of the clearing, the bag of doughnuts and the jug of cider beside him. The ground is covered by a dense carpet of dry leaves and warmed by a patch of sunlight. "Is this spot okay? We can look for another if you want."

I'm standing still with my fists clenched. I want to go back in time and tell my past self that Scott's needs aren't more important than mine. That nobody has ever died of blue balls. That if he needed to, he could always take care of the issue himself. How did I not see that? I force my feet to move. "This is good," I whisper.

"Are you okay?" he asks.

I nod. I don't want to say any of these words out loud. I don't want to talk about him, I don't want to think about him anymore. "This is perfect," I say instead, because it's honest.

Dov rips open the bag. "Do I need to sing 'Happy Birthday'?"

I shake my head as I take a seat beside him. As I grab the doughnut, my fingertips slip along his hand, and I will my body not to shiver.

It doesn't work.

Dov polishes off his doughnut in three bites. "Oh my god, that was good."

"In this area, you *always* stop for stands promising fresh doughnuts and cider," I mumble, my mouth full of sticky dough.

He licks the sugar from his fingers one by one and looks back in the bag. "I'm glad we got enough for seconds."

We quickly polish them off, taking turns scraping the glaze from the sides of the bag and taking swigs from the jug of cider. By the time we finish, I can feel all the sugar coursing through my bloodstream, and it's much easier to push Scott and his crap out of my head.

"I've been wondering about something," Dov interrupts my thoughts. "You said you gave up ballet because you weren't good enough to go professional. But when you talk about it, your whole face brightens. Like when you get really excited about a poem you're reading. And there's this studio, a block from my house, and I constantly see girls running in and out of it, and it made me wonder why you couldn't have kept dancing, even if you couldn't do it professionally. Because they seem like our age, and they can't all be going professional . . ."

I stare at him, mouth open. He'd been thinking about our conversation? Dov picks up a leaf and begins folding it in squares.

"It's funny," I start, "Maple Street Dance—the one near your house—*was* my studio. I started going there the year it opened, a month before my fifth birthday."

"You miss it." Dov stares at me intently.

"I try not to think about it," I admit. "But my body misses it. I miss being able to feel my muscles working. I miss feeling strong. I miss the way the music felt inside my body."

"So why did you quit?"

I play with the lie, prepare to defend my stance, but then I tell the truth. "Last summer," I start, staring at the back of my hands. "I started dating someone. A guy I'd known forever." A guy I'd been in love with forever.

I don't let myself look up because I know that if I do, I'll lose my confidence. "He was a senior last year, and big on the school paper and the debate team, and also the basketball team."

Dov snorts, and I want to stop time and hug him for that tiny sound, but instead I barrel on. "It was hard to find time to be together. And since I knew I wasn't going to become a professional dancer . . ."

"You gave it up for him." His words are quiet.

"It was also more than that. I wound up joining many of the activities that he'd been in. The paper. The debate team. It was a way to spend time together."

"The basketball team?" Dov chuckles.

"Not basketball," I say, "though I did go to every game. I lost myself in Scott, I see it now with perfectly clarity. I gave up me to fit better into his life."

There's silence, and I wonder if I ruined our day.

"So why don't you go back?"

I fill my lungs with air. I slowly exhale. "Even though we aren't together anymore, with my mom out of town so much and college applications, there are a limited number of hours in a day . . ."

I pick up a few leaves, stacking them in my lap by size, the smallest on top. Is it so complicated? I think back to the conversation with Maddie about college and what she said about how I'm always making the decisions that work best for others.

A silence falls between us, and I examine my carefully ordered pile. There's clearly something wrong with me if I feel the need to organize the forest floor. Dov leans back until he's lying in the leaves. I swivel and lie back beside him, the sun warm against my face.

After a while, I roll over to face him. "Do you like being here?"

"I like this." Dov spreads his arms across the ground, like he's making a snow angel in the leaves.

I laugh. "I mean here in Chicago."

"There's a lot I like here." He pauses and brings his arms overhead. Then he covers his face. "A lot I really like. But it's not home. And not only is it not home, but it's an escape from home. I don't know if that makes sense."

The word *home* sticks out to me, like an unexpected burr in a field of wildflowers. My mom differentiates between her Berkeley and her Evanston home. Is Evanston home for me? Or would I be at home in Berkeley if we'd all moved there like my mom?

"I'm not sure." I want to ask more, but I don't know how far I can go.

"I left a lot unresolved when we came here," he continues. "Regular stuff, like getting ready for my own army service and figuring that all out. But also personal stuff."

I push away the question of what personal stuff means, whether it means a girlfriend, and why that thought bothers me the way it does.

Dov falls silent, the only sound now the rustling of the trees as the wind blows. A few leaves rain down on us, some spinning, others gliding gracefully with the wind.

"The decision to come here wasn't handled particularly well." His voice turns harsh. "I wasn't consulted at all. It was announced to me at the last possible minute. I basically had a day to pack everything and let people know."

I can't imagine that. When Mom decided to go out to California it was after months of negotiating and weeks of family meetings. We'd talked for so long about how it could work that by the end I just wanted it to happen already. I can't picture not being part of a decision that big.

"Why did they do that?"

Dov sighs, rolling onto his side to face me. He props his head up on his elbow, and I'm amazed by how intimate this conversation feels, the two of us talking quietly in this empty space. I stare at his eyes, so close, all those shades of blue.

"They did what they thought was best. Nobody was handling Yuval's death well. We were all pretty much flailing. But I guess they saw me as being 'dangerously out of control' and needed to figure out a way to get me out of a bad situation."

My mouth suddenly goes dry. "Were they right? Were you out of control?"

Dov bites his lip, sliding it in his now familiar way back and forth between his teeth. I expect him to scoot backward, to change the subject, to shut down this line of questioning. His eyes dart around. But instead of doing any of those things, he nods, almost imperceptibly. "It was a bad time. Between what I was saying and what I was doing, I wasn't convincing anyone I had my best interests in mind. So, when my mom got the offer to come to Chicago for the year, she jumped on it."

A faint movement in the distance diverts our gaze to the tree line, and we stare as a rabbit hops across the clearing, pausing fifteen feet from us and then hopping into the next set of bushes.

"That's something you'd never see in Israel," Dov laughs, the mood breaking. "See, it's all worth it for this."

The rabbit? I want to ask. Or the two of us lying in the woods?

"Well, I'm glad you're here, even if it wasn't a good way to get here."

The surprise on Dov's face makes me want to take it back, until he smiles gratefully.

"Me too." He rolls back onto his back, arms extended to both sides, his right hand so close to me I could touch it with no effort at all.

I don't.

"You mentioned needing to prepare for the army. But now that you're here, do you still need to go?" I sit up, the effort of not taking his hand is too great.

He moves such that we're now facing one another again. "Everyone goes to the army in Israel."

"But you're here," I offer.

"But I'm Israeli. It's my responsibility."

I think about our argument in class about the war poem. The Auden poem. The idea of Dov being sent home in a box—

"Couldn't you stay here and go to college? Then you wouldn't need to go to the army."

"Lucy," he says, moving slightly closer to me. For a moment I think he's going to touch me, but then the moment passes. "While technically I could shirk my responsibility, I would never, ever do that." His words are emphatic, and they take me by surprise.

I want to call him on it. *The whole system won't collapse because you aren't there*, I want to say. But my upset feels irrational, misplaced, so I purse my lips.

"Do you want to go?" I ask finally.

Dov shifts his gaze back to the trees, squinting his eyes for a moment. "Let's walk," he says, standing up and offering me a hand. His hand in mine is smooth and dry, strong. My stomach drops when he lets go and starts gathering our garbage into his pack.

We walk along the trail in silence, and I wonder if he's going to answer the question. Enormous trees shield us from the sun and all at once I'm chilly. I stop for a moment to put my sweater back on.

"I'm not sure I know anymore," he surprises me by continuing. "When I was young, I was terrified of going to the army. But later, it was all anyone talked about. And while it was still scary, it felt much more like an adventure, getting to carry a gun and run around the country on training missions. So I talked the talk but never really thought about what it would mean to actually do it.

"It wasn't until Yuval was killed that it became real to me. Suddenly, everything was about going to the army, getting into an elite unit, being at the top, proving myself to my parents. But also . . ." He stops walking and stares up at the sky which is barely visible through the treetops. "It was part of this whole pattern of being out of control. Suddenly, the danger wasn't scary, it was enticing, like maybe that wouldn't be the worst way to go . . ."

My chest hurts, and I realize I'm no longer breathing. I take in a deep gulp of air.

"Do you still feel like that?" My voice squeaks.

"No," he says simply and starts to walk again. "Not since I got here. I probably still overdo it at the gym or push too hard when I'm running. But nothing . . . like before. But that doesn't mean I don't plan to serve. I'm going to work like hell this year to be good enough to get into a top unit, just like my brother did. And then during the summer, I'll begin my three-year commitment."

I exhale and follow him, wondering how everything had suddenly changed without my knowing it.

We make casual conversation as we hike, ignoring the big topics—though we carry them with us like extra packs. As we finally make our way back to the car, it begins to rain. For the first few minutes, we're sheltered by the trees, but gradually the rain turns heavier. My hair becomes plastered to my head and my sweater and jeans are drenched. Dov doesn't seem as bothered by it, tucking his hair behind his ears so it doesn't drip into his eyes, but he keeps watching the skies.

My boots slide in the mud, and he grabs my arm before I start to fall.

"I'm sorry," he says, his hand still holding mine.

I'm not sure what he's apologizing for: his hand holding mine, or the rain?

"You can't control the weather," I say, my teeth starting to chatter.

"Shit, you're really getting chilled," he mutters and puts his arm around my shoulder, pulling me closer, as if he can protect me from the elements that way. He's doing it to keep me warm, I tell myself. Getting attached to Dov is a bad idea. He's leaving. He runs hot and cold.

And I'm not getting involved with anyone this year. So this is just a friend trying to keep another friend warm when they're stuck in the rain.

Except, that's not what it feels like.

It feels like comfort. It feels intimate. It feels right.

"I'm really sorry. I should have been watching better. I should have seen the clouds gathering and got you back sooner," he mutters, and I'm not entirely sure who he's talking to. I wouldn't have traded the past hours for anything, I want to tell him, but once again, I keep quiet. I focus instead on the press of his arm around me.

As soon as we make it to the car, Dov opens the passenger door and pushes me inside, cranking up the heat until the windows fog. We both strip off our heavy sweaters, and Dov flings them onto the backseat.

"You okay?" he asks, his forehead creased as my teeth continue to chatter. I nod. "I might have a blanket in the trunk."

"No," I croak. "I'm . . . fine." He takes my hands in his, rubbing them together. I don't realize how cold mine are until they're up against the warmth of his. "How are your hands so warm?" I whisper, and he shrugs. For a few moments, we sit silently in the car. I close my eyes, concentrating on the feeling of my hands in his, the heat blasting through the vents.

"Lucy," he says gently. "What time do you have to be home?"

"Six." I shiver. Even with all the heat, even with his hands, my shirt's too wet. I should have squeezed it out before I got into the car, but now I can't imagine expending the energy. "What time is it?"

"It's after five, and we have at least two hours of driving," Dov says. "And I'm going to need to turn off the heat to defog the windows, but you're not warm enough yet."

I open my eyes and see his face, so close to mine. When had that faint shadow of a beard shown up?

I want to kiss him.

"I'll call my dad. It'll be okay," I whisper.

"I'm going to see what I can find in the trunk," he says, hopping out of the car before I have a chance to object to him getting any more wet than he already is.

I send my dad a quick text as Dov slides back into the car.

"I found a sweatshirt." Dov holds out a dark green hoodie with a yellow Hebrew insignia on it. "Take off your shirt. It's keeping you from getting warm."

He hands me the sweatshirt and turns his back immediately. I rip off my shirt, but then pause before putting it back on. I stay like that for a few seconds, topless except for my bra, the heat of the radiators hitting my body, warming me.

"Are you—" Dov asks, his face still pointed to his window.

"No," I say. "I'm just warming up a bit."

"Great. Tell me when I can turn around."

Turn around, I want to say, but instead I concentrate on the warmth that's starting to permeate my torso.

After a minute, I pull the sweatshirt over my head and the hood over my wet hair. Dov turns around and we start driving back to the city to the sounds of melodic Israeli music.

Dov gently touches my arm, and I wake to find us in my driveway. The clock on the dashboard reads 7:15, and I feel a pang of guilt. The lights blaze from every window in the house, and my dad is standing in the doorway. I avert my eyes, not ready to let go of today.

"Thank you," I say simply.

"What, for getting you drenched and possibly sick?"

"It was a great day." I smile. "If anything, you're the one who would have been safe inside if I hadn't called—"

"Thank you for calling."

"I should go." I put my hand on the door. I have so many questions. What is this? What just happened between us? Why did you want to spend the day with me? Do you feel the same way about me?

"Wait, I have something for you."

I laugh, one of those odd laughs that sounds more like a choke. "What? I already have this awesome Israeli sweatshirt."

Dov smiles. "Actually, I'll need it back. It . . . it was my brother's."

My stomach drops as I smooth my hand over the Hebrew insignia. I don't know what it says, but even if it isn't going to be mine, it means so much that he's even letting me wear it. Dov reaches to the dashboard and pops out a CD. "I don't have a present for your birthday, so—"

"You didn't need to," I blush. "You've already given me this day . . ."

"Please, I'd love for you to have it. I can make myself another one. It's what we listened to in the car, and some more that you didn't hear but I think you'll like. The only thing I ask is don't go looking up the words. I know you like strong lyrics and these songs definitely have them, but just enjoy the sounds for a while first?"

I smile uncertainly. Dov reaches back and hands me my soaking wet shirt and sweater.

"Thank you," I say again. "For everything."

A small grin plays on Dov's lips and I tear myself away, leaving the warmth of his car and heading to the house.

ELEVEN

. . . .

Dinner is not quite the celebration any of us had planned. Dad accepted my excuses and apologies, but Sam and Gabe make it clear that there'd been chaos.

"Everyone was super worried. Dad was calling you, and you didn't answer," Gabe says as he watches me shovel the room temperature Chinese food into my mouth. "Dad had to call Mom, and I heard him get really mad—"

Shit.

"That's enough, Gabe. Lucy didn't do it intentionally. It's all fine. Let's enjoy this birthday dinner."

But there's little enjoyment happening. Dad appears exhausted, and I feel badly that I left him with the boys all day with no relief.

And then I feel like an idiot. It's my damn birthday. It's bad enough I'm always making sure to be home when dad needs me to be. Should I feel badly that I didn't offer to babysit on my birthday?

It isn't until the end of the meal, after Sam and Gabe fight over which corner piece of cake has the most icing and Dad puts them to bed, that I have to deal with the consequences in the form of a phone call from my mom.

"Happy birthday," she says, her voice quiet over the din of other people talking. I imagine her excusing herself from whatever dinner party she's at to go talk to her daughter.

I just turned eighteen! I want to shout. I should get more than a quiet "Happy Birthday"!

"Thank you," I say, swallowing my anger.

"So what happened?"

I let the question hang in the air.

"Are you asking how I spent my eighteenth birthday?" I finally say.

"Well, let's start with that." There's no warmth in her voice. *You messed up*, I hear in her tone.

"A friend took me out for a drive, and then we had a picnic. We hiked and got caught in the rain and then we drove back home."

The words I use don't begin to describe what it was like. The doughnuts and cider, the walk through the trees, the look on Dov's face when he asked me why I don't dance anymore, the pit in my stomach when he told me he was leaving to join the army at the end of the year, the desire coursing through my veins when he held my hand, when I sat in his car, heat blowing on my wet skin. How it was the first time in months that I'd wanted someone to touch me.

"Which friend?"

"Dov."

"The new boy in your class?" she asks, "Where did he take you?"

She makes it sound dirty.

"I don't know the name of it." I'm turning petulant and

I don't even care. This whole thing is bullshit. "It was in Wisconsin."

"You went by yourself," she pauses, "to Wisconsin with a boy we've never met, that we don't know anything about, and you didn't even bother telling your father where you were going?"

I want to unleash my own anger, to throw it back at her. *I'm eighteen, dammit*, I want to say, *I'm an adult now*. I want to say that she might have known more about me and my life if she wasn't halfway across the country. But it's my birthday and I'm too damn tired.

"I'm sorry I worried everyone. I had no idea we'd be gone for so long. Dov is a friend, nothing more. He was a perfect gentleman the whole time. And if it helps, Amy has spoken with him. So he isn't a complete stranger. Now I want to go to sleep. Goodnight Mom, I love you."

I'm about to hang up the phone when she speaks again.

"I love you, Lucy. And I'm sorry this is all happening over the phone. It's just . . . you don't know how scary it is when nobody can get in touch with your daughter, and you're 2,000 miles away. I wasn't prepared for that."

There's so much I want to say, but I don't. "I'm sorry," I say. "I'll see you next weekend." And I hang up. Because if she's going to tell me that she isn't coming, I'll probably lose it.

"She was totally fucking out of line," Maddie insists, this time a little too loudly, judging from the number of people who turn around.

She opens her mouth again, and I give her a warning look as Mrs. Schneider walks past us.

"I was just going to say that I'm glad you had a good birthday celebration with Dov, despite your mom's jerkiness." She grins, her arm around my shoulder as we take our spot on the stairs for lunch. "And that I'm sorry I couldn't hang out with you yesterday. But it sounds like you had a really dreamy day." She wiggles her eyebrows in a way that is a hundred times more comical than suggestive.

"I'm not after Dov," I say, my voice lowering when I speak his name. I don't want to take the chance that someone can hear us. "He's going back to Israel next year. What's the point?"

Maddie's grimace is the same one she makes when Sam refuses to eat ice cream. "The point is, have a little fun this year. You don't need to marry the guy."

How is it possible that this conversation is pulling my stomach into knots even tighter than last night's talk with my mom?

"Maddie, I don't want to get hurt again," I whisper, staring at my peanut butter sandwich. "And I have no idea if Dov even likes me. He's so hot and cold. But either way? I think I should just hold off dating until I'm at college next year. This year should just be about having a great senior year."

She opens her mouth and closes it again, and then says: "OK. But, can I just say one more thing?"

I sigh and roll my eyes. "Fine."

"Can you just think about coming back to the studio? You'll get the workouts you need, and you'll be doing something you love instead of wasting time at a gym."

The gym I'd never even looked into. "I'll think about it. It's going to be hard because I still can't take enough classes to be in the company. I have to be home with my brothers."

"Talk to Ginger. You don't know unless you try." Maddie takes out two containers of sushi and places one in front of me.

"You don't need to share your lunch," I say meekly, barely able to tear my eyes away from a perfectly made inside-out roll.

"I felt guilty that I wasn't there for you on your birthday," she says, breaking a second pair of chopsticks in two and handing them to me.

"It's fine," I say. I don't want to tell her that I can't imagine anything being better than yesterday.

"Are you going to be okay in your poetry class today?"

Crinkling my nose, I shrug. Would it be like after our first talk, when Dov went back to stony silence? Or would it be back to what things were like on Friday, before the intensity of my birthday?

The reality is, it's neither of those. It's awkward, and our conversation is stilted. But underneath it all, there's a fine web that links us. The space between us is warm and alive, filled with the memory of his hand holding mine, our quiet picnic in the Shakespeare Garden, and my body falling into his on the first day we met.

When he turns to me after Mrs. Schneider dismisses us to work in our pairs, his eyes hold mine a moment too long. His look tells me he remembers all those things too.

"Hey." His smile is tentative.

"Hey."

I want to say something . . . profound. Something—

"I brought another Amichai poem. It doesn't really connect to what you brought last week, but . . ." He shrugs.

"I'm sure we can figure out a connection." I press my lips together tightly to keep from smiling.

He reads the poem in his soft lilting voice. The words describe what it feels like to live in a land filled with tourists, where monuments and museums and ancient structures are points of reference rather than real people living real lives, buying fruits and vegetables for their family.

"Is that how you feel?" I ask, interrupting what is supposed to be his chance to explain the imagery, the technical aspects of the poem.

Dov stares at the paper in his hands. His back is rounded, and he lifts his left shoulder and lets it fall.

"Sometimes," he mumbles. "It's hard to live in a city like Jerusalem that's so important to so many people. Because while it has all these holy sites and politically charged spaces, it also has the park I played in where I learned to use the monkey bars. And the pubs and bars I knew would serve me despite being underage. It has the pole on the corner of Kovshei Katamon and Halamed Hey that I ran into when I first tried to drive by myself and took the corner too quickly . . ."

And for the next ten minutes, he paints pictures of the sacred and the ordinary side by side on the streets of his city.

And I say nothing, because that's his home. There. Not here.

That afternoon, I drive out of my way to pass the Maple Street Dance Studio. As the large windows come into view, I try to catch a glimpse inside. I watch through my rearview mirror as a group of almost identical girls, their hair pulled back into neat buns, walk through the door like it's their home. That used to be me. But that doesn't mean I should go back, I tell myself as I drive home. It was hard enough to quit the first time.

That night, I pull out all my ballet gear: leotards and tights, thin warm up skirts and my outlandish collection of leg warmers. I shove them all in a large paper bag, and then place piles and piles of ballet slippers on top—everything except my first pair and my pointe shoes. Those remain in their own closed box, ribbons carefully wrapped in the proper position, the satin smooth and familiar. Those I can't part with. Ginger has a special supply of ballet equipment for students who can't afford the basics, and I'm certain my stuff will be put to good use.

Not surprisingly, the next day it takes less than ten minutes before I'm wearing my leotard and tights, my feet in pink leather slippers. Ginger flings her arms around my neck as I enter, and when she insists I join the lower-advanced class that's about to begin, I can't say no. The class is a few levels below what I'd been in, but given how long it had been since I'd danced, I didn't have a problem easing back into it. Even if just for one class.

"I only came to donate my stuff." My words are swallowed by the empty room.

Ginger moves past me, flicking on the lights in the small studio where the advanced students meet at night. I see myself in the mirrored wall before me. The girl I see is nothing like the one I used to be. Her eyes are uncertain, her shoulders rounded slightly. Her hair is pinned in the familiar low bun, but her neck has lost its familiar length. Her confidence is gone.

How did that happen?

"Lucy?" Ginger is at the far end of the room, pulling down the shades, the whoosh of movement causes the dust that coats the hardwood floor to dance in the light.

To dance. In the light.

I won't be scared of this room, I tell myself.

I take an uncertain step forward, reveling in the familiar squeak of the floor, and then another, and another, until I'm standing in the middle of the room. Until I can see myself reflected over and over again in the clash of the various mirrors.

Ginger flicks some switches and fills the room with the sounds of a piano.

"Finally replaced the old stereo?" I tease, my voice scratchy.

Ginger grins over her shoulder as she fiddles with the dials, slowing the music down almost imperceptibly. "New toy I picked up at the end of the summer. No more fiddling with fraying cables and hoping the music won't cut out. I can program this baby for an entire barre work, pick my tempo and I'm set."

A couple of girls skip into the studio in identical black leotards and pale tights. They'd been a few years behind me, never in the same class but always in the dressing rooms at the same time. Maybe Iris and Lynn? I can't remember and, despite a flicker of recognition in their eyes, they barely give me a glance before finding their places at the barre and starting to stretch. Their conversation doesn't falter as they put one foot up on the barre, their torsos lengthening as they bend backwards and then forwards.

Three other girls join them, two who smile and wave at me, and another who doesn't look familiar. Then I notice a snide look from Iris. That's one thing I don't miss.

"Are you sure it's okay to crash your class?" I ask as another couple of students find their places along the barre.

Ginger smiles and motions to a space at the front of the room. "It's a pleasure to have you back in class."

"This is probably a one-time thing."

Ginger's mouth turns up slightly.

I stare at my scuffed ballet slippers as I make my way to the spot. "Maybe I should be in the back. I don't think I've put my ballet shoes on since I left."

"Well, it's a good thing they fit then," she says and claps her hands. "Okay girls, let's get started. Pliés . . ."

I stop worrying as Ginger runs through the routine, the instructions so familiar I could have given them myself. As I rest my left hand gently on the barre, I pull my shoulders back, stretching my neck. The barre is smooth and cool, but I know it will warm in minutes with the faint pressure from my fingertips. I caress it gently, surprised by how much I missed the familiar sensation.

"Ready? And, one and two and three and four . . ." Ginger intones, and I sink into the bend, my knees remembering their position over my feet. By the time we reach the *grand battements*, it feels like no time has passed at all.

This is where my body belongs. This is what I'm meant to be doing.

Prompted by Ginger's voice, I point and flex and stretch my body in ways it hasn't been in months. The other girls disappear as I lose myself in my own practice, repeating the mantras that accompanied me through the years in this room: shoulders wide, head up, don't grip the barre, hips turned out, don't roll over your arches . . . My muscles are pulled taut, my back rod-straight, my arms strong but graceful as they are put through their workout.

By the time we move to the middle of the room, I'm covered by more than a light sheen of sweat, and my mom and Dov are long forgotten. The music fills my body and I slip into the familiar *adagio*, my core tightening to keep my balance as I stretch into a series of *développés*, *balancés*, and *pirouettes*. And then I follow the others into the corner for a series of *piqué* turns, *pas de chats*, and *jetés*. I spin and leap and balance, entirely focused on the image in the mirror and Ginger's words. My ribs expand to make room for my inflating lungs. I'm loose and relaxed and light as air. And so very happy.

I'm surprised when Ginger takes us through a cool down, shocked when I realize the ninety-minute class is almost done. I take extra care with the closing stretches I used to rush through. Tomorrow is going to be painful.

"Not so bad?" Ginger asks as I walk out of the studio. My body is still buzzing. I can barely keep it still. I know I'll pay for it all tomorrow but today, I feel alive. After the humidity of the studio, the cool reception room gives me goosebumps and I slip on my sweater, already feeling the practice leave me. I long to yank it back, envelop myself in it.

"I miss being here," I admit, tears stinging my eyes.

"Come back," Ginger says as she turns off the lights and quiets the stereo.

Like it's so easy.

"I can't do six days a week," I mumble, hating that the offer will be taken back. "I'm helping out more at home, and it's just not fair to my dad . . ."

I wait for her to tell me I should be taking dance more seriously, that I have talent and I shouldn't squander it, the words she usually uses . . . the words I heard over and over again when I told her I was quitting.

"So don't. Come to my adult class. I have three different ones during the week and, if you have time, I don't have a problem with you joining an upper-advanced class every so often."

"Adult classes?" My nose wrinkles. "Aren't those like fitness classes or something?"

As much as it's embarrassing to admit now, we'd always made fun of the people who came in for the adult classes, their rounder bodies, the yoga outfits most of them preferred to real dancewear.

"Seriously?" Ginger laughs. "Those classes are as intense as the class you just took, if not more so. The people who come have usually been dancing all their lives. They're as passionate and committed as you are.

"You should have seen your eyes when you walked through the door this evening. It was the exact same look you had on your first day of class: a perfect mixture of nervousness, determination and adoration. I don't know what's going on in your life right now, but I think you might need to be here. For you."

I bite my lip and shut my eyes briefly. Ginger could always see right through me.

"Listen, are you free on Tuesday nights?" Ginger asks.

"Um, yeah? I mean, it's not my day to watch the boys so—"

"Great. If you can, would you come and observe the 4:30 upper intermediate class? I'd do it, but I have the company class at the same time. There's a new teacher in there and she seems lovely, but the girls don't seem happy in the class. I haven't had a chance to figure out exactly what's going on."

I hoist my backpack over my shoulder. "Okay," I say slowly.

"Fabulous," Ginger says, pulling me into a giant hug. "Let's not do it next week because I have a sub coming in. Let's say two weeks? And in the meantime, start coming to my evening classes."

TWELVE

. . . .

Dov gives me an odd look when I walk into class the next day. Maybe it's because the way I'm moving can only loosely be characterized as walking. More like hobbling.

"You okay?" he says, when it takes me what feels like eternity to get into my seat.

"Fabulous," I say, and it's funny because it's both sarcastic and not. My body feels like it was hit by a Mack track, but . . . it also feels alive in a way it hasn't in a long time.

"I went to a ballet class last night," I say, trying to grab my bag from the ground and then giving up at the effort.

"You did?" Dov's whole face brightens, and I want to bask in that grin, because it's all for me.

God, I'm in trouble. "It was amazing," I say, and we don't have time for much more because Mrs. Schneider claps her hands and we're back in the world of poetry.

By the end of the week, I'm back to being able to climb the stairs to the attic classes without outward signs of pain.

Though between thinking about the evening ballet class and focusing on my poetry debate with Dov, I'm barely paying attention to Maddie as we eat our lunch on the stairwell.

"Earth to Lucy," Maddie says, interrupting my day-dreaming. "How are things between you and the boy you are definitely not interested in dating?"

I press my lips together so they don't curl into a smile, but Maddie knows me too well. "Just admit you like him," Maddie says. "Any guy that can get you to go back to the studio is A-OK in my books."

I shush her when her voice gets too loud. I don't want the whole school to know my business, again. It was bad enough when Scott and I were dating, and everything happened in a fishbowl.

"I like him," I admit. "And I want to get to know him better."

Maddie rolls her eyes. "That's the most I'm going to get from you? Half the grade already thinks you guys are together based on the intensity of your conversations in class. And they don't even know about your birthday . . . and your special CD."

Sometimes I really regret telling her things. But her comment reminds me of Dov's music that I've basically been listening to nonstop. "I can't tell what's happening," I admit. "In class, he's no longer distant, but it's still different than it is when we're not in school. And part of me thinks those are flukes, that the real Dov is at school . . ."

I let the thought drop because I'm not entirely sure what I want. I still think dating Dov is a bad idea. And yet, I can't deny the pull I feel toward him. But does he feel it too?

"I think you need to find a way to get him alone out of school again. And then you'll see."

"How am I going to do that?" I ask.

"Well, didn't you say that Mrs. Schneider assigned a project? Given how much time you spend after school babysitting, you might have to do the project in the evening . . ."

And then she bats her eyelashes.

"Seriously?" I ask. "He's never going to buy that."

"He might not," she admits, "but maybe he wants to see you out of school as much as you want to see him."

Huh. "I'll think about it."

And I do. All weekend. As I watch the boys. As I attempt to research college choices. Even as I'm falling asleep. It's basically all I think about. And finally on Sunday night, as I fall asleep listening to Dov's music, I come up with the perfect plan.

"So, I have an idea," I say as we're leaving class. I'd been so nervous that I'd gotten almost to the point of writing the whole idea down to make sure it made sense. I press my lips together so I won't break out in one of those grins that hurts my cheeks.

But either I'm a terrible actress or Dov already knows me too well, because he's already giving me that wary look, the oh-god-what-now expression. And yet, he's not backing away. Which I take as a good sign.

"This might be a totally crazy idea," I start.

"*Ra'eyon meshuggah*," he responds.

I start for a moment. "What did you say?"

He repeats the words, enunciating them this time. "It's how you'd say it in Hebrew."

"Again," I command, and this time I attempt to mimic the sounds as he makes them.

I flip to the back of my notebook and write it down pho-netically, and then I ask him to write it in Hebrew.

"Can you read Hebrew?" he asks.

"A little," I say, not meeting his eyes. So many years of Hebrew school wasted. "But it's slow."

I stare at the Hebrew letters and try to match them to the sounds.

Dov gives me a long moment and then asks: "So what's this ra'eyon meshuggah of yours?"

His English words, while fluid, don't have the ease of the Hebrew in his mouth.

Even though everything that has gone on in the last few minutes fits perfectly with my idea, suddenly I don't want to tell him.

Maddie was right. I want to flee.

"Tell me your crazy idea, Lucy," Dov says, and maybe he's just that good at reading my expressions or maybe he thinks I'm embarrassed by my Hebrew skills, but his voice is kind.

Which only makes the words lodge in my throat deeper.

What am I doing?

I can't lie and tell him I forgot it.

I don't want to lie.

"I've been listening to your CD," I say instead, staring at the table between us. "A lot."

"You like it," he says, and I don't need to glance up to know that he's beaming.

"I do," I admit. "I started thinking last night how Idan Raichel blends all these languages together, all these sounds."

"It's like Israel in that way," Dov says, his voice qui-eting. "When you listen to people talk in Israel, it isn't just

Hebrew with a bit of English sprinkled in. You have Jews from all over the world speaking their native tongues and then Arabs and foreign workers, all those dialects and languages blending together."

I swallow hard. This project, this year, is going to kill me. "Right," I force myself to respond. "I was thinking we could do something for our end-of-semester poetry project that links to that idea."

When he doesn't say anything, I continue. "We could take some of the poems you brought in that are originally in Hebrew and the poems I brought either as responses or triggers for your poems. And then we could layer them, the way Idan Raichel does. Like, create a new poem. And sometimes we could read the lines in unison, and sometimes they could be responsive. And . . ."

I'm rambling, so I stop. I'm afraid to glance up at Dov, but I finally force myself to be brave.

What's the worst that could happen?

"It's a good idea," he says softly. "I like it."

Relief floods my body.

"Good," I say. Single biggest understatement in the history of the world.

"I have to go now," he says, "I'm meeting someone at the gym, but let's talk about it later?"

I nod, but I don't think he sees it. Because while he said it's a "good idea," and I said "good," he's fleeing right now. And that's *not* good.

I'm distracted after school with my brothers. I burn their toast, and then burn myself as I try to dislodge the charred remains from the toaster.

"Shit, shit, shit," I mutter, hoping that I'm being quiet enough.

"You aren't allowed to say bad words," Gabe hisses at me, and I want to hiss right back at him. My eyes smart, but if he sees me cry, he'll get worried and that's way more than I can handle right now.

So instead I channel the sadness into anger. "Have you done your homework?" I ask, even though I know the answer.

"I just got home," he says.

"You've been home for forty minutes."

I'm picking a fight. My hand is going numb beneath the cold water, and I'm picking a fight with a nine-year-old. Way to go, Lucy.

"Thirty-five minutes. And you always let us relax after school until after our snack. It's not my fault you burnt the toast, and now it's going to take longer before I can get to my homework."

I wonder if my parents ever got so frustrated with me that they could feel it in their muscles like I can right now. I want to yell at Gabe. I want to scream and scream and scream.

I'm a terrible sister.

"Then go relax," I say because it's the kindest thing I can manage.

Why did I tell Dov that idea? Why risk everything we've built?

The TV turns on in the other room, and instead of finding something else for the boys to eat, I slide down the counter to the floor. Pulling my phone out, I call Maddie and cry as quietly as I can on the phone to her.

"So you don't know whether he's freaking out or whether he thought it was a good idea but then had to leave for the gym?"

I can't help myself. I laugh-snort.

"What a lovely sound. Be sure to do that in front of Dov, and there's no question he'll immediately want to jump your bones."

"I don't want him to jump my bones," I mutter.

"Liar," she laughs. "You want to kiss him, kiss him, kiss him."

I know she's trying to make me feel better, but it's really not working. At all.

"Maddie," I interrupt her. "Stop. I don't even know what I want. All I know is that next year he'll be in the army halfway across the world and I'll be somewhere around here. And that's going to hurt like hell. So it's not in my best interest to—"

"Screw your best interest," Maddie says sharply. "Tell me what you want. You, Lucy. What do you want?"

"It doesn't matter what I want—"

"Yes, it does." Her tone is hard, and I'm full-on sobbing now.

I hope that the boys can't hear me over whatever they're watching, because they'd completely panic. I don't want to be in charge of them anymore. I want to go up to my room and cry in bed. I want to be a freaking teenager instead of a babysitter and a substitute mom.

"I need to go," I whisper. "I need to make sure the boys are okay."

"Lucy," she starts, and then evidently thinks better of it because she stops. "I love you."

"I love you too," I say, and then I try to put myself back together.

After dinner, when my dad is eyeing his office as I encourage the boys to help me clear the table, I don't tell him to go. I'm too tired.

"I'm feeling really overwhelmed," I say after the kids have gone off to take their showers. "Is there any chance you can get someone to help out with babysitting? Just for a little bit as I'm trying to figure out some of this college stuff."

Lie. I've done almost nothing to figure out the college stuff. Which is not good.

Dad frowns, pressing his lips together until the little tuft of beard above his chin flips up. Dad's had a beard ever since I can remember, and that little tuft of hair is my favorite part. When I was little, I remember sitting on his lap and asking him to press his lips together so I could feel that little patch of hair stand up.

I miss being a kid.

"I'll try to find someone who can pick up some after school times," he says finally, and my shoulders sink down.

"I'm sorry," I whisper. "I know I said—"

"We said that if it was interfering with your schoolwork, that we'd find a different solution."

I don't want to bring up the ballet classes I've been taking, don't want to suggest that I give those up to make more time. But maybe that's the most responsible solution.

But then before the words come out, I pull them back. What do *you* want? Maddie keeps asking me.

So instead, I say thank you and give him a quick hug, and then make my way upstairs.

I fall asleep before the boys get to bed.

The next morning, I wake to the sight of a missed call from Dov. And I wear a perma-grin through the day.

"Do you want to meet after school to plan this project?" Dov asks when I see him. We'd had a special college prep session during English class, so no poetry for us. Which sucked. Especially since thinking about college was ramping up my anxiety.

Northwestern or somewhere else? If not Northwestern, how would I choose? All the colleges look the same. American Literature 101 or Eastern European History Between the Wars can't be that different at Brown, Rutgers, Wisconsin, or Northwestern. Can they?

Which means it's really about all the other stuff: the social life, the Greek life, trimester vs semester systems . . . all things I could care less about.

The only thing that distinguishes the schools one from the other are their additional essay questions. I almost want to apply to the University of Chicago just because their essay-topic choices include "What's so odd about odd numbers?" and "Why are you here and not somewhere else?" Though I'm also kind of partial to Brandeis University's "Tell us about an unjust law, written or unwritten, that you believe should be broken." I mean, who doesn't want to write about that?

But apparently I'm not supposed to choose which colleges to apply to based on their essay questions.

"Lucy?" Dov's look is a mixture of concerned and bemused, and I realize that I've been staring into space for a while. "Do you want to work on our poetry project after school?"

Oh Maddie, I adore you. "I can't," I sigh. "I need to help out today with a ballet class at the studio, and then Wednesday and Thursday, I'm supposed to watch my brothers after school."

"Um . . ." He purses his lips. "I guess we could either talk over the phone or meet up after you finish babysitting?" His voice is hesitant, and I stop myself from doing cartwheels.

Maddie is a genius.

"I'm fine with meeting up after babysitting or after class," I say, feigning nonchalance. "What day works for you?"

It takes less than ten minutes for me to diagnose exactly what's wrong in the ballet class Ginger asked me to watch, another half hour to get up the nerve to ask the teacher if I can help, and then three minutes to make it right. Which leaves me forty-five minutes of watching with a grin that rivals Sam's when he thinks he's getting away with watching more TV than he's allowed to. Which is how Ginger finds me standing against the mirror during the final *reverence*.

"You fixed it?" she whispers as the girls clap for Joyce who looks bowled over by their exuberance. Then she opens her arms back to the girls and curtsies, clapping for them, and then for me when she straightens.

"It wasn't a big deal," I shrug. "I needed to rearrange some of the girls at the barre and then again at the center and in their groups. Joyce was alternating strong and weak students, which usually would totally work, but in this case, it was just making the weaker ones more self-conscious and the stronger ones more haughty. They were smirking, which was destroying the confidence of the weaker girls. So I re-arranged the barre and had them go in opposite directions. That way one group couldn't see what the other was doing. Then I stood in front of the group who needed guidance and moved to the other side when we changed sides.

"Same with the center. Joyce had lovely *adagios* and lots of variations for stronger and weaker students, but a student who needs more help can't follow someone who is doing a different variation. It puts them off course, and then they get flustered and start doubting their instincts and these girls actually have great instincts. So I took Lea, who I could tell was the most supportive of the strong students, and placed her in front of the weaker group. She was happy to do the easier variation with them, and I took the opportunity to correct some of her fundamentals, which humbled her a bit, but still left her feeling good about herself because she was leading the others. Really no big deal."

Ginger looks like she's about to speak, but I remember one more thing. "Oh, and I put the stronger students on the sides and the ones who need more help in the middle. That way Joyce could watch them better. And I gave Heather and Marie the barre at the back because their snickering was bothering everyone."

"She was amazing," Joyce says, as the last girl leaves the studio. "I don't understand why I never saw it, but she's right. The girls were totally psyching each other out and making themselves miserable. Just reassigning spots at the barre made all the difference."

"Oh, and one more thing," I interrupt as Ginger once again tries to open her mouth. "Sorry."

"No, please," she smiles.

"Joyce, I love the fact that after you mark out the steps of the *adagio*, you explain the bits and pieces that are from famous ballets." Having spent hours of my childhood watching ballets online, once Joyce mentioned the moment in the ballet that she was copying or adapting for the class, I could immediately picture it. "But while that's inspiring for me, the girls wilted when you mentioned it. As soon as you told them to picture themselves in *The Nutcracker* or in the wedding scene of *La Fille mal gardée*, it stopped them up. Because I think it became terrifying instead of inspiring."

They're both staring at me intently, and all of a sudden I realize I'm talking to a woman who has doubtlessly taught hundreds of hours of ballet. My face flushes and I take a step back, the barre hitting me square in my back. What am I doing here? I have no business—

"I can totally see that," Joyce says, nodding as she stares at the empty studio. "I was trying to show them how much closer they were getting to their dream of being professional dancers, but you're right. I was scaring them."

We chat for another fifteen minutes before Joyce realizes she's about to miss her biology lab. Ginger walks me out to the foyer and through the front door. She'd always had a policy that the studio needed to be closed for a dinner break, because otherwise, dancers were taking class after class, and stopping only to energize with a protein bar. And as she lived in downtown Evanston, she always made a point of running home for the dinner hour to be with her son and her partner.

As she pulls her car door open, she turns back slowly to face me. "Listen, I have an idea. I'm about to lose a teacher for my ten-year-old class, which isn't a bad thing. She's a great dancer but she's old school in her teaching and she makes the kids cry, which is not what I'm looking for. I need a teacher who knows her stuff and inspires kids to try hard, but ultimately will help them fall in love with ballet, not quit halfway through the year. It would be once a week on Saturday mornings and while the pay isn't fabulous, I could also comp you any class you wanted to take."

A class. I picture a dozen girls up at the barre, the same age as Gabe. I'd be their Ginger, gentle and encouraging.

But what do I know about teaching ballet?

"I couldn't . . ."

"I wouldn't ask you if I didn't think you could. Look what you did in there. Not only are your fundamentals solid—"

"Thanks to you," I laugh.

"But you are very aware of class dynamics and the emotional health of your students. And that's what I need for this class in particular."

"Really?"

"Absolutely."

I think briefly about Dad and the boys. He doesn't usually need me on Saturday mornings . . . I could make it work. I desperately want to make it work.

"Yes." Ginger's grin is so infectious that I match it without thinking.

Ginger winks at me and slides into her car. "Let's talk about it in a couple of weeks. The class wouldn't start until after winter break."

I'm still smiling five minutes after she pulls away when I remember I really shouldn't spend the entire night grinning like an idiot in front of the dance studio.

Convincing Dad is slightly more difficult.

"I'm going to need to talk with your mom," he finally says after I argue that in the off chance that he needs someone to watch the kids on Saturday morning, it may be necessary to pay a babysitter.

"It's not that I don't love hanging out with the boys," I insist.

We're in the backyard raking the last of the fall leaves into large piles for the boys to jump into. We'd gone through the schedule of the next few weeks and it felt like every day there was a need for more babysitting time. Which meant that it would be all but impossible to fit in the adult classes that Ginger had offered me.

"I know you wanted a little less babysitting, but I thought you were basically fine with this situation," he sighs, sitting down on the back stoop.

"I am," I said. "Mostly. But I don't think I realized what an impact all this babysitting would have. I feel like I'm missing out on senior year. Plus, it's not like this can continue indefinitely. Next year you'll need to find someone when I'm in college."

I hate that we're having this conversation right now. The sun is shining, the boys are squealing, and I don't want to add anything more to my dad's plate.

But this conversation needs to happen. So I focus on pushing my leaves into a steep mountain. I love the smell of musty leaves and wool sweaters, the slight chill in the air that comes with the advent of fall.

Dad takes a deep breath, and I know if I glance up, I'll see his lips pressed together.

"I wish your mom was here. She'd know the right thing to say," he says, and my stomach muscles tense. "But as I said before, if I need to hire a babysitter, I will. I'll also try to be home more, take some more things off your plate. We'll just have to talk to your mom when she's back . . ."

"Thank you," I start but then an argument breaks out about whose turn it is to jump into a fresh pile, and whether Sam intentionally pushed his elbow out when he maneuvered toward the pile, and we never get to finish the conversation.

The next evening, I make my way to Dov's house after my dad comes home. We'd thought about meeting up at a coffee shop or somewhere else, but then he mentioned that his parents weren't home, and we could work at his place.

And while my first instinct was to suggest the library instead, I forced myself to say yes to his suggestion. Because I'm tired of being scared. I'm tired of always making the "right" choices. I want to work with Dov at his house. I want to see the inside of his house, see him in his element. I don't care that it means that we'll be alone. I trust him.

It seems so long ago that I'd dropped him off here after we walked through campus. When I climb the stairs onto the small front porch, Dov immediately swings open the door, like he was waiting for me.

My heart leaps.

I stand there, my foot about to step into his house and then I wonder if this is what I should be doing.

But I refuse to psych myself out. He leads me past an empty living room, tidy and uncluttered, and then an empty dining room.

"I was just making some dinner and then got worried you'd knocked and I hadn't heard you," he says as he pushes through a closed swinging door. The kitchen is bright and colorful, a sharp contrast to the muted tones of the rest of the rooms. But before I can react, my stomach growls at the smell of fried eggs.

"Are you hungry?" he asks with a grin that says he knows the answer.

"I wouldn't say no," I whisper, and I'm lost in wondering if Scott had ever done anything like this for me. The small kitchen table has two place settings, and while it isn't fancy or romantic it is . . . so much more than that.

"I made some tea, but I also have—"

"Tea is great."

I feel like a little kid playing a grown-up, and I want to stop time and revel in it.

Dov shakes his head when I try to help him gather the food, and instead I take a breath of the minty tea he's poured, trying to figure out why there are actual plant leaves inside the cups.

"It's tea with *nana*," he says. "Regular tea but with sprigs of fresh peppermint. Very Israeli."

I take a long sip, and I'm quite sure that my desire never to drink tea any other way has nothing to do with how I feel about Dov.

It's delicious.

I turn to look around the kitchen. Unlike the rest of the house, this room appears lived in. Based on the notebooks and novels on the counter, I assume this is where Dov does his homework, where he spends a good deal of time. Dov moves around the space gracefully, taking the plates off the table and dividing the eggs between them. A wooden board behind him reveals cut up tomatoes and cucumbers. He pushes half of the vegetables onto each plate and sprinkles them with a pinch of salt.

It's a totally new side of Dov. He's comfortable, more at ease than I've ever seen him. I can't help but stare at his forearms. They're strong, muscular. How come I never noticed them before?

"Don't be shocked," he says, misinterpreting my look. "Eggs and cut up vegetables are pretty easy." He sets the plates on the small table.

"It looks delicious," I say, digging in. The eggs are just the way I like them, firm and buttery, with a hint of a spice I can't place. "What did you put in them?"

"Za'atar. It's a middle eastern spice."

I wolf down the eggs.

"Bread?" he asks.

"Did you bake it?" I laugh.

"I didn't bake it, smarty-pants. Seriously, it's just eggs. It's what I turn to when I need comfort."

I bask in the lightness of his voice. This is so comfortable, so easy. All I can think is that this really could be something.

But I can't go there. I inhale the first slice of bread he gives me and then I grab another.

"My old ballet teacher asked me to teach a class at the studio," I say instead.

Dov's smile is so wide, I can see it through my downcast eyes. "At the place near here?" he asks.

I smile slightly.

"I thought there was something different about you," Dov says. "You seem lighter. More centered."

He noticed?

I mop up some of the tomato juice with my toast to avoid doing something else. Like launching myself across the table.

"Ready to start working on the poetry?" Dov asks when we've finished the food and cleared our plates. I want to say no, to tell him that I want this instead, but I nod.

"When will your parents be back?" I ask and then blush. "I mean, I'm just curious."

He smirks, and I think about calling him on it, but then I let it pass.

"They won't be back until morning."

Holy shit.

"What do they do?" I ask instead of all the other questions I want to ask.

Dov's smile dims. "My mom is a lead headhunter for a big multinational group, and my Dad is a business professor, but he's been working here as a business consultant."

"Are you alone a lot?" I ask, pulling out my poetry notebooks and my computer.

"I am. But I don't mind. I put my foot down when my mom suggested having a college student stay with me while they're gone, but then I think after seeing a few end-of-summer bashes around here, they weren't that excited to have me hang out with local college students. I keep to myself mostly, and the quiet is kind of nice.

"It's funny, this whole coming to Chicago thing started out as a way to get us back together as a family, and for them to keep an eye on me away from all the bad influences in Israel. But I don't think they took into account how much they needed the distance too, from Israel, from our life there, maybe even from me. After being constantly under a microscope for the past year, I'm glad they feel confident I can be trusted."

"I get that." Suddenly a wave of exhaustion hits me, and I yawn.

"Let's get working before you fall asleep on me," Dov laughs, and while I miss the talking and eating, this is fantastic too.

THIRTEEN

· · · · · · · · · · · ·

That night I call Amy before I go to bed. I could call my mom, and I debate it, but right now it's Amy I want.

"You haven't called in a while," she chides. "I can't believe I had to hear about your breakup with Scott from your mom."

"Oh my god, Scott," I sigh. "That was so long ago."

"I think I need to clear my schedule just to keep up with your love life," she says.

In the background, I hear dishes clattering and I can perfectly imagine Amy in her royal blue silk kimono washing dishes while she's on the phone with me. Amy always says that the only reason to live with a man is so that someone can do the dishes and take out the trash. Megan enjoys doing the former, but they have an elaborate system based on bartering salted caramel truffles to figure out who will deal with garbage. "I heard about all the drama around your birthday. And apparently you're taking ballet?"

I don't know how Amy gets her information. I can't imagine that Mom calls her more than she winds up calling us. But I update her on all the specifics, including the evening's egg dinner and study session.

"Dov is the sad one from the car, right?" Amy asks, but it's a formality. We both know she remembers the conversation. She might be older, but her retention of things she wants to remember is unparalleled.

"He is," I say. While things had been so much better between us, I still see that sadness sometimes, usually when he thinks nobody is paying attention. He's so filled with sadness sometimes that it hurts to even think about it. "But he's leaving at the end of the year."

The water shuts off. "So? You don't have to marry him. Hang out, spend some time doing some heavy petting. And if you need someone to take you to get birth control, I'm here for you."

"Amy!"

"Don't be a ninny," she laughs. "Safe sex is the most important thing."

"I'll have a heart attack if you repeat any of this to Mom."

"Remember our rule," Amy says, and I can hear her home phone ringing. "I only tell your parents if I'm worried about your physical or emotional safety. Other than that, I'm your priest. Or better yet, your rabbi. Now go have some fun. I need to get the other line, but I want a full report."

"OK, Ames, thanks."

"You know what, screw the other line. I just had a fabulous idea. See if he has plans for Thanksgiving. I'd like to finally meet him."

Oh god. No, no, no, no.

"I'm sure he doesn't want to hang out—"

"If you don't call him, I will."

No. Way.

"I'll ask," I promise, because otherwise I'm positive she'll make good on her threat.

I wake up a week later to a text from my grandmother.

"You said his last name is Meiri, right?" she'd typed. "I think I found his mom's office phone number. Since your father hasn't mentioned anything about extra Thanksgiving guests, I should probably just call her directly?"

And then she put a freaking smiley face.

Sometimes I hate my grandmother.

The truth is, I did try. Dov must have thought I was a freak for the past few days because I keep opening and then shutting my mouth. Thankfully, we'd already handed in our Personal Poetry Project (Mrs. Schneider loves alliteration) so at least I don't actually need to say words out loud. Because for some reason, all of them are gone.

But I take her blackmail seriously and choose a poem for class that features a batty old lady, hoping that would help start the conversation I was dreading.

And then I email it to her.

I clearly have a death wish.

While my connection to Dov's poem about a young boy discovering the joy in blowing dandelions is tenuous at best, we get into a great discussion about aging, and I'm sure to pepper it with hilarious anecdotes about Amy.

"So," I say as Mrs. Schneider dismisses us. I can't let this moment pass me by, especially after the email I'd sent Amy. "I was wondering what you were doing Thursday night."

Dov glances at me with an odd look on his face. "Nothing?"

"It's Thanksgiving."

He shrugs. "Ordering Chinese food maybe and watching movies."

"You can't forgo Thanksgiving dinner."

Dov laughs. "It's not my holiday, Lucy. I'm not American. For me it's just another Thursday."

"But you're in America now."

"It's really not that important to me."

It's important . . . I want to say, *to me*, but I swallow that. "Come to my house. Your parents could come too."

"We couldn't." He backs away slightly. "It's a big family day for you. I wouldn't want to intrude. Plus, I'm going back to Israel a few days later . . ."

This is why I should stay away. Because every time he says the words "going back to Israel," the lining of my stomach rips away.

It's why I should turn around and shrug like I don't care; find some way to put one step in front of the other. There'll be guys for me at college.

"How long are you going to be in Israel?" Any glee I felt is gone now. I hate this.

"For the month of December."

Shit. Shit. Shit.

I don't bother asking how he's getting away with missing that much school since clearly his parents make things happen.

He takes a step toward me, a reversal of roles that I can't help but note. "I'm coming back in January, Lucy," he says, as though that's important.

I should offer to take notes for him. I should walk away. I should—

"Come to Thanksgiving dinner next week?" I say instead. "Please."

He nods without answering.

I grin, vowing to buy Amy an extra-large Frozen Hot Chocolate from Kaffein. "We start dinner at three but I'll expect you at one to help me with the cookie decorating."

"Cookie decorating?"

"I'll explain later. Actually, come at noon so you can help me with the baking. I never get anyone to help me with the baking."

And then I work very hard at not skipping down the hall, not doing a series of grand *jetés* or even *pirouettes*.

When I get to the bathroom, I sneak out my phone and text Amy.

> LUCY: I love you.
> AMY: What can I say? I'm pretty great.

For a batty old lady, she's kind of awesome.

The butterflies in my stomach are tearing each other apart. They're wild, possessed killer creatures, and I can feel their every smack and jab.

Dov said yes. Not only did he say yes, but his parents are even coming.

Dov and his parents will be at my house. It's ridiculous.

Who cares that the last two days were all kinds of awkward in class? Who cares that Mom called to say that she was taking a flight home Thursday morning instead of Tuesday night? Who cares that I want to puke from the nerves?

For two days, I've done a crazy dance of telling myself the reason I'm excited is because he's a good friend (lie), that I don't want to be dating anyone after Scott anyway (lie), and that I don't want to be dating Dov because he is leaving at the end of the year (half-truth).

But the truth is, when we're in class, things are intense but contained. When we're out of class? That's when the real Dov peeks out.

I'm a glutton for punishment, and I want more.

Thanksgiving morning is cold and overcast, and Dad is stressing about Mom's flight getting in on time. The turkey was purchased precooked. When I'd walked in on the heated phone conversation earlier, Dad's tone had been firm and unyielding.

"Clare," he'd said quietly, "if you aren't going to get here in time to help, I don't see what business you have telling me how to prepare the meal."

I'd exited quietly.

But now, with two batches of roasted potatoes already cooked and ready, I survey the kitchen. We're actually in pretty good shape. The turkey is on the counter, ready to be reheated. Megan is bringing some vegetarian side dishes, and Aunt Joan will take care of the cranberry and lemon sauces. I still have some salads to make and aspirations to bake an apple pie in addition to the cookies.

"I'm going out to the airport to get Mom," Dad pops in. "Do you need me to pick something up? I'll have the boys with me."

I take in the bags under his eyes, the deep creases across his forehead. Going into a grocery store with the boys on Thanksgiving Day is a nightmare. "I'm good."

"Because of the weather, we might be stuck at the airport for a while, but I figure I'll treat the boys to hot chocolate . . ."

"Don't worry. I've got it all under control."

They've only been gone for a few minutes when there's a knock at the front door. I'd just put an apron on over my tank top and PJs to start rolling the pie dough and Édith Piaf is crooning on the stereo.

"What did you forget this time?" I call as I open the door. Dov stands on the porch, a wrapped casserole in his arms.

He looks at me quizzically. "Am I overdressed?" he asks as I take the casserole from him. He sheds his jacket to reveal a deep orange sweater over a checkered button-down shirt and tan Dockers. Even his usual hiking boots have been replaced by dress shoes.

"You look nice," I say shyly, and then look down at the disaster that is my appearance. I can't believe I'd chosen my Dad's "Kiss the Cook" apron over the much more respectable Chicago Botanic Garden apron my mom usually favors.

"I'm sorry I'm early. My parents are coming later, but I figured . . ." His eyes dart around the empty room, taking in the quiet. "I figured if there was too much going on, I'd leave the dish for now, go for a walk . . ." He pauses and bites his lip nervously. I try to think of something to say but words seem to have escaped me. Dov is here.

"Come in," I say finally, even though he's already inside. I pray my voice won't falter. "I'm rolling out pie dough. How are you at cutting apples?"

Within minutes, Dov is settled at the kitchen counter, shirtsleeves rolled, surrounded by apples. I'd offered to change the music, but Dov said he liked it. It's more cheerful than what we usually listen to, and I feel at an advantage because with my years of French classes, for once I'm the one who can understand the words. But I don't spend my time translating the lyrics for him. Instead, we work in silence as I attempt to calm my heart. Dov is in my house. We're alone in my house.

I begin kneading the dough for the apple pie.

"Are these your brothers?" Dov interrupts my thoughts, his elbow pointing to a picture of the boys on the fridge. "Where are they? It's awful quiet in here for a house with two young boys."

We're alone.

"Dad took them to the airport to pick up my mom," I say, begging my voice not to betray me. "Everyone else won't be here until the early afternoon."

"Where is she coming from?"

"San Francisco. She's a professor at Berkeley."

Dov is quiet.

"She just got the job. Last year she was at Northwestern. She was recruited into a tenured job in California."

"Right. I remember you saying that she's not around a lot." He pauses, his forehead furrowing. "Is she your mom or their mom?"

I startle and look over at him, the rolling pin pressing down tightly on the dough. "Both." There's a deep indent in the dough. I'll need to start again. "Why?"

Dov blushes and stares at the apple slices. "I thought," he stammers. "Because of the age difference." He glances up at me worriedly. "I'm sorry, I didn't mean to . . ."

I scowl. The age difference. I hate this topic of conversation.

"I need lemon juice to keep the slices from browning," Dov says meekly, his eyes not meeting mine.

I pass him the bottle, listening as Édith's voice turns more melodic, and longing for her more playful songs. Don't ask about my mom, I plead. The dough in front of me is a mess. I've overworked it now, it's too soft to hold a shape. I push at the edges, trying to dislodge it from the counter but it only smears. I hear Dov's footsteps approach me, but I don't look up.

He clears his throat. "I used to make a dessert where you spread the dough on top of the apples, like an upside-down pie."

I glance up gratefully and try to smile.

"My *safta* taught me. When I was little, I would escape into the kitchen when we were at my grandparents' apartment. The grown-ups would be in the living room, and Yuval would have disappeared into some other kid's apartment, and so I would find my grandmother in the kitchen.

"She was barely five feet tall, but with so much energy and personality that she more than made up for her height. She could make anything out of what she had on hand. She'd dump the contents of the fridge into a pot and make the most delicious soup." He looks over at me quickly. "I can't do that. But this I can do. My *saba* would frequently announce at the last minute that he was bringing home guests for Shabbat and what was intended to be the ingredients for one pie would magically be stretched to fill two or sometimes even three." He shrugs, a half smile on his face, caught in another time.

"She sounds really special."

Dov nods and motions to the pile of dough on the counter. I step back, and he starts to scrape it with the side of the spatula. His movements are quick and sure.

"When I was a year old, my mom got sick." I swallow hard. This isn't the story I usually tell.

"She wound up spending a couple of years basically in bed. It took a while for the doctors to find the right combination of meds to put her back on track, and after that, it took a long time for her to get pregnant again. I was almost nine when Gabe was born. They thought that was it, because of how hard it was, and so Sam was more of a surprise two years later."

Dov stops scraping and listens intently, his eyes on me. I play with a piece of dough, pinching and rolling it between my fingers. I can't believe I'm telling him the real story. I'd only ever told Maddie.

"I'm sorry. That must have been hard, as a kid."

I shrug, my cheeks flushing. "I was pretty young and didn't really know what was going on. It's not like it was serious or anything. Nobody thought she was going to die." I cringe. I shouldn't have used that word.

"Still," he says, his voice quiet and soft. "Your mom was in bed all the time. That couldn't have been easy."

Dov rolls the dough into a ball, wraps it in saran wrap and puts it in the fridge, as I stand there dumbly.

"*Bo'i*," he says, motioning me out of the kitchen. "The dough is going to need to cool before it will hold a shape, and my hands are sore from chopping apples. Can we sit down for a while?"

He rubs my shoulder slightly, his touch warm on my skin, and the world spins out of control.

We sit down in the armchairs around the unlit fireplace, the apron finally discarded. For the first time in years, I try to remember back to what it was like with Mom in bed, but the memories are hazy. The truth is, I can't really remember a time that she had been present in my life. Dad took over when she was sick, and when she got better, she launched herself into finishing her PhD. And then the boys were born.

The anger starts to gather in my back as I think about how many allowances we'd all made for her, even before she left for California. How often she wasn't present, even when she was still in the house. When was the last time she'd made dinner? Been in charge of bedtime? We were always stepping in for her, first Dad and now me. When did that become normal? I draw my legs up until I'm virtually curled in a ball.

"Are you okay?" he asks, and his voice is soft and gentle.

I hate thinking about all this stuff. I hate being angry at my mom. So she wasn't around when I was a kid. Big deal. Lots of parents work or get sick or . . .

I nod, not meeting his eyes. Dov walks around the living room, examining the pieces of artwork, the books on the shelves, the photographs on the piano. He chuckles under his breath at a few, staring for a while at an old photograph of my great-grandparents standing in front of a small house on Chicago's south side, their first home.

"May I?" Dov motions to the piano and then sits down. He lets his fingers trail over the keys, playing what

I recognize from Gabe's lessons to be scales. Dov's fingers are perfectly timed, and even his scales sound beautiful.

"What do you want me to play?"

"What do you know?"

Dov shrugs, picking out "Chopsticks" on two fingers. "Try me."

"'Für Elise'?"

Dov gives me a puzzled look. "Seriously?"

I giggle despite myself, the sadness slowly dissolving. "I can't think of any other classical pieces."

"So give me something that isn't classical. Tell me your favorite song. If I know it, I can play it."

"How about . . ." I screw my face up, exaggerating the motions. "'The Sound of Silence'?"

"Okay," he says, looking at the keys.

"Do you need sheet music?"

"Nope."

He plays a few keys, hitting a false note and starting again. Within a minute, he has the whole thing down.

"How did you do that?" I make my way to the piano and watch his fingers move flawlessly over the keys, his body swaying slightly back and forth.

Dov shakes his head. "Party trick. If I've heard a song, I can usually play it."

I quiz him on different songs, watch him figure it out each time.

"How did you get so good?"

He shrugs, stretching out his fingers. "I spent a lot of time at the piano when I was younger. Truthfully, I think it was mostly fueled by my fear of going into the army. I used to think that maybe, if I was good enough, I could join the army orchestra and then I wouldn't have to fight.

Those feelings changed . . . but piano was still my thing—my place to go when I needed to disappear."

His fingers trail over the keys again.

"It stopped when Yuval was killed. I stopped playing, stopped wanting to. This is the first time I've played piano since then." Dov smiles sadly as he closes the lid of the piano over the keys and stands up. "Thanks for letting me play. Shall we roll ourselves some pie dough?"

I stare up at the clock and startle when I see how long we'd been sitting in the living room. "Crap. We also need to get the cookies ready before they come."

"I know about the turkey from TV, but this cookie thing is new to me." Dov follows me back into the kitchen.

"There are Thanksgiving traditions, and then there are family traditions. Cookie decorating occupies the kids so the grown-ups can cook," I say, taking out the sugar, oil, and flour.

"But you've already done the cooking," Dov says, pointing to the collection of food on the counter and the turkey on the warming plate.

"Yes, well, traditions are important."

"So you have to keep the kids occupied *and* cook the food?"

I think back to the question of selfishness that had come up earlier and wonder how I never saw any of this. I shrug it off.

"Help me find the rest of the ingredients? If we have to entertain the kids without cookies to decorate, we're going to be in big trouble."

FOURTEEN

· · · · · · · · · · · ·

f I'd lain in bed the night before, daydreaming about
how Thanksgiving dinner would go, I would never have
imagined it this good, this seamless. Not that it's perfect.
There's some awkwardness, like when my Uncle Alex corners Dov to talk about human rights violations in Gaza.
But Dov listens respectfully, and when I try to steal him
away, he doesn't take the bait.

Even things with Mom are okay. She masks her surprise
at seeing Dov and his parents at the house (no thanks to
Dad, who forgot to mention Amy had invited them), and
while she isn't helpful, at least she doesn't pretend to be.
At dinner, when we're going around the table saying what
we're thankful for, she expresses her gratitude for the way
we all stepped in to make sure we had a typical Thanksgiving, even without her help. She laughs at what things will
look like next year when I'm off at college, how Sam and
Gabe will need to learn my tricks. But then she dismisses it
all with a swipe of her hand and a "Luckily she'll probably
be only a few miles away." It isn't until she's almost ready

to cede the floor to Sam, who is squirming with excitement for his turn, that she looks purposefully at Dad, and then me. "Thank you," she simply says, and it almost makes it okay. Almost.

Even the addition of Dov's parents feels natural. Dov's father, whom I'd never heard speak until now, apparently has a lot to discuss with my Uncle Mike, while Dov's mom and Megan spend most of the meal discussing the books they'd both read and the writers they'd gone to see.

But Dov is the most unexpected element. Dov teaches the boys simple sleights of hand, grinning at the puzzled looks on their faces. Dov doesn't say a word when Gabe rearranges my careful seating chart, placing him between the two of them, further down the table from me, further from his parents. Instead, he pays extra attention to them, helping to pass the food they want, focusing on them when they talk to him incessantly about sports. And when he isn't doing that, he talks with Amy across the table, laughing at her stories of visiting Israel in the seventies.

So long as his parents aren't in sight, Dov is animated, cheerful, and downright relaxed. It's only when his parents step into his orbit, when his mom tries to place her hand on his back, that his walls slam down. But what he doesn't know, what he doesn't see, are the moments when they watch him and he isn't paying attention. His mom's attention would drift from Megan when she hears Dov's laughter, and she gives her husband the smallest touch to alert him. It happens two, maybe three times, but each time Dov is deep in conversation with my brothers, and each time it happens, Dov's mother's eyes fill with tears.

"He's a sweet boy," Amy says to me later when we're gathering dessert on trays to set up in the den. Her words

are uncharacteristically gentle. In her favorite green cor-
duroy pants and a dark orange top, her hair dyed perfectly black, she almost looks the part of the angelic
grandmother.

I try to hide my smile. "We're friends," I mumble. "And
he's going back to Israel and into the army for three years
as soon as the school year's done."

She slowly cuts the watermelon into strips and curves to
make a swan. It's her one culinary achievement.

"It's funny how things happen. I don't know if you
know this, but your Grandpa Leo's family didn't want to
come to America after the war. They'd only asked for visas
to come to America as a precaution in case they couldn't
get to Israel—well, Palestine at that time. In those days,
it was illegal, and there were all sorts of rumors going on
about what was waiting for them when they got there. But
your great-grandparents were insistent. If there was to be
a Jewish country, they wanted to be there, no matter how
good things were in America."

I don't know much about my great-grandparents and
their lives before they came to Chicago. They were already
old when I was born and died long before I ever wanted
to ask questions. And Grandpa Leo never talked about the
war and what he remembered, saying just "It's better that
you don't know." But I'd never imagined that coming to
America wasn't their first choice.

I swallow hard. "So what happened?"

"The papers came from America. And they were so hard
to come by that they took them. They couldn't stand being
in Germany anymore. They wanted out, and they had a
seven-year-old son, your grandpa. They couldn't wait any
longer."

A seven-year-old. Like Sam. I can't imagine the choice: stay and hope for a ticket to the place you want to go or flee to any place that will take you. And all that with a small child who'd lived through unimaginable horrors already.

"Did they ever get to Israel?"

"No," she says and there's a strain in her voice. "They'd always planned to, but there was never quite enough money, and by the time there was, they weren't strong enough to go anymore."

The silence hangs around us as she threads blueberries onto toothpicks for eyes. "Leo would have liked Dov."

It's so rare to hear Amy talk about my grandpa that I almost don't want to say anything in the hope that she'll say more.

But she doesn't. Instead she peers out the back window. "I think your sweet boy is outside by himself. I'll finish this up. And I'm quite sure your mom is talking about the work she's been doing with the CDC about the ethics of contagion policies, so you've got a good amount of time before anyone notices you two are gone."

It's like every sentence to come out of her mouth makes me simultaneously want to hug her and die of mortification.

"Amy!"

She shrugs. "Or you can go inside and hear your mom talk about . . ."

I grab a small plate of brownies and strawberries and make my way to the screen door. "I love you." I smile.

She winks.

Everyone needs an Amy.

find Dov sitting on the floor of the screened-in porch, his back to the house.

"I can get you a chair," I offer, setting down the plate of brownies and sitting beside him. We'd only just moved the outdoor furniture in, but the truth is, it's probably warm enough that we could have left it out until the snow actually shows up.

"I'm good."

His voice is quiet, with none of the warmth that had carried us through the day. Is he already retreating—

"I like your family."

I chuckle. "They're crazy; Amy most of all."

His smile is fleeting. "They love each other a lot."

I think of my family. Amy with her vaguely inappropriate stories. Gabe, who's right now trying to help Sam demonstrate a magic trick. And for all the craziness with my mom, my dad is probably sitting right beside her, his arm around her shoulders.

"I like your parents. They seem really supportive—"

Dov shakes his head, ever so slightly. "They put on a good show."

I frown. "They seem—"

"Yes, they seem. They aren't nearly as supportive as they appear."

I shrug, not sure if he can even see me in the darkness. "Well, you heard my mom. As many times as I might tell her that Northwestern isn't my only choice, she can't help but—"

"But if you told her you didn't want Northwestern? What would she do? If you, say, wanted to go to school in New York or Los Angeles."

His voice is hard, like he means to prove something with all this.

"She'd let me—"

"Right. She'd let you. And your dad would stand up for you, tell her that just like she followed her dream across the country, you need to follow yours."

I can't figure out why he's so angry.

"Is this about them forcing you to come here?"

He laughs. A deep and angry laugh.

"I wish." He rakes his hands through his hair, yanking his fingers through when they get caught on his curls. His eyes meet mine and he opens his mouth, then he closes it again. "Forget it," he says, dropping his gaze. "I should go home."

I shouldn't ask, I shouldn't push it. We're in a good place. It was a lovely day.

"What's going on?"

The look on Dov's face is enough to tell me I'm right. The lines in his face return to their earlier sharpness, and he looks furious.

I wait, my muscles tense, but I don't move. Dov is focused on the tree line in the distance though I'm pretty certain he isn't seeing anything. "I don't want to talk about it."

My stomach sinks. It's happening again. He's retreating, and then he'll leave for Israel and who knows what things will be like when he returns.

"Please." I swallow hard. "Let me be your friend."

He swings his head to me at the word "friend," and for a moment I think he's going to say he doesn't want to be my friend. But that doesn't happen.

"In Israel," he says, his voice so low I have to strain to hear him, "when a soldier dies, his children and younger siblings are exempt from serving in a combat unit in the army. In fact, they are forbidden from serving in a combat unit unless their parents sign a waiver. You still have to serve, but you do it behind a desk, someplace safe."

He says "safe" like it's a dirty word.

Dov stares at me expectantly, and then resumes when he sees my confusion. "Because of everything that went on after Yuval died, my parents refuse to sign the paper."

I feel like the pieces of the puzzle are all there, but I can't put them together.

"What did you do that was so bad they wouldn't sign?" I finally ask, my stomach churning.

Dov's face is clenched so tightly I long to smooth out the lines etched there, but I don't. I sit very still, hoping he won't bolt.

"My parents thought I was suicidal."

The words hang between us, whole and real. I imagine I can pluck them out of the air, hold them in my hands, squeeze them until they crumble and disappear.

"Were you?"

Dov stares at me and my muscles ache from the effort of not springing forward the eight inches that separate us. "I'm not sure at the time I would have called it that, but looking back, I can see why they did. I took crazy chances. Got in fights in neighborhoods that I had no business being in. I was a mess."

My breath hitches, but Dov doesn't seem to notice. "They freaked out and pulled me out of the country, which they shouldn't have been able to do. Technically, because I was going to get my draft notice, I shouldn't have been able to leave. But my dad has friends in high places and because of Yuval, because of who he was and how tragic his death was, the army made an exception."

"So if they don't sign the paper, you don't have to serve in a combat unit?"

"I know this doesn't make any sense to you, but I want to serve my country. I don't want an exemption because Yuval is gone. My deal with my parents is that if I come here for the year, if I calm down, they'll sign the paper. And then I can serve in any unit I want. I think they're hoping that after a year of being here, I'll decide to stay. Or maybe I'll get soft, see what all of you have, and think twice about putting my life on the line when I can just as easily sit safely behind a desk."

Dov gazes at me intently, his eyes holding mine. "I can't stay here," he says, enunciating each word slowly. "I'm going back home at the end of this year. I need to go home."

I nod, a knot forming in my stomach. I know what he's saying, and I know what he's telling me. Whatever this is, it can't happen. I'm an idiot for reading anything into the time we'd shared.

"I get it." I force myself to break away from his gaze and pull my knees up to my chest. "The only thing that matters to you is getting out of here."

"No," he growls. "It may have been when I started. All I wanted was to make it through the year. But things . . ." He pauses and stares at the space between us. "Things are different. My parents might have forced me to live here, but I'm the one who has been deciding what my life looks like while I'm here."

"What do you want your life to look like?" I whisper.

He stares at me, his lips straight and flat.

"Dov? Are you here?" His mother's voice slices open the silence. "We should go. Our flight is early tomorrow."

"I have my car here. I'll meet you at home," Dov says curtly.

His mother exhales loudly. "Please try to be home soon. We'd like to talk to you before we go to sleep."

Our eyes find each other again. "I should go," he says, leaning forward, and I feel like he's saying far more than just goodbye for winter break.

But I can't let that happen. Not after everything that we've been through. Not with the knowledge that when I see him again, he'll be closed off to me again, that we'll have to start from scratch . . . or not at all.

"You didn't answer my question." It's only the darkness that allows me to be brave, the fact that I already feel like whatever this is, it's slipping through my fingers.

His head drops forward and he leans back. "I don't get to want anything."

This is ridiculous. If he doesn't want me, he should just say it, just end this.

"It's fine if you aren't interested in me," I say bitterly. "You don't need to make excuses."

"What's that supposed to mean?" Dov's voice is quiet, but there's an edge to it.

My eyes fill with tears, and my fingers ache from being held so tightly in fists. "Nothing." I force my fists open and shift my weight away from Dov.

"No, say it."

The air is heavy and electric and more than anything I want to get up and run away.

"You think I'm not interested in you?" he asks.

I stare at my knees, hugging them closer.

"You think it's easy for me to keep my hands off you? That I don't *want* to touch you?" He shakes his head, curls whipping his face. "You think I like sitting here with my hands in my pockets because if I don't, I'm afraid I won't be able to stop myself from reaching for you?"

I shiver. And suddenly the anger I've been holding in my stomach erupts. I'm tired of aching for him, tired of the status quo. "Then why don't you?"

Dov glares at me for a moment, his arms taut. Then he deflates, turning his head away from me. "Because even if I wasn't leaving in six months, I'm not the right guy for you. You deserve better than me. You'll find that guy one day. I wish it was me, but it's not."

His words slice me, sternum to hips, but I'm not going to stop now. Not when we're so close. "What's that supposed to mean?" I say.

For so long I'd planned for the future, lining up my life like dominoes in a row, and what had that gotten me? An ex-boyfriend who dropped me when I became inconvenient, an exit from dance which was possibly the only thing that ever mattered to me, no freaking clue where I wanted to go to college anymore, and obligations at home that threatened to take over everything else.

"Don't make a decision for me. I don't want to walk away just because I can't see a path forward."

"It's not just next year. You don't know everything. You don't know what kind of person I really am. You have to trust me on that. I feel grateful that you're my friend, but I barely deserve that."

"Tell me what you think you've done that makes you undeserving," I say, the calm in my voice masking my dread.

"If I told you, you wouldn't want to be my friend, never mind anything more. I can't do that. I can't lose you . . ." his voice cracks.

"Trust me that I won't walk away. Trust me because I've never walked away from you, no matter what you've told me."

"This is different."

He appears so defeated that I almost put my arm around him, but instead I slide my hands under my legs. This has to be solved with words, not actions.

"Please."

I'm out of reasons for him to tell me, but I know with certainty that if he gets up and leaves right now, it will be over. Everything will be lost.

Dov takes a deep breath. "When I was a kid, I had a best friend, Liat," he begins slowly, his words thick with bitterness. "We grew up together. Every day it seemed Liat was at my house, or I was at hers. Our mothers joked about our wedding from the time we were still in diapers."

Her. Liat is a girl. This is about a girl.

He pauses and while his eyes are on me, he's clearly somewhere else.

"In high school it became clear . . . well, it was clear that we didn't want the same thing out of the friendship, but she never said anything, and I certainly didn't. I was always out doing my own thing, causing my own trouble, and she was just there, always there."

He dips his head, his eyes now focused on his knees. I sit very, very still.

"Everything changed when Yuval was killed. Suddenly I was lost in a whole new way and completely out of control and . . . Liat was there. Liat came to get me when I wound up in dangerous neighborhoods trying to pick a fight. She cleaned me up when I was a mess. And . . . things happened."

Dov focuses back on me and I can see how desperately he wants to look away. "I told you I went through a hard time, but Liat was the one who bore the brunt of it. I knew she had feelings for me, and I used that to my advantage because I thought the world owed me for what happened to Yuval."

His face is a sickly color.

I long for all this to be over. But it isn't.

"I didn't want to tell you because I didn't want you to know the kind of person I'd been." He screws his eyes shut, his hands fisted in his hair. "I didn't want you to know that I'd slept with my best friend just because I knew she'd let me, that while I was picturing nothing at all, I knew she was picturing us together. That she'd been dating a nice guy, a good guy, but broke up with him to be with me, and I treated her like she didn't matter. That I then turned around and slept with other girls, friends of hers, pretending it was okay because I'd never technically promised her anything . . ."

I'm thankful his eyes are closed so he can't tell that I'm not breathing, he can't see the way my shoulders are hunched forward. Suddenly the idea of him not being able to be with me because he needs to make good on his commitment to the army is preferable to the picture I now have in my mind. I want to run. I want to gag.

But this is Dov, my Dov. The Dov who is humiliated by it all. His face is tired and defeated, resigned. Now it's my turn. I can say the words he expects to hear. I can say *I just don't know*, or *I need some time to think*. And he'd let me walk away.

Instead, I slowly unclench my hands and reach for him. He stiffens but doesn't move as I place my hand over his, gently curving my fingers around his. He shivers slightly and stares at me, pleading. Time moves so slowly it's almost painful. "You deserve to be happy."

He shakes his head and closes his eyes. I stroke his cheek, gently. He sits there immobile, allowing me to caress his skin, my thumb finding the small dimple at the corner of his mouth.

"Lucy, please . . ." The beginnings of tears gather in the corners of his eyes. I shift closer, one hand still on his, the other cupping his face, and I let my mouth brush against that corner of his eye, the tear salty on my lips.

"Shhh," I whisper as he opens his mouth to speak, and then I kiss the top of his cheek and his jaw. His skin is warm and flush beneath my lips, and he's utterly still. Until finally he breaks, grabbing the hand cupping his face.

"Lucy, stop," he chokes.

He grips my hand tighter until it's almost unbearable.

"I'm not walking away like you want me to. I'm not letting you take this away from us."

Suddenly, he yanks me forward onto his lap, his hands holding mine down. My heart races, but I hold his gaze.

It's his turn to make a decision, his turn to choose.

"Don't walk away from me," I say, hating that now it's my eyes filling with tears.

For a moment I can barely see him through the tears. I can't tell what he's going to do, whether he's going to shove me off his lap and end it or meet my lips and kiss me.

And then just as quickly, he's pressing me closer and his lips find mine. I'm crying as I hear him whisper my name over and over again between kisses.

The kisses are nothing like I ever felt with Scott, nothing I'd ever experienced before. Our kisses are like the coming together of two magnets. We can't get close enough, can't get there fast enough. It's new and startling and familiar and comfortable all at the same time, a powerful combination of desire and something much stronger, something I can't even name. It's as though I can say everything I wanted to say in a single breath. My fingers slip into the curls I've been daydreaming about since the day he broke my fall at school. And when we stop, it's still a gorgeous fall night in Evanston, the moon high in the sky, the hint of stars above, and I never want this feeling to end.

FIFTEEN

. . . .

I spend the weekend trying desperately to get the ridiculous lovestruck look off my face. My fingers keep finding their way to my lips, as though the imprint of Dov is still there, as though I can capture the feeling again just by touching them.

I can't.

Maddie is out of town for the weekend, so the only people who have to see me are family members, and if my parents notice, they don't say a word.

"He seems like a lovely boy," is all that my mom said after Thanksgiving. My dad squeezed my shoulder. I'm not sure what either of those things mean vis-a-vis Dov, but it doesn't really matter. I have other more pressing issues. Starting with my college choices.

My mom starts up in full force on Sunday morning, as we begin a lovely breakfast at Walker Brothers. Well, lovely if that's how you feel about having breakfast with most of the North Shore.

"So tell me again," she says, her tone sounding more like a mom on a sitcom than a real mom. "You do want to go to Northwestern or you don't?"

As though I constantly change my mind.

I count to ten. And then I try to remember the numbers in Hebrew that Dov had taught me. My old Hebrew School teacher would be proud that I was finally mastering the basics. *'Echad, shtayim, shalosh, 'arbah, chamesh, shesh, . . .*

Well, at least one through six.

"I'm not sure, Mom." I try using my most polite voice but I'm not sure it comes across that way, based on the odd expression on her face. "The truth is, we've never really talked about other options."

"You were never interested in other options," she interrupts. "I'd love for you to consider Berkeley for instance, but I've never—"

"I'm not interested in Berkeley."

I cringe when I hear my voice. But I don't care if they're offering free tuition and any class I've ever dreamed of taking including ballet, I'm not joining my mom across the country.

She narrows her eyes, and I glance at my dad for support. But he's trying to keep Sam from melting down because he's dripped syrup on his favorite Batman T-shirt. I'm jealous. I'd rather be dealing with his meltdown than having this college conversation with my mom.

"I'm sorry, I didn't mean it like that. I just mean that I've been looking around at other college choices. And I'd like to go into all of this with an open mind. It's very possible that Northwestern will end up being my choice, but—"

"Can I just urge you to consider staying in Chicago? If it's not Northwestern then Loyola or the University of Chicago if you *have* to, but we really need your help here next year."

I flinch as though I'd been slapped.

I remember what Dov asked on the porch just a couple of days earlier, about whether my parents would support my decision to go someplace else. Maybe I'd been too quick to respond.

"I thought we were clear that I really want to have a college experience," I say, trying not to let the panic out. "So even if I were at Northwestern or anywhere else in the Chicago area, I'd want to be on my own. I'd come home sometimes, of course, but for the most part . . ."

Thank god I didn't apply early to Northwestern. Thank god Mrs. Schneider said something.

"I get that," my mom says. "And I want you to have that. We both want you to have that. And in an ideal world you would. But this year has been rougher than either your dad or I imagined, and it's been really helpful having you nearby."

This isn't happening. This isn't happening.

"I'm not saying it's a done deal. You can obviously apply wherever you'd like to but, given that you aren't being strongly pulled in another direction, we'd rather you stay local. If you really wanted to study hotel management and Cornell was the only place, then that's a different story. Or if you wanted to become a nurse and the best schools aren't in Chicago. But if you just want to get a good education, why not stick around so you can also help your family when we need you?"

It's like I've been struck dumb.

I'd never really thought of going someplace else, but suddenly the only place I *don't* want to go is Northwestern.

"So, just tell us what you need from us," my mom says, waving at someone in the distance. "And I'm happy to look over any other supplementary essays you might have to do."

I get the impression, though I'm not sure, that she thinks these words are going to stop me in my tracks. Like I hadn't considered that part of applying to more schools would mean writing more essays.

Like maybe I thought maybe that I could reuse my Northwestern supplemental essay question—"Why Northwestern?"—for other schools.

I almost want to feign shock, to see if she really thinks me so flighty that I didn't realize the decision to apply to more schools would result in more work.

"Thank you," I say instead. And then I let my fingers graze my lips to ground me, to remind me of Dov.

That night, I show up at Maddie's door within five minutes of her arriving home from New York. I only know this because I'd been sitting outside her house for half an hour waiting for her to get home. Five minutes is totally enough time when you have big news. Especially after I spent the day trying to forget the horrible conversation with my mom and remember what it felt like to be in Dov's arms.

"I can't believe you didn't call." She stares at me in disbelief. She knows immediately.

"I wasn't ready to put it into words."

She nods, ushering me in. If Thursday night had been warm enough for Dov and me to sit on the screened-in porch, by Sunday night the chill makes it difficult to stand outside for more than a few minutes.

"I'm impressed you waited a whole five minutes before knocking," she grudgingly admits as I pass her my coat.

"I'm a gem that way," I giggle.

"Now tell me everything," she says, and it all comes pouring out. The dinner and the conversation. The way he was with my brothers, meeting Dov's parents. Liat, his ex, and the moment I demanded that he not take the choice away from me.

"Holy shit," she says. "You are badass."

My perma-grin returns, but then the edges begin to fray as I remember where he is now. Where he will be for the next month. Where he'll return to at the end of the school year.

"Tell me what's worrying you." And that's the thing about best friends. They know you well enough to know where your fears live, where your anxieties take root.

What if I've messed everything up?

What if a month from now, I realize that I've built it up into something that it's not? That this was making out on the porch, nothing more.

What if—

"Stop," Maddie says, her hand coming to rest on mine. "We're going to take it one day at a time. You have schools to choose. You have essays to write. And we still have a couple of weeks of school and ballet before winter break. You can jump into all of those, there's lots to focus on there. And in between, you can daydream about Dov."

Right.

And then I tell her about my conversation with my mom, and we spend the rest of our time trying to find a college, any college, that I might desperately want to attend.

With my mom now home until January and Dov in Israel, it almost feels like last year all over again.

I take every opportunity to escape from babysitting. After all, my mom is home. She can play mom.

And to remind myself, I post the old Polish saying "Not my circus, not my monkeys" on my wall. I attach it right by my lamp, close enough that I can see it whenever I need a reminder.

Classes whizz by at school as teachers give us time to make our college applications sparkle. I keep finding new essay questions that make me laugh. Most of them come from colleges I'd never consider. But the questions make me pause. Do I even know the answers?

"Relate a choice that a character in a movie or book made, and whether and why you agree or disagree with their choice?"

"What's the social justice revolution you'd most like to see take place in the United States?"

"If you're looking out a window, what are you seeing?"

"What would you want people who meet you to know about you, but don't want to tell them?"

I begin posting the questions on my wall. Mom used to disparage people who tried to "find themselves" saying that they should just look in the mirror. But glancing over my collection of questions, I wonder for the first time if there isn't something more there, something I can't see.

And when I'm not killing myself in ballet class, I dream of Dov.

He sends a few short emails every day, little updates on his progress through Israeli red tape. Mostly it's clips of songs he wants me to hear and photographs of the places he visits. I see so many pictures of his neighborhood I'm sure I'd be able to find it in my sleep, but still I pore over them, memorizing the details as if they could bring him closer. I begin to feel like everything else I do is an interruption of my real work: learning the landscape of Dov's life.

But what's missing from our emails is any mention of what had happened between us. I try not to read too much into it, try to see his emails as evidence of this new stage in our relationship. I pretend the photographs are the route we walk together, the music—our soundtrack. I create a story of us, placing myself in the photographs, imagining us together. It keeps me from worrying, keeps me from asking him questions that he might not be ready to answer.

The only pause in my routine comes during the week he's at a pre-army training camp. It's a long hard week of complete silence that unnerves me. I dance harder. I read through old messages, study the photographs he sent and envelop myself in his music. I hope that somehow doing this will keep him safe, keep us safe.

It's during that week of radio silence that I write the two essays I'm proudest of.

They come together on the night after school ends, when I'm lying in bed, staring at all the slips of paper on my wall. I laugh at "Not my circus, not my monkeys" and then my eyes follow the poetry discussions to the left. And then all the university essay questions. "Anna Quindlen says that she 'majored in unafraid' at Barnard. Tell us about a time when you majored in unafraid." "If you could enact any law that would make this country a better place, what would you choose and why?"

It had taken me an hour to get the boys to sleep. Mom took them out for ice cream because she announced that she needed to leave a week early in order to attend an important conference, and then left me to deal with the sugar high and the crash that followed. She and Dad went out for an evening alone. As I lay beside Sam, rubbing his stomach, a cold washcloth on his forehead, I felt my anger return in full force. I understand she wants to be the good mom for Sam and Gabe, but what about me? Why am I always stuck picking up the pieces?

And now, staring at the essay topics, it occurs to me that I know the answer. I think about Dov in a desert somewhere doing what's right and Mom out there seeing a movie. And suddenly, I'm typing like mad. About universal conscription and responsibility toward your country. About how afraid I am at eighteen that I'll make a mistake and choose the wrong college. How different that is from Dov who is willing to put his life on hold for three years to be responsible, to do the right thing. I type until my hands cramp, until the anger slowly stills. I write about catching a glimpse of what we could look like as a society if we had mandatory conscription, if before we headed out to games of beer pong and essays about existential crises, we had to stand on guard duty on dark moonless nights. If we had to donate our time and possibly our lives to something bigger.

I write about wanting desperately to learn to be less afraid all the time.

I don't wonder if it's the right essay to get me in the door. I write the right essay for me, and then I send it to Mrs. Schneider. And a copy to Amy, because I think she'll understand.

Over the next week, I churn out a bunch of other essays, but the answers to those two questions are what I keep coming back to.

I want to be unafraid.

I want to be responsible for something bigger.

I tell my parents where I want to apply, but I don't show them the essays.

And when I'm done with it all, I only have a week until Dov comes home. Which is when I start to panic.

SIXTEEN

. . . .

Except, in the end, I don't have a week. It's barely forty-eight hours later when I open the door to find him standing on my porch, his hands buried deep in his jeans pockets. His face is a little more tan, his eyes a little more tired. I lean against the door frame, my arms around my torso. I don't trust myself to speak.

He isn't supposed to be here for another week.

"Hey," he finally says.

"Hey."

He doesn't seem happy to see me. He looks quiet and closed, like he had at the beginning of the year. We stand awkwardly for another moment until finally I find my voice.

What are you doing here? I long to ask, but what I say is: "Do you want to come in?"

Coward. I should rip up that stupid Barnard essay. It'll take more than four years at college for me to learn to be unafraid.

"Ummm." Dov grinds the tip of his boot into the porch.

He's going to say no. I prepare myself, leaning hard into the wood frame. He's going to apologize, say it's all been a mistake, that his real life is in Israel, that he's only here for another few months and this isn't what he should be doing. Maybe there's someone back in Israel. Liat. Or someone he met last week. Everything, everything, is over.

"Do you want to go for a walk?" Dov's tentative voice breaks through my monologue. He doesn't meet my eyes, focusing instead on the bottom of the door frame.

"Sure," I squeak. I grab my jacket. The weather had grown cold over the past week, settling firmly into winter.

As we walk along Lincoln, my steps match his stride, but our bodies remain painfully far apart.

"You came home early."

He shrugs, not meeting my eyes. "I had stuff to do."

Oh.

I hold myself so tightly inside I'm worried I'll break. "Are you jet-lagged?"

"Not really."

"Did your parents come home too?"

Dov shakes his head, his curls flopping in the wind. "They had to stay for meetings."

All those words and yet not a single emotion I can read. I breathe in the smell of the cold and of fireplaces working overtime and try to calm myself.

I will be fine. I will not cry.

Suddenly Dov stops, pivoting to face me so quickly I almost run into him. "I missed you, *motek*," he says, his voice so hesitant it makes my stomach plunge. He's just as scared and nervous as I am, and that's when I melt. I melt and throw my arms around him, relief flowing through my veins.

"I missed you, too," I whisper, my face against his shoulder, breathing in the scent of his skin and his fleece sweatshirt, the familiarity of it making me ache. He wraps himself around me and kisses the side of my face, his nose cold against my cheek.

And then our lips find each other, and it's better than I'd remembered it, better than I'd daydreamed about all month. I'm freezing, but it doesn't matter because he tastes like mint gum, and his hands are cupping my face, and he's kissing me. And when he opens his eyes, I can see all those dark blue flecks beneath his impossibly long lashes, and I don't want to be anywhere else.

"Are you okay?" Dov's breath tickles my ear, and I kiss his jaw.

"I am as long as you don't let go." I bury my face into the crook of his neck, my eyes squeezed shut. Dov hugs me tighter and for a few minutes we stand like that, on the corner of Lincoln and Orrington, the cold park gathering the wind around us.

It's only when we finally reach his house and we're sipping hot chocolate on his pale green couch that I hear about the army training. He's written to me about every other part of his trip, but his army tryouts are the only blank. Our bodies are side by side, almost overlapping. I breathe in the smell of warm chocolate as he tells me about the grueling six days in the desert for the tryout. I slip into Dov's stories about heavy packs that need to be carried up and down hills, about barely edible food that they eat straight out of cans. He doesn't need to tell me about the fear he'd carried around with him like an extra possession. Fear of failure wraps itself around his words like a noose.

"The only thing that redeemed the whole experience was the nights I stayed up on guard duty, when everyone fell asleep instantly, and for those few hours I had the entire desert to myself. I leaned back and watched the stars. In the desert, there's no light pollution so you feel like it's just you and all those stars."

Dov moves me in closer, and I shift so I'm lying across his chest, his arms holding me, his fingers grazing the skin above my jeans. It takes all my energy to push through the intoxication of his hands on my bare skin and focus on his words.

"'I will love the light for it shows me the way, yet I will endure the darkness because it shows me the stars,'" I quote. After being so quiet, it's hard to trust that it's okay for the words to be spoken.

"Is that a poem?" he asks.

I shake my head, a tiny movement but one that brushes my cheek against his shirt. "It's a quote by Og Mandino, an American writer. When I was younger, my mom would put little notes in my lunch. Sometimes they were jokes or reminders, and sometimes inspiring quotes. I remember that one because I liked it so much that I wrote it in pretty letters on a piece of paper and drew a night sky around it, with stars and a giant moon."

"How old were you?"

I elbow him in the side and try my best to give him the evil eye. Which only makes him laugh. "Wait until you see my bedroom. It's filled with quotes and poems and songs . . ."

I lose my train of thought because his lips are on mine again, his hands . . .

Scott and I kissed all the time and I'd thought that it had been good. But this . . . this is like a whole different universe. "Are you inviting me to your bedroom?" he asks, a little hint of the big bad wolf in his voice.

I shake my head, and because our faces are still so close, it brushes my lips across his. His fingers slip down my back, returning to where they'd been tracing tiny circles along my side. My skin is on fire, and it's hard to see straight.

All I know is that I never want to move.

"This is how I kept myself warm on those cold nights in the desert. Thinking of you, thinking of this." Dov dips his head to kiss me again, his hands dancing across my skin. We stay like that for a while, until finally I pull away, get my breath back. "Well, that wasn't the only thing I was imagining . . ."

I shift uncomfortably and inch away. I don't want to have this conversation now, not with everything so good.

"What?" Dov frowns. "What did I say, *motek*?"

"It's nothing," I stammer. "I was just wondering how you say stars in Hebrew?"

I hate this game. With Scott, I practically felt like I had to keep a chart of when I said yes and when I said no. If I said yes on a Monday, I remember thinking all the time, it would probably buy me a few dates when I could say no.

I want to sink into the couch. I adore Dov but the idea of going back to playing that game is so painful. It feels like someone is scooping out my insides with a rusty spoon.

"*Kochavim*," Dov answers.

I take another sip of hot chocolate and pull up my knees. I wish the phone would ring, a cup would spill, something that could distract us from what's coming.

"Lucy, tell me what's bothering you?"

"I'm okay."

"You're curled into a ball."

I shut my eyes. Stupid body. "It's just . . ." I hesitate. Scott knew I was a virgin because I'd known him for-ever, because he was the first guy I'd ever really kissed. Because he was also a virgin, or at least he was while we were dating.

Dov, on the other hand, is different. And knowing how hard it was for Scott to wait, I can't imagine how Dov will react.

"I've never been with anyone . . . I mean, been—been . . ." I feel like an idiot. Why can't I use the word sex? My cheeks are becoming uncomfortably warm and I long to grab the blanket beside us and hide underneath it.

"Shhh, *motek*, that's fine, totally fine. You think I care about that? I don't care about that." Dov's words trip over one another in a rush to get out.

I take a deep breath. "And I probably won't want to . . . you know."

Seriously? It's like I'm ten years old. I'm definitely proving the point that if you can't talk about sex, you aren't ready to have it.

"That's totally fine," he interrupts. "Not a problem at all. That wasn't what I was talking about before." He bites the corner of his lip.

"I mean, I know you've . . ."

He nods, only slightly though, as if he can both answer and not answer the question.

"And I'm not sure that it's something I'm going to want to do, at least for a while." My voice squeaks as I find myself unable to draw in enough oxygen, to replace the dread I'm feeling with clean air.

"I totally understand. And it's good that you don't take the decision lightly. That's a good thing." Dov's voice strains, the words barely able to make it out. "And it's fine if we never . . . if we never have sex, and it's probably better."

He continues to stare at me, willing me not to say anything else, which isn't a problem because I have no desire to continue this conversation. After a moment, he wraps his arms around me, kissing the side of my forehead right at my hairline.

"I don't know how to say this right," he murmurs, "but I want you to know, to believe, that it's all okay with me." He sighs and presses his lips into my hair and then we have no more use for words. But there's a lightness spreading into my chest I don't recognize, a lightness that fills my hands and fingers, that changes the way my body moves against Dov's, that loosens a fear I didn't realize I was carrying.

We practically spend the week on that couch. With my brothers in winter camp, Mom at the conference, and Dad working, there's nowhere I have to be, nowhere I want to be. Especially since Maddie is in the Caribbean with her parents. Dad gives me a pointed stare in the morning as he leaves the house, but as long as I get the kids to camp and I'm home for dinner, he doesn't ask, and I don't volunteer.

After I drop off the boys, I delve back into my college applications, making sure I have everything I need for the dozen schools I'm now applying to. Many of them I've chosen based on distance: a few within a couple of hours of Chicago, a few more a short plane ride away, and then a few that are as far away as I can get without leaving the country. And none in California.

I mix up some public universities with some small liberal arts schools and hope I figure out where I actually want to go before I need to say yes. I hope I find something that I can make a good case for, because I can't believe my parents would really stop me from leaving Chicago.

And then I press send on all of them, because sometimes that's the only decision you can make.

In the afternoons, I drive over to Dov's house, sometimes waking him as I ring his doorbell. We make eggs, the empty house our pretend home, eating together in the sun room or in the breakfast nook, and then all afternoon we lie on the couch talking, our stories weaving a web around our bodies.

At times, the whole day passes without us leaving the house. We occasionally walk into downtown Evanston for coffee, but most days we're happy inside, puttering around the house, our coats hanging on the banister, poetry books in piles by Dov's bed. We've taken to reading together, to each other, huddled under his duvet, music playing softly from his iPod. He pushes my knowledge of Israeli poets beyond Yehuda Amichai, and I introduce him first to Michael Ondaatje and then to more e. e. cummings. By midafternoon, he's discovered e. e. cummings's dirtier poems.

He teases me mercilessly when I can't read them out loud without giggling.

But it is so, so worth it.

There are benefits to Mom having moved across the country.

I ask Dov about his parents one afternoon after a check-in call interrupts our dramatic reading of e. e. cummings poems on the couch. I'd listened to his end of the conversation, which consisted of short answers with long pauses in between. "Does it bother you that they dragged you all the way out here, and now they're always out of town or working late?"

Pulling me closer, he rests my head on his chest, where I can hear his heart beat. I no longer care about the answer.

"I wasn't the only one who went through a hard time after Yuval's accident." Dov's right hand combs through my long hair. "It took my mom weeks to get out of bed, months before she stopped crying every morning. My dad would find her in Yuval's room, curled up on his bed, weeping. In some ways, this year is as much about her as it is about me. So if she needs this kind of traveling, needs to feel important professionally, I can't really get mad at that."

I snuggle closer, wishing I could fill all the emptiness.

The last Friday of break, I come over to his house after spending time at the studio, heavy with the knowledge that our time alone is coming to an end. Saturday night, Dov's parents will be back home, and then we'll be in school. Sitting in my parked car outside his little house, I call Amy.

"I was wondering when you'd emerge from your little love cocoon," she teases.

"How did you—"

"Sam," she giggles. "He said that you come home every night all moony and distracted, and I filled in the rest. Especially since nobody could find either of you guys after Thanksgiving dinner."

That night. The kisses I could feel in my entire body. The way his hands held me as though I was precious. As though I mattered.

"And I lost you again . . ." Amy's voice sounds like it comes from down a long tunnel and it takes a sharp whistle for me to snap out of my memories.

"Sorry," I mumble.

"It's okay, dear. You aren't the first lovestruck teenager I've known. Heck, half the time Megan acts the same way."

I snort. If I had to be compared to a seventy-year-old woman, there's nobody I'd rather be than Amy's partner, who celebrated her latest birthday by getting a tattoo of birds in flight on her back and who, according to Amy, has decided to start penning erotic romances.

But even the image of Megan and Amy doesn't dissolve the knot of worry I'm carrying in my stomach. "I wish I could just be happy, but . . ."

"This is the best stage of falling for someone: the beginning. Enjoy yourself, have fun. Be safe, of course. You know I'm happy to take you—"

"I'm good." I'd roll my eyes, but Amy can tell every time. I don't know how to explain the feeling of foreboding, the worry that darkens the edges of this beautiful picture. "It's just that he's leaving, and nothing can change that.

"I finally got myself back to the studio after essentially giving it up so I'd have more time to spend with Scott. And Ginger just gave me my own class, and I'm taking a bunch of really great ones. And then I have Sam and Gabe, and being around for them in general, especially when Dad needs me. And I have to choose where I'm going if I'm not going to Northwestern, but I don't have any strong feelings about any school because for the longest time all I could think about was Northwestern because that's where Mom and Dad wanted me to go. And then there's schoolwork, and trying to have a great senior year. And—"

"OK, I feel like you're winding yourself up in a tizzy," Amy interrupts. I can hear the sound of water being poured into a mug, and the clinking of a teaspoon, and I can imagine her making her own mocha concoction that hopefully, as it's still before noon, she's laced with peppermint syrup, not peppermint schnapps.

"You're eighteen now. I've always been so proud of you for how caring and giving you are, but sometimes you dip a little into the martyr pot, and that's when I get concerned. Very soon, you'll be responsible for others. You'll have a partner of your own one day—"

"Amy . . ."

"— and if you choose to have kids, you'll have kids. You'll have a job and payments that you're required to make, and real responsibilities. Right now, your responsibility is to discover how best to be you. Your mom chose to take that job across the country, and your dad chose to agree with her. And while I think they made the right decision for her, and ultimately for all of you in the long run, it's causing complications. And as much as you can help, that's great. But it's not your responsibility. You aren't Gabe and Sam's mother, you're their big sister. You are only eighteen. And as for dance and Scott, you need to take responsibility for that decision too. You decided to give dance up, and if you now think that was a mistake, acknowledge that mistake and learn from it. You're growing up into a fine young woman, one I'm very proud to call my granddaughter, but that journey involves learning what you really want, weighing the costs, helping your family and community, but always being true to the voice in your heart. And you will figure out what that voice sounds like. I have no doubt."

It's not that Amy never gives me speeches, but there's something fundamentally different about this one. And I only wish that she was here so I could throw my arms around her.

"I love you, Amy."

"I love you too, sweetness. And I love that you have such a big heart. But I think it would be okay if you didn't give so much of yourself away, if you spent a little more time taking care of yourself. And if you did a little more of that, I think you'll find that the answers to all your questions are a little easier to find than you think."

After a few minutes of sitting in the car and letting Amy's words settle, I walk into Dov's house, knowing I'd find him waiting for me upstairs in his room. He's wearing drawstring black sweatpants and a long-sleeved white shirt. He's lying on his side reading a book, arm bent to cradle his head. He looks perfectly at ease.

When he hears my footsteps, he rolls over so his body faces me and not the window, and the smile that greets me is worth the disruption of that perfect scene.

"How was your time at the studio, *motek*?"

I slip into bed with him, always surprised by how little it took for us to be so comfortable together, for me to trust him enough to simply lie together in his bed. The fear that Dov would ever be like Scott disappeared quickly. We'd started to take naps in the afternoon together, curled up under his covers, my back pressed to his stomach. I learned to lean in, to feel his arms around me, and not worry.

"It was amazing," I say with a sigh, grabbing my history textbook and snuggling back against his open arms. "I bought some instrumental versions of the pop songs that Gabe loves to listen to and figured out some barre exercises I could do with music they'd recognize."

"I'm so glad you're doing this." Dov snuggles around me and I burrow my back into his chest, my head under his chin. He slides the collar of my shirt over my shoulder, his lips drifting across the exposed skin slowly.

Every hair on my body feels like it's rising to meet him. I close my eyes, trying to be present, trying to stay here, with him. I focus on his legs pressing up against mine, his knees in the crook of my knees. I breathe in and out evenly as I concentrate on the pressure of his arm under my side, his hand against my stomach.

Eventually, I drop all pretenses of doing any studying, and instead I roll over so Dov's body is wrapped around mine, as we listened to the music quietly. Until I recognize the song he'd played me on my birthday. "I love this song," I murmur.

"Mhmm," he says sleepily.

"What is it? What does it mean?"

"You never looked up the words?"

I shake my head. "You made me promise. I wouldn't break that promise."

Dov reaches over and flicks the dial on the iPod to replay the song, raising the volume. The beginning music expands through the room, filling all the empty spaces.

"It's called *Mi'ma'amakim*, which means 'from the depths,'" he whispers into my ear. "He's calling out to his beloved, the one who saved him."

I shiver as his warm breath kisses my ear.

"He's telling her, that from the depths, he called to her to come to him, that with her return, the light in his eyes will come back."

I listen to it for a while in silence. "It's as beautiful as it sounds," I say. "Will you write down the words for me, so I can listen to the song more carefully?"

"Will you put it on your wall?"

I nod.

"Then you'll need it in Hebrew also," he whispers. "You need some Hebrew love poems on that fancy wall of yours."

"I have the ones you brought to class . . ."

"In translation, right?"

I nod.

"You can have the real words too. I can teach them to you."

His arms grip me tightly, and I feel like without them, I might float away.

But here's what we don't talk about: We don't talk about the summer when he'll leave. We don't talk about how this is just until then. We don't talk about how after that, he'll be gone, and I'll be . . . somewhere.

We don't forget about it. The knowledge that this is temporary lies between us, even when we're pressed together so tightly. It's etched deep into our frown lines, embedded in our muscles as we reach for one another. We don't need to talk about it because it's everywhere.

SEVENTEEN

. . . .

Luckily, I have the stress of teaching my first dance class to keep me distracted.

"Quick question," I'd texted Ginger during winter break. "They can handle two-thirds barre work and one-third center?"

"Yup," she replied an hour later. "But this class is really into jumps. And I think they want to learn more turns. They're having a hard time controlling their pirouettes."

Who doesn't?

"Have they tried quarter turns?" I replied and didn't receive a text back.

Quarter turns, quarter turns, I daydreamed. They were great for learning technique even though they were frustrating for younger dancers who just wanted to master a double pirouette from the get go. I could build them into their barre routines, practice them again in the center and eventually turn them into half turns and then full.

"It's not all going to happen on the first day," she reminded me when I popped by the studio on Friday. "You need to get to know the kids and take the lead from them. Though you're the teacher, think of them as your partners in this. Watch them, see what they need, what will inspire them. It won't be the same as what it would be for another class, or even this class last semester."

She winked when she saw me gulp. "I know you can do it. In fact, I've known it for a while. I was just waiting for you to realize it."

On Saturday morning when I show up for my first class, I have none of her confidence. The foyer is filled with girls of every height, all wearing regulation black leotards and pink tights, their hair tightly pulled back into buns. Ginger is easygoing about many things, but ballet clothing is not one of them.

"Leave your stuff in the staff room," she calls out as she rounds the corner to ensure the center barres are back in place after a jazz class.

Right, I laugh to myself. That's going to take some getting used to. The staff room is smaller but slightly more comfortable than the regular changing room I'd spent years running in and out of. While I appreciate the personal space, a part of me misses the familiarity of the student room, my locker in the back corner with the door that had to be lifted and kicked in order to dislodge it. I'd taken to keeping supplies in there, deodorant and extra bobby pins, lamb's wool for my pointe shoes and energy snacks to supplement dinner if I was taking several classes in one evening.

I change quickly into my leotard and tights, wrapping a thin sweater around my torso and pulling on plain leather ballet slippers. My hands are so shaky that it takes an extra ten minutes to get my hair into a tight bun, and finally I force myself to leave the security of the empty room. In the reception area, I find Ginger talking with a young girl with the palest blonde hair I've ever seen.

"Lucy," Ginger smiles broadly. "I want you to meet Annabelle Lewis. Annabelle has been coming here since she was in our Mommy and Me class."

The corners of Annabelle's mouth lift, but she doesn't meet my eyes. I glance at Ginger who nods slightly.

"Hi Annabelle," I say, bending down so my eyes are at her level. "I'm very happy to meet you. Ginger has told me a lot about you."

Annabelle's chin lowers until it's pressed into her sternum. Ginger shakes her head sharply.

Shit.

"I have to confess that I'm a little nervous," I continue, my mind racing as I try to think how to extricate myself, "because I've never taught a class. Ginger was telling me that you would be an excellent person to help me for my first few classes."

"Really?" Annabelle glances up Ginger.

"Of course, kiddo. Who else?"

Annabelle narrows her eyes, but a smile is now firmly planted on her face. I'll have to get the story on Annabelle out of Ginger later, but in the meantime, I have an assistant to woo.

"Want to help me get things set up?" I hold out my hand to Annabelle, and she grabs it, her sweaty palm meeting mine. For the next ten minutes she talks nonstop as she assists me in pulling the extra temporary barres to the center of the room. I get the scoop on the other ten girls in the class: which of them are frequently late, which are the ones who get into trouble for talking, which have to be reminded to spit out their gum, and which ones cried when Miss Jacqueline yelled. When she tells me that last bit of information, she glances up at me, worried. She hasn't mentioned her own name in any of the lists she's given me, but I have a feeling I know where she fits.

I smile widely, making sure it reaches my whole face. "Well, that shouldn't be a problem since I don't believe in yelling. But I will need to be reminded about chewing gum because that definitely doesn't belong in a studio."

And then I watch her whole body relax.

The class is a success. If the kids realized I was nervous, they don't show it. Maybe it's because I'm replacing a teacher that scared the crap out of them or maybe it's the massive grin I have plastered over my face for the full hour, but somehow it works. Even when Annabelle has to remind me to do an exercise on the other side when I get distracted. Twice.

By the time I push the barres up against the back wall, the kids have mostly left, and I'm exhausted but relieved. I make my way to the reception area and find Ginger perched on the corner of the sofa.

"Sit," she smiles, motioning the space beside her. Even the slightest movement of her arm is filled with quiet grace.

We talk briefly about the class, the moments I'd felt particularly good about and a couple that had given me trouble.

"I like how you handled Cynthia's problem with holding her position."

My face flushes, and I stare at my hands. "I remember that feeling of swaying back and forth, the feeling I'd never be able to pull everything together. It took me so long to realize that it wasn't only about clenching your thighs together, but also engaging your abdominals. You used to tell me that all the time, and each time I remembered to do it, it made a world of difference."

I glance up in time to see her nose crinkle as she grins.

One day.

One day, I'd like someone to feel about me the way I feel about Ginger. Someone who will remember the words I'd used and hold them inside like I hold hers.

"Well, you should be very proud of your first day. You lived up to my every expectation, and then some."

I take a deep breath, wishing I could bottle the rush I felt at the end of the class when Annabelle hugged me before skipping out of the room.

"Are you coming by for a class this afternoon?" Ginger asks as I slip my wool sweater over my leotard and wrap a thick charcoal scarf around my neck.

I shake my head, wishing I could just watch a few lessons until it was time for the adult class. "I promised my dad I'd take the boys to a movie this afternoon since they're feeling sad that Mom's not around."

"It's great that you're so involved," she says, stacking the dance registration flyers in a neat pile.

I shrug, pulling my strap over my shoulder, the weight of my ballet slippers, leg warmers and extra supplies already familiar again. "My brothers need me."

"What do *you* need?"

The question is so unexpected, I falter. What do I need? "To have this," I say simply, though it isn't really true. I need much more than that. But I'm afraid that if I admit to myself what I really need, what I really want, it will only bring heartache come June.

What will happen next year is a topic that can't be avoided. It smacks into me at the end of the first day of classes, as Dov and I leave Mrs. Schneider's poetry class.

"Do you have a minute, Lucy?"

It's been hard after a week of being so close, so intertwined, to force space between our bodies, to keep our hands apart. Our relationship isn't a secret: the whole senior class knew by the time we made it past homeroom, but there's a difference between what I feel comfortable doing in the hallways and what I feel comfortable doing in class. And even in the hallways, Dov seems to defer to my comfort level, instead of the other way around.

Sometimes it feels like a gut punch to realize that I didn't even know that dating like this was possible, didn't even know that it was okay for things to be on my terms.

But after an hour of sitting right beside him, reading a poem that really isn't as romantic as I was interpreting it to be, all I'm thinking about is catching up to Dov who is one step ahead of me, and sliding my hand in his.

"I just want to have a word with you about the college essay you sent me," Mrs. Schneider says.

For a moment I can't remember what I'd written. And then it comes back to me.

"I found it interesting," she says, seemingly untroubled by my lack of response. Her fingers play with her necklace. "Did you . . . show it to your folks?" Her words push aside my internal high-fives, and I search her face for an indication of what she thought. I'm about to ask, but then I think better of it. It represents me in the best way I know how. I'll deal with the consequences if I need to. I can't even remember now which schools I sent that one to. I stare at her hands resting on my desk.

I shake my head when I realize she's still waiting on an answer.

"Have you talked with them about your feelings?"

Her thumbnail is chipped, and there's a tiny tuft of something in the crack, a snag of her sweater maybe. She has three rings on that hand, all silver, with a variety of stones. Is one of them a wedding ring? Is she even married?

"They've met Dov."

She sighs. "That's not what I meant. Lucy, I know your mom took a new job and it means you have a lot more responsibility . . ." She hesitates and looks at me. "I guess I'm asking if you're okay?"

I stare at her blankly and then a smile takes over my face as I catch a glimpse of Dov's concerned figure in the narrow window of the classroom door.

I am now.

"Have you thought more about next year? Where you'd like to go?"

I swallow hard, my throat closing. "Not yet," I whisper. All those colleges, all those programs and none of them interesting at all. "I mean, I did find a bunch of schools to apply to. And I feel confident that I'll find the right school eventually."

I try to sound confident. The last thing I need is Mrs. Schneider calling an all-faculty intervention to ensure I'm not going to be a blight on Wilmette Academy's perfect college attendance record.

"Or maybe not," she says instead. "Maybe next year isn't the right year for you to go off to college."

My mouth drops open. I remember her mentioning it earlier in the year, but it's just as ludicrous now as it had been then. What am I going to do, get a job at a coffee shop?

"Don't look so shocked," she says. "You could take a gap year—travel or volunteer. There's no sense in going to college if you aren't ready for it. It'll be a giant waste of money."

"Of course I'm ready for it," I bristle.

"I didn't mean you aren't ready academically or emotionally," she says. "For some people, college isn't the best option right after high school. A gap year is a different kind of learning experience, one that can open up new possibilities, allow you to see your life from new perspectives. Remember, President Obama's daughter took one, and everyone applauded her choice. Students who take a gap year often hit campus more focused, directed, and clear on how to succeed at college and beyond."

Not go to college next year? It's unheard of. Even if the president's daughter did it. Everyone I know goes to college. At other schools, kids take breaks. At Wilmette Academy, we're serious about our studies—we don't take breaks. Our education is what's supposed to be meaningful. And if it isn't, we pretend it is.

"But—" I can't.

It's not possible.

"There are many ways of getting to the place you're supposed to be. For some, going to college works. For others? It only locks you in too early. There's nothing wrong with wanting more time to figure out what you want to be studying. In fact, there's something quite brave about it. Think about it. Think about what you wrote in your essay. Maybe you should take your own advice and spend a year making a difference."

My eyes widen at the possibility. What would it look like if I put my life on hold, if I—

No. It wasn't possible. I'd been advocating for our society to change its expectations, not for me to change my own.

"Alright," she says. "You know you can come to me if you need anything. Or if you want to talk. But I'm really impressed with the work that you and Dov are doing in class."

My breath catches at the mention of his name.

"He's really smart," I murmur, trying to cover up the little sigh.

"True," she replies, pulling her bag over her shoulder, "but you were also able to coax him out of his shell, to reach him."

I nod, and then I'm through the door, fitting neatly in the crook of Dov's arm, trying to put out of my mind the idea that my future could be so radically different than what I was raised to expect.

Saturday morning in dance class there are two extra girls lined up at the barre.

But that isn't nearly as startling as the fact that all the girls are at the barre, gum out of their mouths, and ready to dance.

"Am I late?"

The girls titter, but only Annabelle speaks. "We loved that you put some of our barre routine to more popular music, and so we agreed at the end of last class that we wanted you to use more of that music. So we figured that we'd impress you with being on time and ready."

All twelve pairs of eyes stare at me anxiously.

"Are you impressed?" Annabelle adds, her voice quieter.

This is the class that Ginger warned me was compulsively late, girls who were mean to the others, who weren't progressing. And now here they are making this huge effort, just for a change of music.

"I'm enormously impressed," I grin. "And so long as I'm seeing good posture, proper arm placement with no droopy elbows, and big smiles, we can definitely use some more modern music."

For a brief second they squeal, and then they quickly straighten themselves at the barre, first position tight and strong.

"We're going to start with same *plié* combination we practiced last week," I say, standing at my barre in the front. "First position, *demi-plié* one and two, back up three and four, down for two, and then back up. Remember to keep your back straight," I said, bending into a *grand-plié*, "core pulled in, weight evenly distributed between all parts of your foot, and most importantly . . ."

I pause as I pull up, careful to demonstrate it properly.

"Smile," most of the girls fill in.

"Smile," I say.

play song after popular song for my combinations during the class, even reusing some when I run out of options. And when they walk out, they're smiling just as widely as they had been in class.

"I wish she was teaching the Wednesday class too," one of the new girls says to Annabelle. "But I'm definitely going to add this class. You were right. She's awesome. I bet you if we told Cheryl, she'd come back to ballet."

I try to press my lips together so my enormous grin doesn't overwhelm my face. Because what I really want to do is drop my supplies on the floor and *grand jeté* all the way to the staff room.

"I have a little while between classes if there's anything you want to work on," Ginger offers as I exit the staff room, a bulky cream sweater and chocolate brown short skirt over my ballet clothing. "Though I probably should have offered when you were still in your leotard."

I'm about to tell her I can't, tell her that I have plans to meet Dov, when he walks in. His eyes immediately find mine and his lips are a close approximation of the goofy grin I'd left the studio room with.

"Go," Ginger laughs. "Looks like you have someone waiting for you."

"Ginger, this is Dov." I'd told Ginger the basics after the last class, so I felt comfortable slipping my arm around his cold jacket, letting him kiss the top of my head.

"*Naim me'od*," she says, surprising us both.

"*Naim me'od*," he replies.

"How . . .?" I stutter, and she laughs.

"I spent a summer at an international dance festival in northern Israel a million years ago." She blushes, and I wonder if there's more to the story. "I've always thought saying *naim me'od* sounded so much prettier than *pleased to meet you*."

Dov nods before turning to me. "Good class?" he asks, pulling me into a hug.

"Great class," Ginger answers for me. "Lucy has become a superstar in just two weeks. I'm already getting kids who dropped out last semester coming back to join her class."

"Really?" Dov asks, squeezing my shoulder. "I have to say, I'm not surprised."

My cheeks warm as I hide my eyes in his jacket. "They had a crappy teacher before, so I look fabulous by comparison. And plus, it's only class two. Who knows how much they'll hate me by the end of May?"

Even only seeing her out of the corner of my eye, I can tell Ginger is giving me a look that communicates that I'm about to be in a lot of trouble. "Get your stuff before I really embarrass you with praise," she warns.

And then the two of them ignore me as I pull on my coat and tall boots, their conversations focused on the places Ginger visited, her memories of touring through the area. But it's still less than a minute before I'm ready to go, Dov's arm around my shoulder, his lips on my forehead. Where they belong.

EIGHTEEN

· · · · · · · · · · · ·

The first major snowfall of the winter hits Chicago the first Monday in February. The flurry of excited phone calls with Maddie start the night before as weathermen start breaking into regularly scheduled programming with dire predictions of epic snowfall, warnings of the perfect storm, of a lack of preparedness on the part of the city, with lake effect snow that could top historic records. Flipping channels in tandem from our two houses, we giggle like little kids as we watch reporters standing outside on a perfectly clear night, alerting us of the coming Snowpocalypse.

The next morning, I wake to the sounds of Sam and Gabe yelping about the thin layer of snow on the ground, arguing about how to check online to see whether school has been canceled.

"Stop jumping!" Gabe yells from the study, and I leave the warmth of my thick comforter to mediate the fight.

"It's not my fault. He's bothering me," Gabe grumbles when I remind them that it's just after five, and that Dad won't appreciate being woken this early.

"He's spelling academy wrong," Sam says, trying to shove Gabe aside and get his fingers on the keyboard. Gabe pushes back, and I can feel the morning unraveling.

I take a deep breath and hold it, trying to recall being a little kid, the joy of the first snowfall. "If you quiet down, I'll look it up," I promise, sliding my body between theirs.

"I'm positive it's closed," Sam whispers as I scan the list of school closings.

Gabe sighs dramatically. "How would you know?"

"Because they always close when there's at least three inches."

"How do you know there's three inches?"

"Stop!" I whisper loudly. "School isn't closed, but there's a late arrival."

They both open their mouths to argue—either with me or with each other I'm not sure. "Go get dressed in warm clothes, and I'll make you something to eat. If you're quick enough, you'll have time to play outside before school."

Dov arrives at school in his usual leather jacket with a thick hoodie underneath it. He has snowflakes in his eyelashes and his curls look frozen solid. Suddenly, all of the morning's arguments about how long the boys could play outside, whether they *really* needed hats and gloves, why Gabe got to wear the only neck warmer, dissipate in his presence. I run my fingers through his frozen mess of hair until he gets a sly look and shakes himself out like a dog, showering me in the process. Squealing, I jump out of the way, but he grabs my hand, keeping me in place.

"Mr. Meiri, Miss Green, please behave yourselves," Ms. Ross, the math teacher, warns us as she passes us in the hallway, and Dov's mocking look is replaced by a contrite one. As soon as she makes it around the bend, Dov pulls me closer.

"Please let me go?" I beg, giggling.

Instead of shaking his head again, Dov puts his freezing hands against my warm cheeks, and I yelp again.

"What a freaking cold city," he complains as I struggle to get his hands off my cheeks. "Warm me up?"

By third period, Chicago is buried under a thick blanket of snow, and the city begins the process of shutting down. Trains warn of delayed service. Lakeshore Drive turns into a parking lot. But Wilmette Academy remains open.

"When are they going to cancel school?" Maddie whines in her best imitation of a little kid, a slip of a giggle punctuating her question. I laugh and then wrap her in my arms, squeezing her tightly. It should be illegal for me to be this happy.

The academy remains open for another hour beyond the airport closures. After a school assembly that reminds us about safe driving and how dangerous conditions are outside, they cancel after-school activities and let us loose. The school hires a private snow removal company to make sure the parking lot is accessible, and between the staff and seniors, it takes less than an hour to clear the snow from the cars.

"Come into my car," I offer Maddie, who frowns at her tiny compact car. My car is a hand-me-down from Amy, large and clunky, but with the essential Chicago feature of all-wheel drive. Maddie and I may teasingly call her The Boat, but she doesn't slide. Unlike Maddie's cute little Bug.

"I'm sure it's fine . . ." But the hesitation in her voice doesn't match her words.

"I'm leaving mine too," Dov says. "Don't take a chance."

Maddie glances over at me, and I can tell we're both thinking about Dov's brother, about how life can change in an instant.

She nods, following me to my car.

It takes almost forty minutes to drive Maddie home, four times longer than usual. The roads are slick, and at times the safest speed is with my foot barely pressing the gas. Even after Maddie makes it inside, I keep the car in park, my hand on the gearshift, my fingers aching from gripping the steering wheel.

"You okay, *motek*?" Dov asks, placing his hand on mine. "I can drive if you want."

"I learned to drive in snow," I say with more bravado than I feel. "There's no way I'm trusting you, desert boy."

"Oh you think driving in the desert is so easy," Dov teases. "Let me tell you, you wouldn't last five minutes on some of the drives I've done through the Negev."

I laugh. "Let me just phone my dad and check in, and then we can be off."

It takes a call to the house, his office, and finally his cell before I find him. "Where are you?" I ask.

"Sorry," he says, his voice distracted, a sound I know means that he's still reading whatever paper or book he's in the middle of and hasn't yet transitioned to focusing on me.

"Dad!"

There's a sigh and then I hear the snap of a heavy tome being shut. Busted. "Sorry. Everything okay? Why are you calling in the middle of the day?"

"Uh, there's a major snowstorm and school's been canceled?"

There's a long silence.

"And I wanted to check in with you?"

"Okay," he says slowly.

"Are the boys taken care of?" I ask slowly like I'm speaking with a small irresponsible child. Which is not so far from how I feel.

"David's mom is picking them up and bringing them home."

"And you're at home."

"No, I'm at the office. I figured with them closing the university, I'll be able to get a bunch of work done that's been sitting on my desk for a while."

There's another long pause and irritation makes my limbs jumpy.

"Aren't you going to be home if school is canceled for you too?" he asks, as if this is the most ludicrous conversation.

"I was planning to go to Dov's," I say.

"Well, could you go home and meet your brothers?" What irritates me most is the way he's acting like this is the obvious thing. Because that's what I'd led him to believe, I realize.

"Dad," I say, trying to warm up my tone. "First of all, you didn't ask, and if I hadn't called, you would have wound up with two little kids standing on our porch, locked out of the house. And second, I don't want to come home this afternoon. I've been working really hard for the past couple of weeks and, if there's an unexpected break from school for a couple of hours, then I want to spend them with Dov."

Dov frowns and mouths what I assume is "We can hang at your place with the boys." But that isn't what I want. I don't want to have to play endless board games or watch the kids in the snow. I do plenty of that. I want to recreate a small moment from our delicious winter break and snuggle into the couch in Dov's sunroom or on his bed. Not constantly be worried about some small child walking in on us.

Dad sighs. "Lucy, it would help a lot if—"

"Dad," I say, forcing myself not to acquiesce and to think about Amy's comment during break that this was ultimately not my responsibility. "If you're really stuck, I'll definitely come home. But if you aren't, if there's any way you can work from home, I would really appreciate it."

I don't say what I really want to say. That the assumption that I'd spend any spare minute I have watching the boys was taking advantage of our agreement for me to help out "when needed."

"Okay," he says, and to his credit he doesn't sound resentful. "But please call me from Dov's house and make sure your phone is on so I can get in touch with you. And be careful."

I promise, though I'm not sure if his comment to be careful refers to me being home alone with Dov or me driving on snow covered streets.

"Okay, we're good," I smile as I toss my phone onto the console between our two seats. "Ready?"

"Are you sure—"

"I'm sure. Just entertain me to take my mind off the stress of this crazy drive, and I'll be fine."

"Oh, I'll take your mind off the stress," Dov teases.

I swat his encroaching hand. "I need to pay attention to the road. Use your words to entertain me."

And for the next hour, he does. He fills the car with stories about growing up in Israel, the hiking trips he'd go on with his family as a kid. And suddenly the glittering snowy Chicago streetscape is replaced by a picture of verdant lush forests in northern Israel where his family would stay during Passover break, the desert canyons and wadis they'd climb through in the south. After I was treated to a host of embarrassing stories about his adventures as a kid, he switches over to his teen years, when he was in Israeli Scouts.

"You need to know it's nothing like American Boy Scouts," he laughs. "Our *madrichim* were only a year or two older than us, and we'd go out on these *tiyulim* with no real supplies. We'd do our *tiyul* and camp and nobody would say a word about safety, least of all the counselors. Two years ago our group was in charge of building the campsite for the younger kids, so we went up a week early. Can you imagine? Sixteen years old and we were expected to be setting up a whole campsite, with a separate sleeping area for boys and girls, a kitchen, all sorts of things. It was crazy. I loved those hikes."

He laughs, and I glance over at him, warmed by the grin on his face. I love hearing about his life before Yuval was killed. It sounds so normal, so happy. Once upon a time he had a family that did normal family things.

"Wait, write down those words for me. For my list." I point to my backpack. "Just grab a sheet of paper, I want to keep track of the Hebrew words you're teaching me."

"Really?" Dov asks, his body twisting to reach my bag. "You're doing that?"

I nod. "I want to learn."

And then we go through his story again, and I learn the relevant word. *Madrichim*, counselors. *Tiyul*, hike. *Shemesh*, sun. *Midbar*, desert.

I grip the wheel a little tighter as we skid slightly. Dov stops his list and raises his eyebrows, but I shake my head, calming my own breathing at the same time. "Keep going," I say, and he does, moving into a story about the year all the kids came home with lice—*kinim*—after a week at the makeshift Scouts—*tsofim*—camp. Eventually I tune out the story as I focus more closely on the side streets that aren't as well plowed. It's his tone of voice I cling to instead, the lightness in it. That's all I really care about.

By late afternoon, after we make quick work of shoveling Dov's short driveway and walkway, we move inside, the snow now coming down fast and furious. According to the news report, it's only set to get worse. Dov's mother calls from her office downtown where she's stuck, not used to the snowstorms that Chicago residents take for granted. It only took a few minutes of skidding down Michigan Avenue before she turned around and circled back to her office.

"I'll be home by dinner," she promises Dov, but unless she's one very powerful executive recruiter, there's little chance of her making it through the snow until late at night, if at all. For all our laughter, Snowpocalypse turned out to be an accurate name, as the speed of the snowfall combined with sharp winds made plowing challenging. Photos online reveal highways that look like parking lots, and the first order of business is rescuing those who are stuck. Thankfully, it isn't that cold. At least while there's still daylight.

"When will your dad be home?" I ask when Dov pulls me into the kitchen with the promise of food.

"He's in Denver for a meeting, so I'm guessing not for a while. But don't forget to call your dad. He'll probably want you to go home before it gets too bad out there," Dov says as I sit down by the heating vent.

I love these old Edwardian homes with their antiquated heating systems. While they never really heat up the whole house, there are delightful pockets of warmth you can find, like jets of hot water in a swimming pool.

"Can we eat something first?"

Dov parts the window curtains and frowns at the sky.

"It'll be fine," I say, pulling up to face him. "Or rather, no more or less fine than it is right now. So let's eat something."

Dov drops the curtains and shrugs. "I don't think we have much by way of fresh food."

We make pizzas, dumping whatever vegetables we can find from the panty onto pita breads we find in the freezer. Dov sprinkles Za'atar on top.

"This reminds me so much of home," he says, sniffing his fingers.

I ignore the flip in my stomach at the word "home" and instead trail my fingers down his arm, taking the spice container so I can smell it too. "I still think of those eggs you made me in the fall. I don't know if it was the fact that you'd made them, or the Za'atar, but they were the most delicious eggs I'd ever eaten."

The corners of Dov's mouth curl up, and for a second he presses his lips together. "I was so nervous, you being in my house. I only cooked the eggs to give my hands something to do."

I pull him toward me, the spice container forgotten. "I didn't know that." His lips drift against mine as his hands slip under my top, sliding over my skin. And then there's no more talking until we smell our makeshift pizzas burning.

"You thought the pizzas would be gross," Dov reminds me when I polish off the last one.

I laugh. "I was hungry. That was a lot of shoveling."

"Come, *motek*, let's go to the couch."

I call Dad, who confirms what I expected. Now isn't a good time to venture outside, the wind gusts are too strong. I promise to keep my phone on and to check in with him in a couple of hours. He'd try to see about getting his truck out of the driveway to come get us.

We leave the dirty dishes on the table and drag ourselves over to the couches. The food makes me sleepy, and as soon as we get to the couches, I collapse beside Dov, my head resting on his shoulder.

"You make me so happy," he whispers. My limbs grow heavy, and I sink in deeper beside him.

"You too," I say, too tired to think of something more intimate to say.

"I don't know what I'll do without you next year," he starts to say, and I burrow my head further into his chest. *Don't ruin this*, I beg him silently. *Don't talk about what will happen.*

We sit like that for a few more minutes, and I shut my eyes, allowing my thoughts to wander.

Until Dov starts speaking again.

"I don't know if you're awake, *nishamah*, and I almost hope you aren't, because I don't want this to be a big deal, but I need to tell you something, and I need to tell it to you in Hebrew. And I know that makes me a coward, but it's the only way I can really have the courage to say this.

"*Ani choshev sheani mitahev bach. Ani lo matzliach l'hotzi otach meharosh sheli. At nimtzeit b'chol hacholamot sheli. Bechayim lo chashavti sheargish kach k'lapei af achat, ubevadai lo chashavti shezeh yikreh kan. Aval* Lucy, *at habenadam hachi madhim she-i pa'am pagashti. Ani ohev otach* Lucy, *v'ani lo yodea mah la'asot b'kesher lazeh."*

My ears perk up as I hear him move into Hebrew. I listen quietly, the seriousness in his voice, the raw edges like the music we listen to. And I hear him use the words *ani ohev otach*, and while I know very little Hebrew, I know what those words mean.

When Dov quiets, I reach up slowly and kiss the hard edge of his jaw, my eyes closing as I sink into the moment and hold on. "I love you too," I whisper, my chest filling and expanding until I feel like I almost can't handle the love I feel.

"How did you—" he starts.

"Hebrew school was good for something," I say. And then I close my eyes again, and he holds me, and I sleep.

When I wake up, it's dark outside, but it stopped snowing. Dov is asleep beside me, one arm still around my shoulder, his other hand holding mine. Careful so as not to wake him, I extricate myself gently and make my way to the living room window. I watch the neighbors shoveling their walks, the pristine layer of snow that covers Dov's front lawn. Sam would have a field day here, I chuckle to myself.

I'm so distracted by the picturesque scene I don't notice Dov until he's right behind me. "Why did you leave, *nishamah*?" he complains, his voice thick with sleep. "You made the couch cold."

He wraps his arms around me, his hands now warming my stomach, and I lean back. This is love. The heat of his hands through my shirt, his body pressed against mine. A less controlled version of me would imagine this as permanent, as forever.

"What does that mean? *Nish*—"

"*Nishamah*." The word brushes my ear and I shiver. "It's like *motek*."

I dip my chin. "I like when you call me *motek*."

Dov's breath hitches and he pulls me tighter. "*Motek* is like sweetie. *Nishamah* is hard to describe, but it's stronger."

I can feel my heartbeat quickening. My cheeks grow hot. "What does it mean?"

"Literally, it means soul. It's like saying 'my soul,' but that's not really it either."

"Like angel?"

"Yes, but more. Like saying 'my love' I guess, but that doesn't feel right either, because people say it to strangers too, but not the way I say it to you."

I watch us in the window reflection, watch as his lips brush my temple, and it's hard to believe this is my life.

In the end, Dov walks me back to my house at eight, my car abandoned close to what I hope is a sidewalk. There's virtually no traffic, and for the most part we stick to the middle of the road where it's at least slightly plowed. It feels like one of those scary apocalypse scenes, cars abandoned on the road, haphazardly parked near the curb. The chilly air penetrates through my clothing, but remembering Dov's words on the couch, the picture of us framed in the window, I feel immune to its bite.

Reaching the house, we find Dad at the window, watching the street. The relief on his face is clear, and he insists Dov not go back outside.

We eat more at my house. Dad pulls together a chili with all the canned beans and vegetables he can find. In the living room, Dov endures round after round of checkers and Connect Four with Sam and Gabe, sometimes both games at once. When Sam falls asleep on the couch waiting for his turn, it's Dov who carries him upstairs.

Later, much later, after Dad goes to sleep, we sit on the couch, bundled under heavy blankets, watching a movie. I can tell by the vacant look in Dov's eyes that he isn't here at all, he's remembering other days, other games in other places, and I hold his hand and wish I knew what to say. After I leave him in the guest room downstairs, I pen my first poem and stick it on my wall. I place it next to another new scrap of paper that reads "Nobody, not even the rain, has such small hands," a line from my favorite e. e. cummings poem that Dov apparently added when he was upstairs depositing Sam in bed.

My poem's paper overlaps at the edges with Dov's. The words had come to me as we sat on the couch, and I repeated them over and over again in my mind so as not to lose them, because I refused to make a move that would jar us out of the moment.

Nishamah
When you told me
I was your angel
I believed you
If only because
You deserve to have
An angel
Fall in love with you

NINETEEN

· · · · · · · · · · ·

Within a week, winter is in full swing. After the snow-storm, Dad and I create a week-by-week schedule so he knows when I have dance and when I'm teaching, when I'm available to help and when I want some time to spend with Maddie or Dov. And he promises that we'll talk through things on a more regular basis so I won't feel like all the responsibility of the house and watching my brothers rests on my shoulders.

I don't know if it's the conversation, Amy's influence, or what things are like with Dov and ballet, but suddenly I don't feel selfish when I ask if I can start taking an additional class on Mondays, or when Ginger asks if I could teach a Wednesday night class as a maternity leave replacement. We talk it through and compromise on my teaching an additional class on Wednesday after the class I'm already taking, but not on Monday when Dad usually has faculty meetings.

And my Saturday morning kids are soaring. That class is now packed to the gills with sixteen girls filling all the available barres—all girls whose parents heard about the class from other parents of girls in the class—and Ginger is thrilled. Between Dov and the classes at Maple Street Dance, I feel like my whole world is in alignment. As long as I don't think about June.

Luckily, in the midst of a cold Chicago winter, June feels like the very distant future.

"We should stop," Dov groans, shifting slightly.

We're lying in his bed, the room darkening around us. We've buried ourselves under his thick duvet right after school, creating a steady rotation of studying and taking breaks; though as each rotation progresses, we race through the former in order to justify going back to the latter. It's just after seven, but already the world feels like it has fallen asleep. Dov's parents are at a dinner downtown, and I have almost three hours before I have to be home.

"Why do we need to stop?" I pout. Resting my cheek against his bare chest, I stroke his skin with my fingertips, skirting around Yuval's dog tags.

"Because if we don't stop now, it's going to be even harder to stop later."

I feel possessed and wild and free, fully inhabiting this body that is loved by this beautiful boy. "Well," I say slowly, trying to sound as seductive as possible as my fingers sweep across the bumps of his ribs, "maybe we shouldn't stop."

I feel exquisitely powerful.

Dov's eyes widen, and then he grins lazily, reaching over to sweep his lips over mine, grabbing my wandering hand in his. "Not an option, *nishamah*."

"Why?" I tease, breaking my hand free. I trace slow figure eights along his side until he stops me again. "Come on. We love each other. Nobody's home. Nobody's coming home. Maybe it's time."

Dov pulls away from me. I inch closer but the arm he'd draped around my shoulder holds me back. "One day, *nishamah*, maybe. But I don't want to make the decision like this. I don't want you to regret it."

"I won't regret it." I wriggle closer to him. My whole body feels charged and loose, and I don't want to lose this feeling. I didn't plan it, didn't know it was going to happen, but it feels so right. The polar opposite from the way it did with Scott. Every cell in my body wants to be closer to him. How can this be wrong?

"No," he says more forcefully and sits up, moving further away. Cool air fills the distance between us.

"Don't you want to?" I know I'm not playing fair, but I want this. I need this. I need more.

"Don't do that." Even in the half-light I can see the plea in his eyes. "I'm doing this for you."

I'm doing this for you. My body changes course in a split second, like a giant metal garage door slams down, separating this moment from all the delicious moments before it.

"I didn't ask you to make this decision for me." I turn my back to him, rooting around on the floor for my sweater. Screw my shirt and bra. Tears fill my eyes, and I don't want Dov to see them, don't want him to comfort me. I want out.

"Please, *nishamah*," he whispers, his arms wrapping around my waist. He kisses the curve of my back. "It's not just about you. I'm . . . I'm not sure I'm ready."

If anything, that's way worse. Who'd ever heard of a guy not being ready, not wanting sex? What's wrong with me?

I wrench myself out of his grasp, sliding off the bed completely. I pull on my sweater. I yank a hair elastic off my wrist and twist my hair into a messy bun, anything to distract myself from remembering how Dov had combed through it with his fingers. Grabbing my bag, I ignore the sounds of Dov pulling on his shirt, and I mumble a quick goodbye, racing down the stairs. I know I'm overreacting, that he's doing what's right, that we should talk about it first when we aren't in the heat of the moment, that it's just as much about what he wants as what I want. But I can't control the feeling of shame rushing through me.

I fly down the stairs, shove my feet into my snow boots, and try the front door. It doesn't budge. I twist the lock as far as I can one way and then the other, jerking the door. I can hear Dov coming down the stairs, and I beg the door to open, to let me out before he reaches me, to stop us from having to talk about this. Tomorrow I'll be better. To-morrow I'll apologize and make some excuse for my crazy behavior.

Just as I hear the bolt finally click back, I feel Dov's body behind me. I debate yanking the door open, but in the small vestibule, I would either slam the door into my head or crash into Dov. So I stop, leaning my head forward on the glass, the window cool against my flushed cheek. It's too late.

He stands behind me for a moment without touching me, and I breathe in and out, my eyes screwed shut. I wish I could go back in time, erase the last few minutes, return to the warmth of his bed without having to talk about any of this. I can't believe what a fool I'd made of myself.

"I'm sorry," I whisper into the window.

"Please don't leave," he mumbles. "Please?"

I bob my head stiffly, my forehead still pressed against the glass. Then I turn, slowly, head still down.

"I—"

"No," I interrupt, trying to put on a brave face without looking directly at him. I focus instead on his shirt. I stare intently at those pearly white buttons, ignoring the swathes of Dov's skin that their haphazard fastening reveals. "You were right. I'm the one who was wrong. You have every right to say no."

Dov takes a small step toward me, his face tilted down. "I didn't want to hurt you. I just—"

I close the space between us and put my arms around his shoulders. "It's okay," I whisper in his ear, willing the shame to die down.

"Will you stay a bit longer?"

I can't say no. I can't walk away like this. I nod and let him snake his arms around me.

"Thank you," I think he whispers, but I'm not entirely sure it's directed at me.

I slip my boots back off, allowing him to lead me to the darkened living room, onto the couch. He pulls me close, and I let my head drop onto his shoulder.

"It's not that I don't want to," he starts, and I close my eyes again, wishing this conversation was already behind us. "It's just that I'm scared. I'm scared it's already going to be impossible for me to leave you at the end of the year, I'm scared that if we . . . take this further, then it'll be even harder . . . and when I . . ." He swallows hard.

I think about all those college applications I filled out, all those decisions that are coming soon. How even if my parents might make it hard for me to go someplace other than Northwestern, it's not the same thing as what Dov is facing. How it will be years before he's free to make his own decisions about his future.

"What do you think you'll do when you finish the army?"

My body shifts with his as he shrugs. He unwraps my hair from its bun, combing through it again with his fingers. It's so soothing; I almost forget I'd asked him a question.

"Not sure," he mumbles, his voice caught in my hair. "I hadn't really thought that far in advance. Probably travel, that's what most people do after the army. Go off to the Far East for six months, unwind, let my hair grow out again."

"Wait, what are they going to do to your hair?" I gasp, knowing the answer even as the words come out of my mouth. I straighten and take his hair in my hands. I love this hair. For a second, I try to picture him without it, with a buzz cut, and I push the image out of my head forcefully. That's not my Dov.

"It's just hair," he whispers as I poke my finger through the loose rings.

No, it's not! I want to scream, but I swallow it, burying it beneath my ribs. "What about after?"

Dov gazes over my shoulder. "School, I expect. Find something I can do, make some money. The usual. Maybe move up to a *kibbutz* in the North, or out to the desert. I don't really see myself living in a city."

A kibbutz or the desert. Which means—

I take a deep breath, letting my eyes close. "Do you think you'll always want to live in Israel?"

His chin moves across my forehead, up and down, the move so slight but unmistakable. "It's my home, like this is yours."

The chasm between us widens so far I'm afraid I'll topple inside the ravine. It isn't just the next three years. It's every year after that. It's forever.

"I know to you it seems like just a country, a place you can move away from. And it is, to many people. But not for me."

He pauses and leans forward, my body suddenly chilled as air replaces the warmth of his body. He roots around with his right hand in the backpack he'd dumped by the couch when we first came in, his left arm still around me. He finally pulls out his dark leather planner and returns his body to mine, flipping it until he picks out a black and white photograph.

It's old, printed on thick card stock almost like a post-card, its edges a decoratively cut white border. In the picture, a young couple stands in the middle of what appears to be a garden. They're smiling, a real smile, one I can see in their eyes. They're well-dressed, the woman wearing a double strand of pearls and the man sporting a white hat, the type you see in old-fashioned movies. Her hair only just covers her ears. Her short-sleeved dress doesn't hide the tan marks on her upper arms, as though she's used to working outside.

"These are my *safta's* parents, my great-grandparents," Dov says softly. "That building you see behind them was their first real home. It was 1949. She was seventeen, he was nineteen. They'd come together on the same boat two years earlier. They found each other after the war. They'd grown up in neighboring towns, and while they hadn't been friends, the fact they'd known each other's families bound them together.

"My *safta* was born a year after this picture was taken. She was the first child in the family to be born on Israeli soil. And it was a similar story with my *saba*, her husband.

"I know it sounds like nothing. Who cares? But for both my *saba* and *safta*, their births in Israel were considered miracles after what had happened in Europe, after all that had been lost." He stares at the smiling couple. "My great-grandparents on either side never left Israel. They lived in the same small apartments where they had raised my *saba* and *safta*, two blocks away from one another by the port in Haifa. I couldn't understand it when I was little. 'Don't you want to see other things? Other countries?' I'd ask them. 'We've seen so much more than we ever wanted to see,' they'd say. 'This view from our living room window is all we want to see now.'"

"But that's not it," he says. "It's also the place where my *safta's* brother was killed during the Yom Kippur War and the place where my brother is buried. And I know that makes it sound depressing, but it's not. In some ways it's the opposite. It's more than just where I live, and the place where my grandparents and their parents lived. It's a place they built with their lives."

His words trail off and the silence of the house settles around us. There's nothing more that needs to be said.

A group of people passes the house, their voices loud enough I can almost hear them word for word. I wonder if they know, walking past us, that we can hear their conversation. I wonder if they care at all, as they jostle one another and call out to someone else across the street. I want to shout at them, tell them to shut up, to keep their happiness to themselves, to stop shoving it in our faces.

Dov kisses my forehead, and I wish again that I'd never said anything upstairs, never run down here, never led us to this conversation. I would trade all this knowledge for the playfulness we'd had upstairs in a heartbeat. I can't pretend anymore that if we can make it through the next three years, we can be together. He'll join me at college, and I'll wait for him to finish and we'll figure out our lives together. But I can see now that that isn't going to happen. There will be no happy ending.

TWENTY

. . . .

The next week, Maddie and I sit across from each other at the Coffee Lab doing our homework. Between the trees bared of their leaves, the chill in the air, and the lack of sunlight when we leave school, it feels like every day is lowering us deeper and deeper into a cave. I wonder how I'll remember all the facts for tomorrow's history quiz, and finally I slam my book shut. Senioritis, I tell myself. None of it matters anyway.

Maddie glances up and then quickly finishes the math problems she's been blowing through. She closes her notebook carefully, making sure none of the pages are bent.

"March blahs?"

"I'm tired. Ready for warmer days."

"What poem did Dov bring in this week?"

My irritation must be written all over my face because Maddie laughs.

"Mrs. Schneider isn't having us exchange poems anymore. We're now working on poets who've influenced each other."

"Why don't you just tell her that you and your boy-friend really liked that assignment, that it was super sexy and deep? It made you fall in loooovveee . . ."

I choke as my scowl transitions to laughter. "I'll be sure to do that."

"Is Ginger doing a dance recital this spring?"

I grimace. "Thankfully no. She strongly believes that re-citals are good for very few kids, and it just derails class for the months leading up to it. And now that I have my own class, I agree completely. I don't know if half of them could deal with the anxiety of being on stage. And then there's the question of who gets which parts . . . I think it would just erase all the good work we've been doing."

I can't imagine having to choose between the girls: who would get the bigger part, who would stand in front.

Maddie is staring at me, and I realize I've missed some-thing. "Sorry, I was just distracted."

"You really love it."

Nodding, I shove the textbook back in my bag. It's a good thing I'm known as a hard worker, because I'm defi-nitely coasting on past impressions to excuse my work these days. "I do. At first it was all about being able to be in the studio without having to be the best dancer, but something changed. I care about these kids a lot. I've loved watching them learn new things, the moment when something finally clicks and they can hold a pose they'd been struggling with, or execute a series of movements flawlessly. Sometimes I think I get more excited in those moments than they do."

I remember back to the previous class when Simone, a quiet girl who always took a position in the back of the room, nailed a routine that nobody else could get. The look in her eyes, the smile that overtook her flushed cheeks, was priceless. I had her demonstrate the intricate series of moves to the rest of the class. I was so proud of her I wanted to bring Ginger in to witness it, wanted to call people in off the street to see an example of pure joy.

Maddie's gaze holds mine. "I hope it's something you can continue, even after school is over."

I wrinkle my nose and stare at a couple holding hands at the table beside us. Their fingers are intertwined, his thumb rubbing hers as they whisper in low voices.

I hate thinking about things ending.

Maddie's eyes follow mine, and she presses her lips together. "Spring is going to be hard, isn't it?"

My stomach flips, and I feel nauseous. "Can we not talk about it?" I force a smile on my face. "I heard that Katelyn is dating a sophomore boy. Quite the departure for the girl who only dated seniors, even when she was a freshman. Do you think—"

Maddie's face doesn't register. She drains the rest of her hot chocolate and puts down the cup. "Yes, it's hilarious. But that's not what we're here to talk about. We need to talk about you and Dov. I've been watching you fall deeper and deeper into this, and I haven't said anything because you're so happy. But at a certain point we need to talk about what will happen when he leaves."

"I don't know," I mumble. "It's not like I don't think about it. I just don't like talking about it."

The coffee shop barista sets up the coffee cone and beaker to our left. I stop and watch him pour the hot water, swirl it through the cone. An old Regina Spektor album creates a calm undercurrent through the noisy shop as he prepares the coffee. There's no rush, no deadline in sight. A young woman waits patiently for her coffee, checking her phone for messages.

"Is he definitely going back?" Maddie asks, and I swivel back to face her.

I nod silently, not looking at her face.

"He won't change his mind?"

I shake my head, thinking back to last week's conversation, the sad look in his eyes. "He sees going and serving in the army as an absolute obligation."

"What if you asked him—"

"No," I interrupt, my voice harsher than I meant it to be. "I can't ask him, and even if I did, he wouldn't say yes. It's too much a part of who he is." I swing my empty mug back and forth in my hands until Maddie grabs it, placing it in front of her.

I stare at our coffee cups. I have two drip stains on mine while Maddie has three, one of which has almost reached the table. That last drop is barely moving, but it's so close to hitting the tabletop. I root for it, hoping it will make it, escape to the table.

"Lucy." Maddie's voice cuts into my escape fantasy. She takes my hands in hers and I blink back tears. "What are you going to do?"

"I don't know."

"Do you think," she pauses and pinches her lips together. "Do you think it might be easier if you stopped now, if you didn't wait until—"

"Until what?"

"Until you fall in love with him."

I glance back down at the coffee cups. The drop on Maddie's mug made a last-ditch effort to reach the table. It seems almost possible that it will make it. It's hard to see because my eyes are filled with tears, but I don't let go of Maddie's hands. I blink and one tear escapes, sliding down my cheek. If only the drop on the coffee mug could move so easily.

"It's too late, isn't it?"

I free my right hand and grab my chocolate stained napkin, use it to wipe away the tears. I feel like an idiot, crying at the Coffee Lab.

"Have you guys . . ."

I shake my head quickly.

"Well, that's good, at least."

Define "good." Since that night in his room we agreed to hold off on going any further than we had already, and while I think it's the right decision, I can't help but worry it isn't so much waiting as closing that door. Because what will ever make it the right time to say yes? I stare miserably at the table, crumpling the napkin in my fist. The drop on the coffee mug hasn't made it to the table. It's never going to make it to the table.

"Can we stop talking about this, please?" I beg. "I know it's going to be shitty, and I know it would have been easier if it had never happened, but right now I can't do anything about it." After feeling trapped in the silence for so long, my words tumble out. "I'm not going to leave him now. It wouldn't make things any easier. If anything, seeing him and not being able to be with him would be worse. When he leaves, I'll deal with it."

I stare at Maddie intently. "I know you're saying this because you care, because you want to make sure I'm okay, but this is the only way I can do this. And in the summer," my voice shakes, and I take a deep breath. "In the summer, when Dov leaves, I'll fall apart. And then I'll go off to some college, or maybe take a year off . . ."

"Take a year off?"

I drop my gaze. I'm not really thinking about Mrs. Schneider's suggestion. It's too ludicrous. But somehow the idea has implanted itself and sometimes, every so often, I turn it over in my mind and wonder if it really is so crazy.

"It's a stupid idea," I mutter. "Mrs. Schneider mentioned it a few months ago and . . . I don't know why I brought it up."

"Do you think your parents would go for it?"

"My parents?" I choke. "Have you ever heard of someone from the academy not going to college directly after high school? I think the school would disown me before my parents got the chance."

"Maybe. But at the end of the day, it's your life. Maybe you could go to Israel for the year."

"No!" The vehemence of my answer shocks us both and, from the startled looks at other tables, it's clearly louder than I had intended. I take a deep breath. "I love Dov. But I can't keep doing the same thing over and over again. I did it with Scott. I let Scott's story become my story and stopped knowing what I wanted. And same with my parents. There's a reason they're balking at my desire to go off to college somewhere else. I don't know what I want. I've never known what I want. I wanted Northwestern because that's what my parents wanted. I thought about bioethics because my mother pushed it. I thought about poli-sci because Scott thought of it. The only thing that was mine was ballet, and I dropped it to stay with Scott. So while I desperately want Dov to be a part of my future, I can't lose myself to make that happen. I need to do what's right for me, as hard as it is to figure out what that is."

On March 25th, I receive two thick envelopes and one skinny one. The following week, another four go into the *yes* pile and one in the *no*. Mom is home for a break that week, and she meets me at the door every day with another unopened envelope, evidently watching by the window for my car to appear.

"We're in at Penn, Michigan, Duke, NYU, Northwestern, and Barnard," I hear her tell my grandmother on the phone. "Princeton and Williams are our only rejections, and we're still waiting on Smith."

We're in? I go upstairs, pulling off my sweaty workout clothes. Now that the weather is getting warmer, Dov and I have started running together, and between that and my dance classes, I feel the difference in my body. I flex my muscles trying to control my irritation.

As I go to turn on the shower, I hear her carefree laugh tinkling up the stairs. "Oh, I don't know what she wants. She's a teenager. She probably doesn't know what she wants. Hopefully she'll just stay at Northwestern . . ."

I twist the water faucets with such force that the water comes shooting out, drowning out her words. I plug my iPod into the bathroom speakers and turn up one of Dov's more hardcore Israeli playlists, blasting it over the sound of the water—and her voice.

The worst part is, nothing has changed since the conversation with Maddie. She's right. I have no idea what I want. I'm happy when I see the thick envelopes, but there isn't one I'm hoping for any more than the others. After all those years of dreaming about leaving the academy, the victories feel empty. I don't care that I was rejected by Princeton or Williams and can't really tell the difference between the places that accepted me. I only applied to all those schools because it seemed like the safe option; I'd hoped it would buy me enough time to figure out where I really wanted to be. I'd hoped that by the time it came to say yes, I'd know what I wanted.

I don't.

And even when I allow myself to think about gap year programs, it doesn't make it easier. I could go the noble route, volunteer in some underprivileged area or spend the year in Eastern Europe teaching English. I could participate in a cultural exchange, work for a year in London or Tokyo or Johannesburg; or make the time educational and take Spanish in any number of Latin American countries or continue my French courses in Paris or Quebec City. There are so many possibilities, so many options for next year that I often shut down my computer because of the headache blooming between my eyes.

I'm lobster red from the shower before I'm calm enough to get out. Hopefully Mom has moved on to some other issue, like what Dad is putting in the boys' lunches or all of our summer plans.

I don't count on the fact she might be waiting for me in my room.

"I want to talk with you," she says, her back turned so I can get dressed. She'd sighed one of those long-suffering sighs when I'd asked her to look the other way. "I thought maybe you and I could disappear for dinner since I'm not leaving until tomorrow. Girls' night out?"

My body is still wet, so it's hard to tug on my jeans. "I'm meeting Dov since he's been away all weekend with his parents. I told Dad this morning."

It doesn't seem fair that on top of having limited time together, he also has to go away during the time we have. Though I guess I can understand the appeal of a long weekend in California, even if it's with his parents.

"Oh," she says, her voice thin. "Dad didn't mention it."

I remain silent.

"So, you and Dov," she says, her voice brightening. I know that if she'd been facing me I would be able to see the coy look on her face. "I have to say I'm a bit surprised by it all. I mean, I thought you and Scott were really sweet together. Do you ever see him anymore?"

I try to keep myself from gagging. "Thankfully no."

"So, what happened?"

"Enough!" I say sharply, flipping my hair back up so I can look at her directly. "You're six months late on this. I don't give a crap about him. I'm only sorry I wasted so much time being with him to begin with."

"I always thought he was nice," she mutters, smoothing out my bedcover.

I grit my teeth but don't answer. It's easier this way. She'll grow bored with mothering, and then I can get ready in peace.

"Well, be careful with Dov," she says, standing up. We're so close to being done. I have to keep my mouth shut for another three minutes and she'll leave. I can do it. "Remember you guys are moving in very different directions. You'll be at college next year, and he'll be in the army. And from everything I hear, that's an experience that really changes people."

Stop. Talking. Now.

"Who knows what he'll be like when he gets out?"

Stop.

"You're lucky you can go to college, not have the crazy military expectations that he does, be forced to carry a gun . . ."

I'm squeezing my fists so tightly I think I'm going to lose feeling in my hands.

"You and Scott were so alike, going in the same direction, planning for the same type of life. Dov isn't like that. He's going to be a soldier and having that kind of power changes a person. You see these Israeli soldiers on the news—"

"You have no freaking idea what you're talking about!" I snap, my rage out of control.

"Don't talk to me like that, young lady. I'm still your mother."

That's debatable.

"Stop!" I yell. "Don't come into my life at this late date and start pretending you know what's going on."

I stop myself from saying more, from itemizing all the things she's missed. I take a deep breath and calm my voice. "You're doing what you need to do right now, and I'm doing what I need to do. You needed to follow this opportunity that took you away from us, and I get that. But you can't pretend it doesn't have consequences. You don't know anything about what kind of person Dov is, or what kind of jerk Scott was. Dov is putting his life on hold to serve his country. All Scott cared about was drinking and having sex. And what am I doing? Following everyone off to college like a good little lemming because that's what's expected of me? That's nothing to be proud of. I wish I was brave enough to do something important next year instead of just saying yes to some school because that's what everyone here does."

Her face blanches. I think about the other things I could say, about Dad, about the responsibilities she left me saddled with, but then I let the anger slip out of my body. It isn't worth it.

"It's okay, Mom. It'll all be okay. But I need to go meet Dov now."

I grab two socks—sadly not a pair—from my laundry basket and move to the door.

"Do you really not want to go to college right now?" she asks, her voice tiny and sad. I hate the fact that she has no idea about the world of possibilities out there, that her words sound so much like mine had.

I stare at my wooden door, my hand so close to the knob, so close to being able to leave. In front of me are the series of tick marks she'd used to chart my growth. I'd stood with my back to door, hoping every year that I was taller, bigger, closer to being grown up. I wish fleetingly that I could shrink myself back down to the time when my biggest devastation was not being invited to a birthday party.

"I don't know," I admit, but as I say it, I realize it's a lie. I *do* know.

There's a silence that seems to last for days as I stand there with my back to her as she continues to sit on my bed. "I love you," she says quietly.

"I love you too," I whisper, and then I walk out of the room. For a moment, I stand outside my room and listen. She doesn't move. The wooden floor doesn't creak, and I wonder how long she'll remain seated on my bed.

TWENTY-ONE

· · · · · · · · · · · · · ·

D ov tries to be interested in my college options, but I know it's hard for him to relate. All around us, the senior class is brimming with anticipation. Next year! Graduation! Summer trips! The prom! It swirls around as everyone but us seems to get caught up. Skirts get shorter, sandals show up even before the last dregs of snow are really gone. Everyone is looking forward but us.

I catch Dov staring at me several times, not with the intensity that usually marks his looks, but rather with concern. I avoid his eyes, pretending I don't notice. For once in my life, words are my enemy. Words mean conversations, and conversations mean decisions. I want to pretend we have all the time we need, that there's no deadline.

Only once do I approach the topic, and then only circuitously. We'd gone for lunch off campus with Maddie who'd been talking about her travel plans for the summer. She was thinking about backpacking through Europe. Did I want to join her? If I choose a gap year program in Europe, it could make sense. There were some options that were interesting, study/travel programs that could be the right hybrid to convince my parents. I look over at Dov casually, just casually, my fingers brushing against his thigh.

"Maybe we could both go?" I laugh. "Israel is close to Europe."

Israel is close to Europe. Israel is close. Maybe if I go to Europe. Maybe.

His face stiffens as I watch the same thoughts swirl through his mind. Israel is close to Europe. We'd be close. Maybe. And then his hand comes to rest on mine, his smile sad. He keeps his voice even. "Once I begin my army service, it'll be a long time before I'll have any time off."

Instead of letting despair swallow me, I slip my arms around his neck and kiss him gently.

But I can't keep reality at bay for long. I feel like I'm trying to keep a sandcastle standing, but it's too close to the shore, and the water is constantly lapping at the base. Graduation! Next year! My arms ache from the effort of pretending nothing is crumbling.

And then it happens.

We're sitting on Dov's porch, stealing an hour before I have to be home for the boys, the first genuinely warm day of spring. The swing is narrow, but I've angled myself to face him, my legs balanced across his lap, and I almost don't feel anxious. We both hold reading material in our hands: a book in mine, an Israeli newspaper in Dov's. But neither of us is paying attention: Dov's fingers are stroking my bare legs beneath the paper, and I'm pretending to do something other than focusing on that feeling.

When Dov's mom walks up the porch steps, his fingers stop moving, and his hand rests on my knee instead. Her perfume displaces the smell of the buttery toast we'd been snacking on, and I wiggle my nose to try to keep myself from sneezing. It doesn't work.

She wears a tight chocolate brown cashmere sweater over a short navy wool skirt. Between her outfit, her cropped hair and her sleek high-heeled brown boots, she always gives the appearance of being closer to thirty than fifty.

"Lucy, it's so nice to see you," she gushes as she settles herself on a rattan chair next to us. "Such a beautiful day."

Dov scowls.

"Dov, *slicha*, can you get me a glass of water? And maybe a pear?"

Dov's eyes narrow, but after a moment he slides my legs gently off his lap and leaves me on the porch.

When the screen door closes, Gal turns to face me. "I'm glad we're alone, Lucy," she starts, a smile plastered on her face, "because I need your help. Shimon and I have decided we are going to stay in America for another year, and we think it would be great if Dov delays going to the army. I know there's not a lot of time for applying to college, but it would be wonderful if he applied to one or two schools."

I stare at her in disbelief. Dov here? Dov, my Dov, with me? The idea is intoxicating, but I push it away. "He wouldn't," I say finally. "Plus, I'm not sure I'm going to college next year. I might take a year . . ."

It feels strange to tell her before mentioning it to my parents, but the words are coming out fast as my mind tries to process the idea of Dov not leaving.

"That's perfect. I'd be fine with him taking a year off. And he would do it," she insists, "if you asked him. We were going to tell him ourselves, but then we realized this was much better. He'd reject the idea if it came from us. But if it came from you . . ."

No. No no no no no. But—

"Going to the army is important to him. He won't postpone it."

She rolls her eyes, and I have a flash of impatience. Now I understand why it annoys my parents when I do it. "Important to him? Everything is important to him until it isn't." She shrugs, and I can almost see the teen version of Dov's mom, the insolence she must have mastered then. "You're important to him. The question is, how important is he to you?"

She pauses.

I press my fingers into the swing's seat and look toward the front door. Where's Dov?

"I thought you loved Dov. I thought you cared about him." She leans toward me and I force myself to stay where I am, not to curl up into a ball. Her eyes, so much like Dov's eyes, are flashing, and she has nothing but scorn for me written all over her face.

"I do," I whisper.

She gives no indication that she hears my words. "If you loved Dov, you would do this. You would do whatever it took to keep him safe. But I think maybe I was wrong about you. I see how my son feels about you, how different he is with you in his life. But maybe for you this is nothing. Maybe this is just some fun you're having."

Her words cut into me, and I struggle to stay calm. It doesn't matter what she says. I know the truth. Dov knows.

"I love him," I say. "I love him so much it seems impossible that he could leave and that I could keep going."

Gal takes another deep breath as she grips the arms of the chair. "You don't know what it's like to have to keep going."

"I didn't mean that."

Gal sneers. "But that's what I'm talking about. You use all these pretty words about being in love, but when I tell you that if you truly cared, you would do whatever you needed to do to keep him safe, you balk. I can't bear the thought of losing another child. And you can't inconvenience yourself to ask him to stay?"

I lick my lips, hoping my words come out cleanly. "He says he'll be safe. He says it's not really dangerous." The words sound useless and I wince.

The look of disgust on Gal's face makes me feel like a small child. "Of course it's dangerous," she says "It's the army. Even if he never has to fight. You didn't see him last year. It was terrifying." She wipes a tear that has escaped from her eye. "He almost killed himself. I can't imagine how he would have survived if he'd been around any real weapons."

She takes a deep breath and relaxes her face, closing her eyes momentarily. "He loves you. He'll listen to you."

I think back to Dov's comment about how much she suffered after Yuval was killed, how she didn't leave the house, how she'd lain in Yuval's bed weeping. I can see the sadness that still lives behind her eyes, can see the way it hasn't disappeared, how instead it's been pulled and twisted into a fine rope of anger, and maybe fear. Suddenly the idea of a piece of paper that protects parents from having to see another child go into combat, from having to face the possibility of losing another child, seems like an incredible innovation.

But how to balance that with Dov's need to lead his own life?

Should Dov be chained to a desk for his parents' peace of mind? Or should his parents be expected to live with the fear of re-experiencing a life-altering knock on the door?

Her jaw is stiff, and it's clearly taking a great deal of energy for her not to fly off the handle again.

"Please," she says instead, the word seemingly stuck in her throat. "I can't lose him again."

Not *I can't lose another child*. I can't lose *him*.

Dov appears at the door. He glances from his mom to me, and back to his mom. "*Eema*, what's going on?" he asks, not kindly.

She stares at me, and my eyes drop to my book. She sighs. "Dov, your *abba* and I have decided to stay in Chicago for another year."

"What?" Dov towers over his mother. His back is stiff, his muscles taut. I long to pull him to me, wrap my arms around him, but I don't. I stay in my seat.

"We're going to give it one more year," Gal says, her hands shading her eyes from the sun. "We have so many opportunities here. It would be a shame to leave now."

Her voice is flat, her face neutral, but I can tell she's working hard to keep it that way.

"We had a deal." Dov's words are sharp and his breathing is erratic. "I did what you asked of me. I came here. I behaved. I did everything you wanted."

"And we'll still hold by that deal. But maybe you don't need to go back this year either. Why not stay a little longer? You have friends here. You could do your army service later. Plenty of people do."

Gal stands up and inches toward Dov. She stops and looks over at me. "You could go to college here in America. Or take a year off. Instead of doing it after the army, you could do it before. Only this way you could do it with Lucy."

With Lucy. I can't breathe. With *me*.

I hadn't let myself really think of what her words would mean. I hadn't let myself focus on a vision of us working side by side in some remote location. I hadn't let myself dwell on the thought of us walking through a new city, holding hands, or the image that comes to mind first: a room where he sleeps beside me.

Dov pivots to face me, but I'm so lost in those images, I don't catch his eyes when they search for mine. I force the pictures out of my head, focusing instead on the sharp points of his shoulders as they arch up. But I don't move.

He turns back to his mother.

"Think about it," Gal pleads.

"I'm not going to think about it," he growls. "You promised. You swore to me it was one year and then I could resume my life. What's the threat now? Are you postponing signing the paper until next year? So if I don't stay, you won't sign?"

Suddenly no matter how warm the sun is, I can't imagine ever being warm enough.

"I didn't say that," Gal mutters, but her eyes are down, and even I know that she's lying.

"*Shtuyot!* I don't know why I believed you in the first place. You never had any intention of signing it. I should just go back to Israel now and enlist. What's the point of even being here? I'd be happier wasting the next three years behind a desk rather than being here with you."

And with that, he spins around and runs down the stairs, crossing the street without even looking.

Go back to Israel now?

What's the point of being here?

Without knowing why, I turn to Gal, whose face is just as white as mine.

I follow her gaze back across the street where I can see Dov pacing back and forth at the back of the playground, his nervous energy so strong I can practically see it sizzling around him.

"Go to him," she whispers, her eyes trained on him. "Please."

And so I do, as my heart scatters in my wake.

By the time I reach Dov, his fingers are gripping the chains of the swing at the back of the park so tightly that I almost imagine he could pull it off the metal swing set.

"I don't believe them," Dov spits. His voice is sharp.

I don't know how to respond, how to make this better.

"What does it mean if they aren't going back?"

Dov sighs, an angry gust of breath. "It means I'll be a *chayal boded*, a lone soldier, someone the state has to take care of because my family isn't around. Like a foreigner who is volunteering for the army. It means there'll be no one cooking up a storm for me when I come home on leave, nobody waiting for me."

I can't lose him again.

I think back to that picture, the one of us discovering new sites together, knowing it would lead to all the other pictures. Why can't we have that? Maybe this is the answer. Maybe this is our chance.

"Would it be so bad to postpone?" I play with the question for a moment before I say it, turning it over again and again in my mind, searching for traps. "Maybe for a year, you could come with me wherever I'm going, we wouldn't have to end things. And then if—"

"What?" He stares at me, his eyes flashing. "You too? How can you say that? You know how important this is to me. Of all people, *you* know! What, I'm going to tell all my friends, all my classmates, everyone I know that I'm not willing to serve beside them because my girlfriend doesn't want me to go? Everyone I know, Lucy. Everyone. I'd rather sit behind a desk than get out of my service like a coward!"

I recoil, my cheeks flushing, the swing tipping back as I knock it with the back of my knees. "But I thought maybe . . ."

I think of the word love, so whole and full, the way it feels when he holds me in his arms, the beat of his heart against my ear, a hidden music that only I can hear. I think about how right it feels when we're together, how different it is than when I was with Scott, how much I want to take this to the next level. Maybe if he isn't leaving, maybe there's the time to discover more.

For the first time, I understand what it means to be ready to have sex, what it means to make love. I want that. Even more than I did on the evening in his room when he said no. That had been about hormones, about passion. This, right here, this is about love. I want more. I want it all.

I shift my eyes back to Dov's, half expecting to see the same love shining back at me. But that isn't where he's at.

It's like he heard all the thoughts I had and saw my realizations. But his answer is no.

"I was always honest with you, Lucy," he whispers. "I told you I was going. I told you there was an end date, that this was never going to be more than just this."

The agony on his face is nothing close to the way my body splits apart bone by bone, muscle by muscle.

I want to scream at him to stop calling me Lucy, that that isn't who I am. I had been his *motek*, his *nishamah* for months. Each time he says Lucy, it hurts.

"Dov." I try not to plead, try not to beg.

He stares straight at me and I want to look away. I want to, but I can't. The mask he wears hides the face of the boy I love. It hides even the face of the boy who I met on that first day at school, so dismissive. It hides every face of Dov I've ever seen.

"Maybe it would be best if we ended this now," he says coldly, stepping back from me. "We both knew this would end one day, and this is as good a time as any."

"No," I whimper, sitting down heavily on the swing to avoid falling. "Dov, no."

"Lucy," he snaps. "My future is in Israel, not here with you. I'm sorry if you misunderstood the last few months to mean anything but that. And anyway, now it looks like I'll be going home sooner than I expected."

I gasp. And then he turns and walks away.

I don't say anything.

I watch as he walks away from me slowly and deliberately. Then he picks up the pace and starts running. I watch him head down the street, watch him cut around the corner without giving me so much as a glance. I watch until I can't see him anymore and then I continue to stare at the place where I'd last seen him. Until finally it becomes clear he isn't coming back and I force myself to leave the swing and make my way to the car.

If the drive home is a blur, being at home is anything but. Everything hurts. The white noise in my head is so loud I can't think. I yell at Gabe when he rejects the snack I prepare and snap at Sam when he can't find anything to play on his own. My eyes hurt from the brightness of the overhead lights, and I long to turn them all off, burrow deep into the couch and pretend none of this is happening.

Instead, I hide in the bathroom, begging the tears to come so I can find relief, but there's nothing. Crouched on the ground, my head knocking against the pedestal sink, I curl into a ball.

He was always going to leave. As much as I knew that, I realize I'd never really believed it. In the future I created for us, there was always some way to divert him from going, some twist in our story that took us off this certain path and moved us to a safer one, one where Dov could stay here, one where we'd be together.

I'm so stupid. He'd been given his excuse from the army, he'd been given his way out, and he wasn't going to take it. No matter how much he loved me, he wasn't going to take it. He was never going to choose us.

TWENTY-TWO

. . . .

For the next few days, I barely speak.

I stay in bed throughout the weekend, skipping my ballet class with the excuse of a sore throat and a fever. Both are true, though unlikely caused by a virus, as I claimed. I pile on the covers until the weight of the blankets is soothing, until I can almost feel my body again. I sleep as much as I can, and when I'm not sleeping, I listen to Dov's music until I can't stand it anymore.

I rip down the poems I'd tacked to my walls and crumple them, shoving them at the last minute into the bottom of my closet instead of into the garbage. Even Dov's papers: the Yehuda Amichai poems, the line from e. e. cummings, the words to *Mi'ma'amakim* in Hebrew and English, the poem I wrote for him.

I have no more use for words.

Luckily my mom stays in California for the weekend so nobody calls me on the medical necessity of my confinement. When Maddie phones, Dad says I can't talk, and I guess whatever lies I told him are believable because he convinces Maddie, and I make it a couple of days completely alone.

By Tuesday I have to appear to be on the mend or I'll be forced to go to the doctor, and so the following day, I drive myself to school. My limbs are heavy, as though my muscles have atrophied. Thankfully everyone else is experiencing senioritis, so my symptoms appear normal.

Except to Maddie.

"What did he do?" she asks the moment she sees me come in the building.

"Not here," I whisper.

She grabs my arm, pulling me across the school until we're in the foyer, the foyer where I'd first seen Dov. I shake my head and Maddie overrules me. "You look like death warmed over. You don't want to go into any of the areas where other students are."

There is no part of me that cares what they think or what they say.

Except . . .

I don't want to ask.

I don't want to care.

Except . . .

"Is he here?"

Maddie's face is completely blank, and if she makes me spell out who I'm talking about I'll lose it. I'll walk away. I'll run. I'll run like Dov did five days ago. Tears burn in my eyes.

"He's been gone for as long as you have. I just assumed you were both pretending to be sick together . . ." I shake my head, and Maddie's face falls. "I'm going to kill him," she whispers. "What the fuck did he do to hurt you like this?"

"It wasn't his fault," I whisper, and the story comes out in fits and starts as I stare at my clasped hands and try desperately to sob quietly.

"Oh honey," she says and pulls me into a tight hug. "I'm so, so sorry."

And then she leads me out of the building, and I don't protest. What are they going to do if I skip another day? Rescind my graduation?

don't show up to Ginger's classes all week, ignoring the concerned text she sends. I can't.

The only time I feel conscious of what's going on around me is when I'm at school, when I expect to see Dov at any moment. I scan the hallways as I walk, half terrified, half desperate to see him.

But he isn't there.

The following weekend, I push past the ache and return to the familiar: studying. I write my English paper and then my history project. When I run out of assignments, I do extra work. Instead of choosing one essay topic, I do three. I have nothing better to do. I bury myself back into my head, into the parts of me that are familiar and safe.

Working can't hurt me.

When I show up for my ballet class, it's clear I'm going through the motions. I ignore Annabelle when she tells me the other girls are still chewing gum, and then I snap at her when she reminds me I promised to download new music for their *adagio* routine. I apologize at the end of class, but she just nods without meeting my eyes.

I feel like shit for a moment until that's replaced by nothingness again.

On Monday, Dov shows up at school again, and in response, I stay as close as possible to Maddie when I'm
not in class. Though while Dov is present, he's only barely
there. He's gone back to being the last one in the classroom
and the first one out. His body is tight, wiry. The easy grin
that unwound me has been replaced by a permanent scowl.
In the hallways I keep my head down, my body skirting the
walls so I don't see him. I can't look at him. I'm broken.
Everyone can see it.

I need this year to be over.

He was never going to choose us.

That week, I dance every night, twisting and leaping and
spinning until I can feel every muscle individually. I bring
my pointe shoes, ignoring Ginger's concern that I should
take it slowly. I dance until my toes bleed, soaking through
my tights into the lamb's wool. I dance until I can barely
walk to my car at the end of class.

I say nothing to anyone in my family. The only person I tell
is Amy, and really only because she calls on a day I'm alone
in the house, cocooned in heavy blankets on the couch.

"How is your sweet boy?" she asks innocently, and I
can't help it, can't control myself. The tears burst through.

For once, she doesn't have an easy answer, doesn't even
have a funny quip. She listens to my heart shatter and tells
me that she loves me.

Every day, another one of my classmates announces their
college decision. After that, it's as if they have an endless
supply of paraphernalia from their chosen school. I don't

know where they get it, whether it's picked out hurriedly from the website when they return their acceptance letter, or whether it shows up once the check is deposited. There are cupcakes and decorated lockers and squeals of joy on a regular basis, and I turn away from it all.

My acceptances stay in a pile on the coffee table, untouched by me but rifled through by everyone, including Sam and Gabe who have their own opinions on the subject. I only have a few more weeks before I have to make a decision, and I'm no closer to caring. I keep track of who's going where, especially if it involves my seven schools, but that's really it. When teachers or other students ask me, I play the part I'm expected to. I smile so widely, I'm worried I'll tumble out.

It's been more than two weeks since Dov even looked in my direction, and it's difficult to muster a smile. The only thing that actually makes me happy is Ginger's classes at the studio. Between the music and the strain on my body, I can lose myself for a few hours.

But Friday, Ginger corners me after class, asking me to stay to help her set up for the next session.

"I've been really pleased with your teaching this term, but I hadn't had a chance to talk to you about teaching this summer." She doesn't look at me as she shifts the barres into the center for the next class.

I take in a deep breath, filling my lungs to the point of bursting. "Sorry," I whisper.

Ducking out at the end of each class was probably the coward's way out. The truth is, I don't know what I'll do without my classes at the studio. Especially now that Dov . . .

"I'll do anything."

She smiles, but the movement of her mouth isn't reflected in her eyes. "What are you thinking about for next year? I remember you were thinking about Northwestern, but I don't know where things are at now."

I wish I could lie.

"Truthfully, I have no idea. I've been accepted to a bunch of colleges, including Northwestern. But I just don't know. I'm not sure what I want."

Understatement of the century. I have no idea at all.

"But if I'm at Northwestern, I'd love to continue teaching," I say, and the thought only slightly warms my heart to the possibility of remaining in Evanston.

I hate the idea of staying here.

"You don't seem particularly excited."

I shrug, pointing and flexing my foot over and over instead of meeting Ginger's eyes. "They're all good choices. And they'll all lead me in the right direction."

"That's good," Ginger starts. She motions to the last barre, and I help her carry it out. I stare at the barre legs intently, shifting them back and forth to make them perfectly parallel to the side wall. "But sometimes it's as important to see the possibility of what's in front of you, where the next step lies. Take that opportunity and trust the right path will build itself with the steps you take."

Her words jolt me out of my numbness. I'd always been so good at following the path, looking ahead to the final goal.

Until this year.

This year, I'd stepped out of that planned track. And as a result, I picked up Dov in the rain that Sunday morning. I called him on my birthday. I invited him to our messy

Thanksgiving dinner. I kissed him, even though I knew the whole thing was temporary. Each time I took a step without knowing where it would lead, what story it would create. And it was the same with dance. Would I have ever discovered how much I like teaching kids had it not been for the single decision I made to walk back into the studio?

I think about the line from a Mary Oliver poem that always felt off but now makes perfect sense:

It is better for the heart to break, than not to break.

As painful as the past two weeks have been, the idea that had I stayed with the script I never would have experienced the past few months makes my stomach clench. It's shocking, but I realize I'd take this heartbreak any day if it meant the gift of falling in love with Dov again, or of coming back to the studio.

"What do *you* want to do next year?"

My first thought is the quote. Part of me wishes I'd never torn down the wall of poems and quotes and stories, but I couldn't have left them up. They were too much. I needed the blank walls to give myself a chance to build something new. I wonder about buying a blank journal where I can write the words that inspire me. Where I can play with words without them quite being so public.

"Lucy?" Ginger asks again, and I realize I never answered her question.

I bite my lip, hard. Outside of buying a blank journal to fill, I need to move on from what I actually wanted, which was the possibility of a life with Dov, and start thinking about next year, about my life without Dov.

"I want . . ." I place my fingertips on the barre and do a series of *dégagés*, forward, side, back, side, forward, side, back, side, over and over.

"I want to take a year off from worrying about my future," I say slowly, the movements of the *dégagés* calming. "I want to try stuff out, see what feels right. To stop worrying about making the wrong decision. I wish I could keep dancing, keep teaching. But only if it isn't here in Evanston."

I switch to a series of *grande battements*. Ginger's hands come to rest on my hips, steadying them, reminding me with the pressure of her fingertips that even when I'm playing at the barre, I need to have correct alignment.

"What about doing an intensive dance program?"

My leg stutters mid-*battement*. I hold it there for a moment as the idea fills my body, blossoming. God, yes. How had I not thought of that?

"I can see by the look on your face that you like the idea."

"I do," I admit, without meeting her eyes. "But there's part of me that also wants to use the year to do good in the world." I dissect the words as they come out of my mouth, search for hints that I'm just trying to do what someone else wants me to do, but I don't feel it. This *is* what I want. I want to do good in the world. I want to put my life on hold for one year to give back.

Ginger's hands leave my hips, and I pull in my abdominals, making sure my hips stay in the position she'd left them.

"I know of two programs that could be of interest," Ginger starts. She moves to the other end of the barre so I can switch to the other side, do the routine again with the other leg. I love that she knows I would do that, love that she doesn't need to ask. "One is a high-level dance internship at a studio attached to a dance school in London. You'd be in your own dance classes all day and then teach the girls in the evenings. The girls the school attracts are all pre-professional, committed to ballet. Definitely focused and driven.

"The other is a lesser-known program. You'd be dancing during the evening, and teaching during the day. But the program is based in a less economically rich area, so your teaching would be more outreach work, going into schools that ordinarily don't have dance programs or even arts programs in general. You'd need to teach a variety of forms of dance, and you'd have students who've had little to no experience. The program is much less expensive than the London school, and it attracts a much more diverse group of girls from all over the world. That said, it's not as fancy as London, the accommodations aren't as nice, and it's probably much harder work."

I finish my set of *grand battements* and stay in place, my fingertips still grazing the barre, feet in first position. Students who've never danced, who've never had the means to dance. There's something about the idea that feels right in a way that nothing else has. I'd be able to dance, be able to continue to teach, but I'd also be volunteering, bringing the possibility of dance and music to kids who need it.

"Are you sure the deadline hasn't passed?" I hold my breath as I wait for Ginger's reply, the certainty that this is the option I want filling me. She wouldn't have told me about it if it was too late, right?

I turn to face her when she doesn't reply, and she smiles thinly. "The London program is open to applications until

June. The other one I'll need to check on. I can talk to my friend Devorah Ben-Dov. It's a pretty flexible program so my guess is they can fit you in."

Dov.

My breath hitches at the sound of his name. I know the answer to the question I'm going to ask before I speak it, know suddenly why her smile is tight. "Where's the program based?"

"In Northern Israel," she says, and just hearing the words make my muscles clench.

No. No. No.

"I think I told you about the dance festival I'd done in Northern Israel? I met Devorah there, back when we were both students. She'd grown up nearby, in a similar situation to the kids she now teaches. She only started dancing in high school, and because of that, she'd never had enough years of practice to go professional. She's been working on her school for years, bringing in dancers she can teach, basically in exchange for their help bringing dance into these poorer communities. She's an excellent teacher, and I think you'd learn a lot from her."

I hug her, promise to think it over, and I grab my stuff and walk out the door. I try to focus on the first program, the one in London. It's still dance, it's still teaching. But my mind keeps returning to the second one, the one where students have no access to the dance classes and studios I'd grown up with, wishing Ginger had said it was located anywhere else. South Africa, Italy, Russia, Cambodia. I'd go anywhere for that program.

But I can't go to Israel.

bemoan the unfairness of it all to Amy, sitting in her sunroom. Maddie is on her way to meet us, we're planning to spend the day downtown with her and Megan, some window shopping for graduation gifts and then a fancy lunch at the Palmer Hotel.

"Why not do it?" she asks, face tipped back as though she can catch a tan through the glass windows. While it's unseasonably cold outside, between the sun and Amy's need to keep the temperature high, I want to purr like a cat in the warmth.

"Are you crazy?" I choke. "People will think I'm following Dov. Worse, Dov will think that."

"Are you?" Her voice is so even, I almost wonder if she's asking me seriously.

"Of course not," I scowl. "Even before . . ." I can't say the words so I fake-cough. "He made it clear my being in Israel wouldn't change things. When you're in the army—at least the type of army unit he wants to be in—it takes over your whole life. He'll be spending all his time in the army; it's more important than anything else."

More important than me.

"Tell me why you'd want to do this program."

I take a deep breath and allow myself to imagine it for a moment. When I finally get to college, I'll be a full year behind everyone else. They'll have moved on without me.

But then I think about Annabelle and the other girls in my class. I picture them in the landscape Dov drew for me, the lush verdant hills of Northern Israel. The Mediterranean Sea steps away. I picture them growing up without the opportunity to discover the joy of letting yourself go in the music, letting your body move. The joy of working on a series of movements over and over, until it's all you think of, until it's all you dream of, until you can feel it in your muscles when you get it right.

And then I imagine myself there, in Israel. I push past Dov's Israel and think about Amy's comments on Thanksgiving, how it had been the place Grandpa Leo's family had longed to go, and how they'd never made it there.

And before I can open my mouth, Amy stops me. "Don't bother. The look on your face is enough, and you know it. And if you know it, then who cares what anyone else thinks?"

As I'm about to reply, Megan interrupts by ushering Maddie into the sunroom. "God, I think this is my favorite room in the universe," she mutters, flopping down onto the couch. "But what's with the long faces?"

Amy leans over and kisses her on the cheek. "Lucy is just complaining that if she does the dance program in Israel, people will think she's following Dov."

Maddie rolls her eyes. "Who cares?"

"That's what I said!" Amy coos like a little girl. "See, we agree. Who cares?"

Maddie sits up, takes a deep breath, and then lets it out all out in a gust. "You've worked so hard to be this perfect daughter, to make sure your brothers are taken care of, that things at home are normal despite your mom's absence. You've earned all the top grades you were expected to earn, did everything they wanted. Now it's your turn. If you want to go to college, then more power to you. But if you don't, or if you don't want to go right now, you don't owe them anything. Not your parents, not the school, not anybody."

"Agreed!" Amy raises her fist in the air. "And you can tell your parents I said that."

"They'll kill me." My eyes widen at the possibility.

"Eh," Amy shrugs. "Tell your mom you were inspired to follow your heart after watching her do the same thing."

I giggle, nerves shaking my insides. Can I really do this? "Everyone will freak out."

"Which will be awesome," Amy promises.

Except evidently when it comes time to tell my parents.

I'm surprised to see them both at the dining room table the next morning. Usually Mom's gone by now.

She reaches for my hand as I walk by. I glance at them quizzically. They both seemed alright, no red eyes, no tense shoulders. I relax for a moment. Until I see the pile of college catalogs on the table in front of them.

"So, what are you thinking about? Which choice are you leaning toward?" Mom asks. Dad takes her hand and squeezes it, and I hate that I have a momentary flash of anger at him. *Don't be nice to her*, I want to yell. She's made our lives impossible because . . . she needed to do what she needed to do. Amy was right.

I think about Annabelle. I think about the picture of Israel in my mind, a country I'd never dreamed of wanting to go to, but now one that I dream about all the time. It's okay that in some ways Dov inspired my interest. As much as it hurts to go without him, as much as it hurts to do anything without him, this is ultimately my decision, my choice. "I'm not sure I want to attend any of these schools."

Dad opens his mouth, but Mom shakes her head ever so slightly. "I know it's hard to imagine yourself at these schools; they look so different from the academy. But trust me, they're all good choices. Any of them would be a dream school. It's really a matter of choosing between a bunch of really good options. But if none of them appeal to you, or none stand out, then I'd ask you to choose Northwestern. Because if they are all the same to you, it would make a big difference to us."

My shoulders curl in as I stare at the pictures on the covers of the brochures, stalling. Maybe this isn't the best time. If I make the decision and then tell them, they can't do anything about it.

But that isn't fair to them. I can't lead them on.

I have to be brave.

I pull out a chair and sit down a few seats away from both of them. I focus on the grain of the wood table, sliding my nail back and forth across a small groove in front of me. "I was serious about taking a gap year," I say slowly, dreading the words that I'm sure will come. "And I think I've found a good program for me."

I press my fingernail in deeper, until my nail turns white. I imagine the looks that are being exchanged over my head, but I keep my gaze focused on the table. It's silent for a moment until Dad clears his throat. "What is it?"

I press my lips together, stalling again. Now is when it's going to get bad.

I tell them about Devorah's school. I show them the program's website on my phone, the description of what I'd be doing, pictures of the types of students I'd be working with. I hold the little screen between their two bodies, praying that in these images they see how right this is, how perfect it is for me, given everything I want.

But I don't look at their faces. I'm not that brave.

"What, now you want to become a ballet teacher? You're giving up college to be a ballet teacher?" The disdain in Mom's voice is so thick I recoil.

"No," I say, trying desperately to keep my tone calm. "This isn't about what I'm going to do for the rest of my life. This is about next year. I've been so focused on—"

Mom pushes her chair back and it scrapes along the floor. "You aren't following some boy to Israel and giving up on college. I don't care what kind of freedom you think you have here. That's not happening."

"Clare, calm down."

"Andrew, I don't want to hear a word from you. Clearly the way you've handled things here hasn't been terribly successful." She turns and glares at me. When she speaks, every word is carefully enunciated such that it sounds like its own distinct sentence. "You are not going to delay college to spend a year in Israel. And that's final. If you really have no idea what you want to do, go to Northwestern. There are plenty of people in the world who would give up everything to go to such a good school."

Anger courses through my veins, but I breathe deeply, trying desperately to keep it at bay. Anger isn't going to work here. I need to stay focused. "I'm not sure I understand why this is such a big deal," I say carefully, trying to remember the words I'd read on the gap-year program websites. "Taking a gap year is considered a great learning experience, leading to more mature students who attend college. I don't want to waste next year trying to figure things out while you're paying over $60,000 a year. I'd rather take the year to figure out what I want and go to college clearer and more directed."

"Seriously?" Mom glares. "You seriously think I'm going to buy that? You don't think I was once a teenager?" She shakes her head dismissively. "If you wanted to take a gap year to broaden your horizons or because you really weren't ready for college, I could understand that. But you're not delaying college and putting your future in jeopardy so you can take ballet classes and continue screwing your boyfriend!"

"Clare, that's enough!" Dad shouts.

"No, Andrew, I don't think you understand what's happening here. Before I left, she was getting good grades. She knew what she wanted, and she had a nice boyfriend. All I've been hearing over the past few months is what a mess everything has become with this new boy. I'm not letting this get any worse. Someone clearly needs to step in here and be the parent."

Dad flings his chair back as he storms up to her. "Really, Clare? Really? You're going to play the 'good parent' card? Maybe you should have thought of that before you disappeared this year. What was supposed to be three days a week in California has taken over our lives. You're barely here for more than thirty-six hours on weekends, and that's when you even bother to show up."

"How dare you? If you weren't so selfish in demanding we stay in Evanston, we could be together. You think your career is so much more important than mine, but let me tell you—"

"Stop!" I yell. They turn slowly, barely able to take their eyes off each other, mouths open and ready to argue. I forge on, trying to keep my tone level. "I've always been the good girl. I've done what's right. I've never been the one to make decisions based on what's best for me. I never make a fuss, not when Mom left, not when I had to take on more work at home, not with anything." I take another breath. "Now I want to make decisions based on what's best for me. I know this isn't what you want, and I know you're afraid that this will make me lose my way. But here's the thing: when you don't know where you're going, you can't get lost. I've been holding onto the paths that everyone else wanted for me, but I realized this year that that's been cowardly on my part. I should be trying to figure out where *I'm* going and who *I* want to be."

I stand up slowly, preparing to leave, hoping beyond hope they aren't going to stop me. "And while it's neither here nor there, Dov and I aren't together anymore. We haven't been for several weeks. But I'd be lying if I said this wasn't inspired by Dov, because it is. Even though it's over between us, he taught me that it's not just noble but necessary to sometimes put what you want on hold to do what's needed. But if you want to know who really made me feel like this is the right choice, it was Amy. Amy and her stories about Grandpa Leo's family who always dreamt of going to Israel, but who died before they got a chance to make it there. I want to do good in the world. I want to be able to dance and teach, and I want to do it in a place that has a connection to my family. And I'm really not sure why that's not something you're proud of."

And with that, I take advantage of their frozen faces and walk out of the dining room and out the front door.

I walk for hours around the neighborhood, wishing I could make my way to Dov's house. That I could tell him about this crazy plan. That I could tell him what I'd done, what I'd said. But instead I leave a message for Maddie and then Ginger. I call Amy, who out of everyone is perhaps the most excited, immediately promising to take a trip to visit me there and see what has changed since she was there so long ago. I walk and I talk with them and I remember that I have so many people who love me. Who support me.

I come home to find Dad reading the paper on the front porch. For a moment I just watch him, his combination of Patagonia fleece top and thick socks with sandals and shorts make me laugh. He'd never be able to make it in California. He's comfortable in his flannel and wool, the cool air, the lakes and the changing leaves of the Midwest. But then, what do you do? What do you do when your wife gets a great job across the country? When do you follow, and when do you admit that your feet are planted in the ground here?

Dad puts down the paper and waves, smiling. I make my way slowly, as he moves his coffee cup from the chair beside him. He angles his chair to face the one he's cleared for me, and I sink down into it.

"I'm sorry," I say quickly, staring at the scuff marks on the porch floor, the residue of chalk marks on the brick facade that Gabe left when he'd "painted" the house two years ago. "I know you wanted me to go to Northwestern—"

"Honey," Dad interrupts, moving his head so it's in my line of vision. He presses his lips together, and I watch the familiar movement of the little patch of beard below his bottom lip flip up. "I want you to be happy. I only advocated for you to stay here when I thought that was what you wanted."

"I don't know what will make me happy in the end," I say.

"The end isn't important right now." He puts down the paper. "You've been forced to be much more responsible than most eighteen-year-olds. Given all that, I'm even more impressed that instead of running from more responsibility, you're embracing it. I think it's good you're taking this risk. That's the only way you truly learn about yourself."

I forgot, in my rush to prove myself responsible and self-sufficient, that I still have people who can help me. How much easier would all this have been if I hadn't tried to do it all by myself?

I must be looking worriedly at the door because Dad puts his hand on mine. "Go talk to her," he says firmly. "She'll be fine with your decision, in the end. But this is hard on her. Even though she's been back and forth, she hasn't really been here, and she's only now realizing the cost of her decision. This was your last year at home, and not only has she missed being here for it, but she's also missed seeing you go through this intense period of growth. Seeing you now, making this decision, I think only served to bring that home for her."

"I didn't ask her to—"

"I'm not saying it's your fault. I'm saying she needs a little more time to get used to the idea of who you've become. I've been proudly watching it all year, but she hasn't been here to see you in action."

I stare at the wood slats peeking out of the chipping grey porch floor. I need to make sure I help Dad repaint it before I leave. Otherwise it's unlikely it will get done until next summer when I come back. Next summer, Gabe will be ten and Sam eight. Maybe by then they'll be helping Dad paint the porch in the early summer as I've always done. We'll be able to video chat, email even, but what details will I miss seeing from far away? What am I giving up by following my heart?

What will be the cost of *my* choice?

"I know it's none of my business," I say, not looking up from the porch floor, "but what's going to happen? With Mom? Will you guys be okay if she keeps going back and forth?"

He doesn't respond, and I finally bring my eyes to his.

"I don't know," he says, and his smile is sad. "Sometimes it's easier to take things one year at a time. We made it through this year, and she'll be here all summer. And next year will be hard, because both of you will be gone. In an ideal world, she'd be happy here or I'd be willing to move there, but I think you already know that sometimes we have to live in a world that is not ideal. But we love each other, and we love you kids. And right now, we have to keep hoping it works.

"In a lot of ways, what you're going through is not unlike what she's going through. And just as I couldn't ask you to give up something you truly need to do, I can't ask her either. Because as much as making the decision has consequences, giving up what you need has far greater consequences."

I think about Dov and his need to go to the army, to have the type of service that is meaningful to him.

I give Dad a kiss, his beard scratching my cheek, and walk more calmly into the house.

The decision has been made, and as Amy likes to say in a faux Southern drawl: it's all over but the shouting.

TWENTY-THREE

· · · · · · · · · · · · · ·

The sky is dark and ominous on the day I say no to all my college options. The type of day you know in your bones will lead to a bad storm. My parents agree that there is no point in deferring my acceptance if I don't know where I'll want to go after this year. But still it feels crazy to commit to going through all this again. But I don't need a quote in my quickly-filling journal to know that it's the right path.

Next year, I'll be in Israel. And while I know from Dov that the country often suffers from a lack of rain, there'll be something nice about not staring at a sky like the one above me right now, worrying about tornado warnings. Slowly I've allowed myself to daydream about being there. After the months of hearing about Dov's Israel, I can't wait to discover my own Israel. Even if I can't experience it with Dov.

While May might bring torrential rains and the tornado watches, it also brings lighter days at school, like today, the official Senior Skip Day (how laughable to have our day of defiance planned by the administration). Which means I'm turning the car around in the parking lot after dropping off the boys and leaving a gift for Mrs. Schneider, when I catch a glimpse of someone who looks like Dov through my rearview mirror.

I blink. That can't be. Dov is basically gone. In the last couple of weeks, he'd barely been in class, and every time I'd seen him in the hallways, he had his earbuds firmly lodged in his ears. This week, he hadn't been in class at all.

One day I'll stop thinking I see him in every runner on the sidewalk, in every guy drinking coffee in a café.

Given that he's already probably in Israel, I should start now.

"Lucy!" Mrs. Schneider yells to me from the doorway of the side door. I roll down the window, and she darts toward me. "Thank you so much! It's a lovely present and I'm thrilled with your decision."

I'd given her a book of Yehuda Amichai's poetry, a copy that matched the one I'd bought myself.

"I've never read any of Amichai's poetry, but it's funny that you dropped this off, since Dov also gave me a copy of Amichai's poems, but a different collection. I imagine you two coordinated it—"

"Wait, Dov?" I interrupt. Could it really have been him?

I don't care. I don't care.

"Yes." She seems puzzled. "I assumed you'd come in together—"

"Just now?"

She frowns but her chin moves up and down. The wind is gusting, whipping her hair around. "He dropped by and said he was going on a run along the lake."

On a run. During a tornado watch.

"But there's a tornado warning," I whisper.

"I told him that, but he seemed distracted by something," Mrs. Schneider says and now even she's scanning the parking lot.

Shit. Shit. Shit.

"Go inside," I say, and scan my rearview mirror.

"Drive carefully in this weather!" she yells over her shoulder, darting back into the school, her long skirt flapping in the wind. I check the weather app. It's just a warning I know, it's probably nothing but . . .

Dov.

I glance back through my rearview mirror, scanning for a glimpse of his red T-shirt through the trees as the rains begin.

True, tornados are rare in Chicago, but definitely not impossible. Best case scenario, we're in for a pretty crazy storm right now and he's walking home.

I shut my eyes and take a deep breath. Not my circus, not my monkeys, I remind myself. He's eighteen, he can look after himself. And next year . . .

I start up the car and push away all the thoughts that are swirling. I'm not responsible for him. He doesn't want my help.

As I drive, I watch the trees around me sway from the force of the wind. I tell myself I feel anxious because one could snap and hit the car, but I know the truth. I can feel it in the pit of my stomach when I get home and pull into my driveway.

I want to back out and drive around Evanston. Find him. Tell him he's being ridiculous. Tell him he can't . . .

One step in front of the other, I make my way into the house.

By the time the doorbell rings, I've almost succeeded in letting go of the fear in the pit of my stomach. Until I see Dov.

And even though I've spent the last two hours pretending not to be worrying, it still takes a while to process what I'm seeing. Dov is panting, his clothing is soaked, water is dripping from his hair. His body is hunched over slightly, like he's protecting a part of himself or too tired to care. I stand there for an uncomfortable minute, startled more by his closeness than his appearance.

After a particularly loud crack of thunder, I snap out of it. "Are you okay?" I whisper, ushering him in without touching him.

"I've been running." He struggles. "My parents are out of town, and I couldn't handle the idea of going back to my empty house. So I ran."

All this time?

The tornados hadn't materialized, but it had been bad for the last hour and a half. He was out there all this time.

"Let me find something," I start to say but he grabs my hand, his touch cold, and I startle. It's been twenty-nine days since I last felt his body touch mine.

Tears gather in my eyes. His teeth are chattering hard, and I remember when we went hiking, how we got caught in the rain, and I was so cold, and he took care of me.

"Lucy," he pleads. "Lucy, I'm so—"

I shake my head. "You need to get warm. Everything else is secondary." I don't wait for his reply before sprinting to the laundry room to find towels. In seconds I'm back, cradling a small pile. Gently, I dry his wet face, knowing it's only cosmetic, that it's about making me feel better. I need to touch him even if it's through a towel. His eyes close as I wipe his forehead, light strokes across his cheeks and nose. I brush the tendrils of wet hair behind his ears, trying to slow the rivulets of water soaking his shirt.

My hands shake. I can't believe I'm touching him.

I wrap his shoulders in a thick blue towel, and then crouch in front of him and use another to wrap around his legs. He shivers uncontrollably, and I don't know if it's my touch or the chill.

"I need to get you into a hot bath," I say, more to myself than him. "I don't know how else to warm you up."

I undo the laces of his sneakers, and he places his fingers on my shoulder, barely touching me, as I slip off one shoe and then the other. His socks are soaked through as though he'd been walking shoeless through puddles, with nothing to protect him. I tug them off clumsily, and this time he puts his whole hand on my shoulder. I try not to react, try not to give him an excuse to remove it. His feet are so wet his toes are white and puckered. They're not the feet that played with mine as we'd snuggled in bed so many times.

"I'm so sorry." His whisper is still hoarse, but his words no longer sound as though they're stuck in his throat, as though he hasn't spoken in days. "I'm so sorry, *nishamah*."

I gasp. It hurts to hear him call me *nishamah* again. "Shhh, everything's fine." I get the second sock off and stand up, noticing how red his eyes are, the pained look on his face.

"I never should have said those things . . ."

I place my hand on his cold cheek, my thumb grazing the side of his nose and look at him intently. He doesn't flinch.

His eyes shift away from me, and he stares at the puddle accumulating on the floor.

"Did you mean what you said in your essay?"

My stomach tenses and I drop my hand. My essay?

"Mrs. Schneider," he says, answering my sharp intake of breath as I realize what he's referring to. "I saw her today and she said how moving it was, how proud I must be and . . . she assumed I'd read it. And then I needed to see it. I didn't want to at first, but then I couldn't stop myself. So I lied and said I hadn't seen the final version, and she gave me a copy."

I think back to the words I'd written so long ago. Why hadn't I shown it to him, even back when we were alright, back when I'd dreamt about our future together?

Would it have made a difference?

"Why . . ." I shrug my shoulders. There's something I'm missing, something that isn't making sense.

"I need to know if you meant what you wrote there, about me," he says, his voice pleading. "I was so angry at first, so angry you'd sided with my mom, but when I read your words, you made it seem like you respected my decision—"

"Of course I do."

"I know," he says simply. "That's why I needed to see you. That's why I kept running and running, and I couldn't make myself go home. I needed to see you and tell you how sorry I am."

His words hang between us, and I think how easy it would be to take him into my arms, how much better it would make everything. "I meant it when I wrote it."

His eyes find mine. "But not anymore?"

I squeeze my eyes shut, shifting my weight so I'm leaning against the door. The rain slides down the house, the backyard filling with water that the soil can't absorb quickly enough. "I think," I say slowly, opening my eyes but not looking up, "your commitment to put your life on hold for three years to serve your country is selfless and admirable. And I think this country would be a better country if eighteen-year-olds were expected to make that commitment."

I pause, regretting my decision to go down this path. Why risk losing it all again? I clench my fists until my nails dig into my palms.

"But . . ." I drag the word out, knowing I can't keep the rest in, can't forget the picture of his mom sitting on the porch. I think about the conversation I'd had with my mom after I'd talked to my dad, how she listened to me talk about what this year had been like, what had drawn me to the decision to go to the dance program. How it pained her that she'd missed out on being my mom not only for the bad moments but also for the good ones. I take a deep breath and force the words out. "But I also think there's something really selfish about you. You're so wrapped up in what you need that you don't consider how your decisions affect others. You don't let yourself hear the fear in your parents' voices when they talk about the possibility of losing another son. Their only other son. And you don't care how . . ."

Dov opens his mouth and then stops himself, nodding back to me as he closes his lips tightly.

"I love you, Dov. I still do, despite what happened. Maybe I always will. And I know I'm only eighteen, I'm only a kid. I know the chances are that we . . ." I shake my head, "would not have lasted forever."

I take a deep breath and hold it for a moment, knowing I'm about to let out all the words I'd hidden deep in the bottom of my lungs. "Somehow your act of selflessness, of wanting to make a difference, became more selfish than anything else. When I wrote that essay, I could only see the admirable parts. I couldn't see how it had stopped being a sacrifice for you anymore. It became everyone else who needed to sacrifice so you could have your dream. And maybe that's fine. Maybe you're allowed to want something so badly that nobody else gets a say in it, but you can't then claim you're doing it for the greater good. Because you're doing it for your own good, that's all. If you wind up protecting your country in the meantime, that's an added bonus."

I stare down at his feet; his toes pressed down hard. Was he about to take off?

Dov clears his throat, and I move my gaze to his Adam's apple, watch it bob. When he runs from here, will he grab his shoes or leave them behind?

"You're right, *nishamah*," he whispers. "You were always right." He starts to sway, and I grab his hand, shocked by how cold he is even in our warm foyer. He grips mine tightly.

"I didn't want to be that guy. I said I would never hurt you. I promised you. But hurting people is all I ever seem to do," he says, his voice so miserable it cuts through me.

I lift my face, forcing him to meet my eyes. He stares at me sadly.

"I would not give up a single moment we had together," I say fiercely. "Not a single minute. Even if right now you walked out the door, and I never saw you again. Every single moment we had was worth it. Every moment."

He opens his mouth to speak, but I shake my head.

"Come," I say, wrapping my free arm around the rough towel that envelops him. "We need to get you warm."

He lets me lead him upstairs.

I bring Dov into the bathroom and crank the hot water in the tub. Our claw-foot bathtub is great to soak in, but it takes a while to fill up. "I'll put your stuff in the dryer later," I say as steam begins to rise toward the ceiling. "Stay in here, near the tub, but don't turn off the water until it's really high, until it will cover you completely when you finally get in." I pour some of Sam's favorite bath soap in the water.

I peek at Dov and I'm relieved to find that a little color has returned to his cheeks. He nods mutely but grabs my hand as I start out the door. "Come back?" he pleads.

"I promise." I walk out of the bathroom, the cold air of the hallway shocking me. Good, at least that means the bathroom is getting warm. I run downstairs, clean the mess of water on the floor and put Dov's discarded shoes and socks on the radiator. And then slowly, I make my way back up the stairs.

When I reach the bathroom door, I pause and listen for a moment. The water is no longer running. I rap softly on the door. "Dov," I call. "Can I come in?"

The door swings open with a squeak, and my heart jumps. Dov is still sitting on the closed toilet where I'd left him, the bath now filled with water and piled high with bubbles.

"Why didn't you get in?" The air is thick and wet as I walk in and the steam makes it hard to see anything clearly.

"I wasn't sure . . . I wasn't sure it was really okay."

I close the door swiftly so as not to lose the hot air and kneel in front of him, taking his hands in mine. Thankfully they're warmer, and I rub them gratefully.

"What will your dad think?"

"I'll figure it out. Right now it's you I'm worried about."

"I don't want to do anything that will get you in trouble."

I lean forward, take the bottom edge of his T-shirt in my hands and pull it up, slipping it over his head in one graceful ark. His chest is still cold and clammy beneath Yuval's dog tags. While I long to put my hands on his shoulders, to climb onto his lap and wrap myself around him until he's warm, I stand up instead. "I'm not going to do the rest, but I'll turn around until you get into the tub."

I move to the corner of the bathroom and lean my head against the wall. I let my cheek rest against the cool tiles. I don't know if it's the heat of the bathroom or the sound of Dov removing his pants, the water sloshing in the tub as he steps inside, but I long to lie down on the floor, my head on the cold ground, and go to sleep.

"You can turn around." Dov speaks softly.

I move slowly, my gaze staying near the floor. Maybe this is a terrible idea. How can I really have Dov, this boy I love, this boy I would do anything for, naked in this tiny room with me? Even from the door, it would take only two steps to reach him, only a moment to step inside, slide beside him in the giant tub, clothing be damned.

I walk over to him, staring at his right arm that is extended across the lip of the bathtub, not looking up at his face. I sit down beside the tub, his arm at eye level.

I lean over and take his hand, disengaging it from the rim and holding it in mine. I need to think of something else, something that has nothing to do with nudity and comfort and what could happen if everything was different. "I'm so glad you're here," I whisper, my voice sleepy. "I thought you were gone, that I'd never see you again."

"I am so sorry, *nishamah*," he says, and I tighten my grasp, ever so slightly. "I've been so lost these past few weeks . . ."

Dov's voice fades, and we sit in silence side by side, his hand still in mine, my face pressed against the side of the tub. There will be time for talking later.

TWENTY-FOUR

. . . .

When Dov is finally warm enough to exit the bathroom, I leave him to get dressed in some of my dad's old clothing. Even once he's dressed through, his breathing is labored. He leans heavily on me, and I wonder how badly he hurt himself on his run. I motion him to my bed, but he pauses as he scans the walls.

"What happened to the poems?"

I shift nervously beside him. "It was hard to see them after . . . There were too many words and they were all meaningless—"

"I'm so sorry," he says, pain streaked through his words.

I shake my head. "Come on." I lead him over to my bed. He insists on lying on top of the covers, so I find an old blanket in the closet to drape over him. He touches the place on the wall where he'd tacked his paper, and I force myself to breathe.

"The boys will be home soon. I need to meet them downstairs and open the door. I'll be right back."

"Will you come back upstairs?"

"I'll come back up."

I pace across the living room as I wait for them to show up. When the carpool finally drops them off, I need to clench my teeth to avoid yelling at them to come into the house more quickly.

"Hungry?" I ask, already halfway to the kitchen as they're taking off their boots.

"Starving!" Gabe yells. I settle them in front of the TV, glasses of milk beside plates of snacks. Then I head back upstairs to Dov.

I stop when I reach my door. Dov is lying still on my bed, beneath the empty wall. What good were all those other people's words? Did they really know more, or understand more, than I did? Part of me is relieved they're gone. It's the boy who lies there now that matters.

The words we use are the ones that have power.

"*Bo'i nishamah,*" he whispers groggily, his eyes still closed. He reaches his fingers toward me. "Can you sit with me for a few minutes?"

I nod. I want to lie down beside him, fit my body around his, hold him until he falls asleep, but instead I simply sit down on the bed. He lifts his head and I scoot closer, until his head lies in my lap, my hand resting on his hair. He snuggles closer, and I rake my fingers through his curls gently.

"*Nishama, ani lo yodeah ma ha'iti oseh biladayich . . .*" he mumbles, and while I don't know what most of what he says means, I understand. There's no clear path, but we're still here.

"Shhh," I whisper. Holding one of his hands, I continue to stroke his head with the other, my fingers playing with his curls until his body loses its tension, and his breath calms and deepens. I sit with him like that, his head cradled in my lap, as tears stream down my face.

"Take care of him," I repeat quietly over and over again to nobody and everybody all at once. "No matter what happens, just don't let anything hurt him. Keep him safe. Keep him whole."

That's how Dad finds us when he comes home.

In my defense, the kids were still only on their first video, and there'd been no mess as a result of their eating their snacks on the couch. That said, I can also understand that that's not really what he's upset about.

"He took a bath here?" he says a few times, his eyes darting back and forth to the bathroom door from the hallway, as though it would give him an indication as to what had happened.

"He was hurt."

"And the boys? Were they here when your boyfriend was naked in our bathroom?"

I bristle at the word boyfriend but try to ignore the subtext. "They weren't here then. He's not my boyfriend. And I kept them downstairs since they came home because I didn't want them to get scared. Dov wasn't in good shape."

Dad stares at my closed bedroom door. "Is he on something?"

"Dad! No. He got caught in the storm. He was soaked through and just needed to warm up."

For a moment he's quiet, his gaze still on the door.

"Dad, I know you're mad. And I understand what you're feeling—"

"No, Lucy, I don't think you do. You didn't just walk into your home to find that while you were gone, your daughter and her boyfriend took a bath."

"Dad! I didn't take a bath! It wasn't like that. He took a bath. I was fully clothed." I say, trying desperately to keep my voice calm. "I told you, nothing happened. He was hurt, he needed help. You always taught us we should—"

"Don't treat me like an idiot," he interrupts, his face drawn and his eyes flashing. "Especially since you told me you guys had broken up. Was that a lie too? Were you saying that so we'd let you do this program in Israel?"

The program. Dov doesn't know about the program.

I recoil. "No, no, no," I gasp, my words becoming more emphatic as they trip out. "This is the first time I've seen him since we broke up. And he doesn't even know about my plans . . ."

"Why should I believe you?" He grips my doorknob tightly. He seems to be forcing himself to look at me, while desperately wishing to be as far away from this conversation as I do.

How did we come to this point?

I stare at my hands clasped in front of me and tighten them.

"I trusted you, Lucy. I trusted you when I allowed you to spend time at Dov's place, when I allowed you to invite him here. Is this how you repay that trust?"

"No!" I take a deep breath, hoping and praying Dov can't hear all this. "But let's face it. You didn't give me all this freedom because you trusted me. You gave it to me because you had to, because Mom's been gone, and you needed someone to look after Sam and Gabe. You needed to focus on making sure they were okay, so it was convenient for you to give me freedom."

I try to take a few more deep breaths, willing the anger to dissipate. I glance up at Dad. His expression has moved from fury to shock, to something much worse. Something that looks tired and old, defeated almost.

A choked sigh escapes from him, and he lets go of the doorknob, slowly moving toward me. "Lucy," he whispers, his voice so sad I wish none of it had happened, that I hadn't said a word. I want to go back and fix it, change it, erase it all. He reaches out to touch my shoulder and then in a second, he's wrapped himself around me. "I'm so sorry, Lucy, I'm so sorry."

"It's fine, Dad." As the words come out, I realize I mean them, truly. "You gave me your trust because you knew I was responsible. If you didn't think I could handle it, you wouldn't have done it. You would have figured out something else. I don't feel like you abandoned me. I knew if I ever needed anything, if there was anything I couldn't handle, you'd be there in a second. But you have to trust me now. When I say nothing happened, I mean it."

His grip is so tight it's hard for me to breathe, but there is no place else I'd rather be. I think of Dov lying in my bed, how alone he is all the time. I rub my cheek against Dad's wool sweater, breathing in the musty scent.

After a moment I pull away, and he lets me, though he keeps his hands on my elbows as though he doesn't want to let go. I choose my words carefully. Nothing feels more important than this, and I can't mess it up.

"Dad, can Dov please stay here for a bit?" He opens his mouth and I barrel ahead. "His parents aren't home, and I don't think it's a good idea for him to be alone right now."

Dad lets go of my elbows. I hold my breath, praying. *Please*, I beg silently. *Please don't make him go back to an empty house.*

"He can stay for a couple of days, until he's feeling better." Relief floods my body but he swings back to look at me fiercely. "But he's staying in the guest room, and you're sleeping in your room. All night. Do I have your word?"

I nod and keep my face serious. *Anything,* I want to promise, *I'll do anything.*

Dov stays with us through the weekend. He offers to leave on Saturday morning, but Dad really steps up to the plate. I catch him watching us, the look of sadness still appearing when he thinks I don't notice, but he insists Dov stay until his parents come home. I know he won't say a word about next year; I don't even need to ask.

Sam and Gabe skirt around Dov at first. But when Gabe catches Dov eying the piano, he begs him to play. I'm about to protest, but the look on Dov's face is enough to keep me quiet. Dov needs Gabe as much as Gabe needs Dov right now.

I take Sam on my lap, and we sit quietly on the couch watching them. At first, Dov and Gabe fiddle with the keys. Dov must have shown Gabe a trick or something because Gabe keeps playing the same series of notes over and over, as Dov smiles widely. "See, you can do it," he whispers, and even I can hear that he hit all the right keys.

And then Dov plays. He plays some of Sam's favorite songs from *Joseph and the Technicolor Dreamcoat* and more popular songs for Gabe, songs I had no idea he knew. And then he turns to oldies, hitting the Beatles and Simon & Garfunkel and even Dad comes to sit with us in the living room. And then old Israeli songs that none of us know, but it doesn't matter. Nobody leaves, not even Sam. And there's something extraordinary about the moment, the music and the singing, the kids happy and Dov so whole it breaks my heart. I weep quietly, Sam's head my shield from being seen. Or so I think until Dad hands me a tissue.

The only problem is, we don't talk. Not really. Apart from my Saturday morning dance class, we spend every minute together, but there's always someone else there, someone keeping the conversation from going anywhere. Dad even stays up late on Saturday night to watch a movie with us. At first he'd said he would be working late, but when Dov suggests an old James Bond movie, he agrees to stay. It isn't clear to me who's insisting on the chaperon, Dov or Dad. But either way, when the movie is done, Dad and I walk upstairs together and Dov stays downstairs in the guest room.

I don't tell Dov about next year.

Everything that's happening is so firmly in the present, in the now, I don't want to do anything to lose it. To lose him.

I want this, whatever it is, to last as long as it can.

But finally on Sunday morning, it's unavoidable. The boys have to go to Hebrew school, and I don't offer to take them, even when Dad looks at me pointedly.

I need to be brave.

"I should get some groceries anyway," he mutters, staring back and forth between the two of us.

"We'll behave," I say sweetly. Dov looks pale, but he nods as well. We listen to the kids get into the car, arguing about having to go to Hebrew school.

We don't move until we hear the car back out of the driveway, see it pass the front window. Only then do I shift my position so I can look directly at him.

I have to tell him.

"Hi," I say quietly. Despite how warm the house is, I grab the blanket beside me and cover myself up with it.

"Don't hide," he whispers.

I press my lips together for a moment. "I'm scared," I say. "I think we need to talk, but I'm afraid if I tell you a few things, that you'll leave again."

Tears start to fill my eyes, and I blink them back.

"I'm not going anywhere." His words are easy but forceful.

But you are.

"What happened with your parents," I struggle, "and the form they had to sign?"

Dov's eyes stay on me. "They signed it." He speaks the words clearly. "Even though they won't be in Israel next year."

I nod, the tears making it hard to see clearly.

"I need to tell you that I hate that you're going to be in a combat unit. I know you'll go, that you feel like you have to. But I can't lie and say I'm okay with it."

He swallows. "Actually, I've spent a lot of time talking with my parents over the last few weeks, and we came to a compromise. I'll still be in active duty, but it won't be in a combat unit. Luckily, with my dad's connections and the testing I did during winter break, they were able to get me into an intelligence unit."

Intelligence. Intelligence means that he might just stay on a base. Or at least he won't be running into danger.

He pulls me onto his lap, and I lean into him, relief filling me. No matter what happens, he'll be safe. I let my head drop onto his shoulder. I miss his shoulder. I miss the smell of the side of his neck, that soft, soft spot. I don't want to talk anymore. I just want to kiss that spot.

"I'm sorry," I say, my tears dripping onto his T-shirt. "I don't know what's going on."

"Talk to me, *nishamah*." He pulls me back so we can see one another, and I want to lose myself in the look he's giving me. *Don't let this end*, I beg.

I slide off his lap, breaking away from him. I feel like a coward. "I need to go. My dad will be home soon, and I should clean the kitchen . . ."

If I walk away now, we won't need to talk about it. He won't be able to say the words that I'm dreading. That my coming to Israel for a year changes nothing. That we only have the next few weeks, if that. That some problems can't be solved. Because our lives, the rest of our lives, are clearly in different countries.

"Don't leave," he begs, pulling me closer.

"Please," I say, more harshly than I wanted. "I'm not ready for this."

"*Nishamah*, I'm not letting you walk away. Talk to me."

Why haven't you kissed me all this time? I want to ask, but I don't want the answer.

Maybe that's his plan: we can be close but not get involved again, hold each other without really touching.

If I push him, what will happen? Will he push me away again?

If I tell him about next year, will he think I'm trying to follow him?

I allow myself to lean back against him, pretending to have all the bravery I don't. "I know we can't make it through your army service, but I can't bear to think about not being with you," I whisper. "I'm scared to lose you again." I can't be any more direct than that. I can't use any other words. These words already feel like they've taken chunks out of my throat as they come out.

"I'm scared too," he says, taking my arm. "But I don't know for sure that this will end. Maybe it won't."

The conversation is so heavy I can't get enough air into my lungs. I need to get the words out. I'm only eighteen, I want to yell at someone. I shouldn't be dealing with this. Neither of us should. We should be planning for prom or worrying about our last summer before college. I feel the urge to be like Sam, to whine that the whole thing isn't fair.

Me being in Israel for a year will change nothing.

Even if things are good between us, he said that being in the army is all-consuming.

"Of course it ends," I say bitterly. "Everything ends. This is real life. This isn't some fantasy we created. In real life, things like this end."

"Why?"

I stare at him in disbelief. "Why? Because you're going to the army, and even if we make it through that, Israel is your home. And this is my home." My stomach pitches and rolls, and I wonder if all this sadness can make me throw up. I move to shake off his hold.

Dov tightens his grip on my arm. "No, that's a cop-out. Don't turn your back on me because it's hard."

What the—

"It's not hard, Dov," I yell. "It's impossible. You said it yourself."

"I was angry."

"But you were also being realistic. What fantasy world can we create where this won't end? I know what this feels like. I've lived through it for more than three weeks. My best-case scenario is we can stay together while I'm in Israel next year but then what? You'll have two more years and what will I do?" I bury my face in my knees, unable to watch it all fall apart.

"*Nishamah*, I love you. I've loved you ever since that first day of school, when you were so unbearably kind to me, you . . . wait, what did you say?"

I lift my eyes when he stops talking, knowing my words finally registered. For a moment I can't look at his eyes, I'm too scared to see whether they're showing happiness or frustration. I focus on his mouth, watching him flatten his lips and roll them back and forth.

"What did you say?"

He sounds . . . hopeful?

"I'm not going to college next year. I signed up for a gap year program." I say, my voice barely over a whisper. "It's in Nahariya."

He nods slowly as though he's having a difficult time understanding the words. "You're going to be in Nahariya next year? For the whole year?"

I smile meekly, hoping the shock is a good shock. "It's a dance program. I'll be working with underprivileged teens."

"When did you decide?"

I can't tell what he's thinking. I can't tell, and it's killing me.

"A few weeks ago. It's a program run by a woman Ginger knew from that Israeli dance festival she went to. It'll let me both volunteer and dance, which seemed like the best of all options. And after all your talk about Israel, the landscape and the food, I couldn't resist. It didn't matter to me if I'd be with you or not." I try to make my voice light, but I can hear the cracks. "I didn't do it for you. We had already broken up. I did it because my great-grandparents dreamed of going to Israel and they never made it there. I want to fulfill that dream. And I don't care what you think because it's already decided. I'm not—"

"*Nishamah*. You'll be in Israel? Next year? With me? I don't care why you did it; I'm so excited. It gives us another year to figure out how to make it work." He smiles, a smile so warm and loving it can't really live in the same category as other smiles.

Suddenly I can't hold it in anymore. The tears come rushing out, and Dov holds me tighter as I sob. It's only when I start to hiccup that he pulls me back so I'm facing him. His eyes are also filled with tears.

"I'm not giving up on us," he says. "I tried, and I never want to feel like that again. I know it's hard, and I know it'll be crazy hard even with you in Israel. I know everyone will tell us we are being ridiculous, and I know I should let you go because being committed to someone who will be in the army for three years is hardly fair. But I'm selfish, Lucy. You're right. I'm selfish. And I don't want to let you go. And the only thing that makes that okay in my mind is that I love you. And I need to believe that makes it okay."

I kiss him, not caring anymore. What starts gentle turns more insistent, more intense, as Dov's hands snake under my shirt, warm against my back as he pulls me closer, my fingers fisting his curls. We kiss as though it could seal us together, as though it could connect us forever. When our faces finally part, my lips are sore, but I reach forward and kiss him again quickly. "I don't know how we'll make all this work," I whisper, and his smile fills my entire view.

"We'll do it one day at a time," he laughs. "Because I know I can't live without you, so we have to figure it out. I'll have some weekends off, and days every so often. And my base isn't far from Nahariya. And maybe it's a good thing I'll be a *chayal boded* because it means the government has to give me a month off every year to visit my family. We'll come here and spend every minute together. And when I'm done, I won't go to the Far East. I'll come here, or wherever you are. I'll do whatever it takes. I just don't want to lose you . . ."

We sit like that for a while, weaving dreams tightly around us. Dreams where I will be the one cooking up a storm for him when he comes home on leave, where I can replace the family that will be absent.

TWENTY-FIVE

. . . .

My ticket for Israel is booked for June 29th. I'll begin in Jerusalem with three weeks of learning Hebrew in *ulpan* and living in Dov's old house as he finishes things up here. Then he'll join me in Jerusalem for three more weeks of intense Hebrew for me. After that, I'll have a couple of weeks to tour around before I need to start in Nahariya. Hopefully Dov will be able to take me around, but we still aren't positive when he'll need to report for his army induction.

The last month of school speeds by in a flurry of graduation-related parties and events. I'm careful not to devote all of my time to being with Dov. Maddie and I plan our schedules like army generals, sneaking off together. We take long drives just the two of us, skipping many of the "senior half days" the school gives us to drive up to Michigan or down to Indiana. The destination is the bonus; the real appeal is the drive. One Sunday morning we try to drive to the Iowa border, just so we can get a picture with the sign that reads: "The people of Iowa welcome you."

But we get detoured by an ice cream parlor in western Illinois and a discussion about whether Dov and I will finally have sex in Israel. By the time we talk it through, it's too late to get to the border and back home.

But most of all, I want to make sure I have time alone with each of my brothers, time when I'm just focused on them. I take each of them to a Cubs game, spoiling them with soda and special treats. I make sure I'm available to take them to their Little League games, cheering them on loudly, even when they strike out. I often find Dov there already, and he grins sheepishly. He isn't there for me.

At first Sam and Gabe were angry when I told them I was leaving. I tried to explain that I would have been leaving either way, but Gabe glared at me until I apologized. I was taking away our summer together, and I was going much farther than any of the colleges I'd applied to would have taken me.

They listened when I told them stories about where I was going and showed them Dov's pictures that he'd sent me over winter break. Mom and Dad had promised that they'd all come visit over winter break, and for a while I thought that the thrill of an overseas trip would overshadow my desertion. Until one night I overheard Sam ask Gabe if one day he'd also leave, just like me and Mom.

And I cried.

I'm not like Mom, I remind myself when a dull ache blooms behind my eyes. But maybe I'm not that different either.

I glance around my room one last time. For all the crazy packing, the bags waiting downstairs, my room is virtually unchanged. I stare at the books piled beside my bed, the bare walls that remind me of the poems that kept me company all winter. In a year, when I come home, who will I be? Will all of this seem foreign, like someone else's life? I'd been so insistent on opening myself up to new experiences, new possibilities, the opportunity to discover what is important to me, yet what will happen when I come back? Will I slide back into everything with ease or will this year be the year that everything changes?

I have an hour to go before breakfast, so I do something I've been thinking of doing for weeks. I grab all the poems, all the crumpled pieces of paper, and I cut and paste them into the blank journal. They might not all represent me anymore, but I want to be able to look back at them. I want to be as open to my past as I am to my future.

It takes me almost an hour and a roll of tape, but I cram all the poems into the journal. I don't put them in any order. I don't even put the poems that Dov and I shared in order. The order isn't important. Their presence is. They are a part of me.

Once downstairs, I pause before entering the kitchen. For Gabe and Sam, I need to keep it together. I swing the door open and find Dad at the counter, making pancakes, Mom at the computer and the boys at the kitchen table, drawing robots.

"I'm making this one for you, Lucy," Gabe calls, barely looking up from his drawing. I ruffle his thin brown hair and watch him shake it off, his marker never drifting from the page.

Sam is writing what appears to be a letter, his tongue moving back and forth as he carefully draws out the letters, some overlapping, capitals interspersed with lowercase ones. By next year his letters will be more consistent.

Someone will have told him that stronger sounds don't mean that the letter is bigger. I swallow hard. I don't want to miss that. My eyes fill with tears, and I blink them away. I take a deep breath, preparing to walk out if I need to.

I glance anxiously at Dad preparing the pancakes. Dov is going to be here soon, and then there'll only be a couple of hours before I need to leave for the airport. As much as I want to eat leisurely with my family, I need to deal with leaving Dov as well, need to leave time for that goodbye, even though I'll see him again in a few weeks.

"Go make sure that nothing is missing on the table, hon," Mom calls without looking at me. "We're going to eat in the dining room."

I push the door out and see the table set for six, orange juice and croissants already on the table. And just past the dining room table, sitting calmly on the couch, is Dov.

My heart quickens, and I skip over to him. "I wasn't expecting you for a while," I sit down beside him and lean in to kiss him. Instead of moving my head back though, I stay there for a moment longer, my lips on his, my eyes closed, trying to be present, to remember this moment.

"I can only stay for a minute *nishamah*," he says once I've pulled away.

My heart sinks. "But I thought . . . with the six places set that maybe you were staying for breakfast."

He smiles and shakes his head. "No, I think that place is for Maddie. I have to go home and spend some time with my parents."

I press my lips together, trying to push away the disappointment. I'm glad he wants to spend time with them, but couldn't he see them later, once I'm gone? Once again I feel tears come to my eyes and I brush them away, annoyed with myself.

Stop being so overemotional. It's only three weeks.

"I'm coming with you *nishamah*. That's why I have to go home." Dov's words are so quiet that I think I've misheard him.

"But how—"

"I can't let you go to Israel without me. So I changed my flight. Or rather, my parents changed my flight for me. I only just convinced everyone, so I spent most of last night packing up my stuff."

"On my flight?" I ask, feeling foolish but just wanting to make sure.

"On your flight, *motek*," he smiles. "Right beside you. All through the flight, both flights actually, and on the stopover in London. I'm not going anywhere. I'll be right beside you. And I'll be there when you see Israel for the first time. And then when we land, we'll be together in Jerusalem until I need to go to my call-up. You'll need someone to show you around, help you discover the city's hidden treasures. How else will you find the anglo bookshop and the best place to hear music late at night?"

"You'll show me around?" I tease.

"I'll show you everything," he promises.

"Your parents aren't mad?"

Dov shrugs. "You're the one who stood up to your parents to be able to come to Israel this year. I just changed my plane ticket. They'll live."

I lean over and hug him tightly. "You're sure?" I whisper.

"You can't get rid of me that easily," he whispers back.

"Never," I say, pushing the curls from his face.

And then we stop talking. And I stop worrying about my parents and the boys and everything that will happen when we get on the plane because I know I'm heading in the right direction.

TWENTY-SIX

· · · · · · · · · · · · ·

We sit in silence in the middle of the large white bed as the Jerusalem sun sets. The scissors in my hand are heavy, uncomfortable, and every time I use them, I clench my teeth. Dov's curls are scattered around us. They slide down his bare chest, finding their way into my tight black camisole. I know wisps of hair will cling to me for days and that even after I wash this top, I'll still find them caught in the elastic, tucked into the strap. I'm counting on that.

For a moment I think of the lyrics to a Regina Spektor song I've always loved, about a woman cutting her lover's hair in the middle of a bed and I want to look it up and see if it explains all this, if it will help me understand what I'm feeling. But I know it won't. Nothing will explain this.

It's the end of the summer, a year to the day since I first met Dov at school. To celebrate, I cooked him eggs with Za'atar this morning, here in our little cocoon. While my parents weren't pleased that we were staying in Dov's house in Jerusalem together all summer, they were appeased by his parents' presence in the house, our separate bedrooms, and the possibility of supervision. But Gal and Shimon left a few weeks ago as my intensive Hebrew language courses finished. And so for the past month we've been playing house here in Baka, a neighborhood of Jerusalem. Each night we sleep entwined, the sound of Dov's heartbeat against my ear the perfect music.

That is, when we aren't touring the country in Dov's decrepit car, compressing years of experiences and favorite spots into a frenzied crisscrossing of a tiny country. I've met his old friends, had dinners with his family. We even had coffee with Liat in a cafe on the Tel Aviv boardwalk, the brilliant blue of the Mediterranean distracting me. He drove me to the northern tip of the country where I'll be dancing for the year, the wooded hills and valleys a sharp contrast to the southern desert. I held his hand as we visited Yuval's grave in the crowded cemetery on Mount Herzl, with white stones and blue and white flags as far as the eye could see. He'd brought rocks with him from Lake Michigan and we placed them on the grave. On the way back to Dov's house, I drove. Dov clenched Yuval's dog tags in his right fist, like he had almost a year ago when we sat in the Shakespeare garden on campus. But this time his left hand rested on my thigh, and I'd like to think that made a difference.

Tomorrow, I will drive Dov to the bus that will take him to basic training. By then, I will have cut off all his curls. He will be wearing the army uniform he's already picked up, the one I won't let him put on until he absolutely needs to. All of his stuff will be packed in an oversized duffel. We'll get there early, have a few minutes in the car alone before he has to unfold his body, sling the bag over his shoulder, and walk to the bus. I've played the scenario out dozens of times in my mind to prepare for it. I've imagined the sight of his retreating back, imagined him disappearing from view.

Before the bus starts up to leave, I will drive away. We've talked about this. Just as he can't bear standing with me outside the bus, saying goodbye over and over, I can't watch the bus drive him away from me. I will turn the car around and leave the parking lot, drive past his empty house without stopping, and begin the three-hour trek to a kibbutz outside Nahariya where I'll be living. Where I'll spend the weeks before he gets a day off, and all the rest of the time we're apart.

I've now cut all the curls I can reach from where I sit in front of him, so I climb onto his lap to reach the ones at the back. Dov's hands pull me closer until I am too close to wield the scissors anymore.

"I found a poem for you," he says quietly. "I even memorized it."

"English or Hebrew?" I've been practicing my Hebrew by reading poetry and children's books, but still I half hope it's in English. My heart is too heavy to translate words.

"English. I thought you needed some American poetry to keep you company. And then, if you want, you can send me a response poem."

I laugh and squeeze him closer, tears filling my eyes. "Tell me."

"It's by William Carlos Williams," he says, his voice the only sound I can hear. "It's called: 'This Is Just to Say.'"

And then he recites it to me, his words fluid like it wasn't a different language at all. A silly poem about eating all the plums in the fridge, but it's so much more than that. It's a poem about home and love, comfort and affection. At least to me. And the last stanza brings up every image of Dov and I walking through the shuk, eating ripe fruit, kissing the juice trailing down each other's chins.

"Why don't we take a break, *nishamah*?" he whispers, his breath warm against my neck.

"Your haircut is uneven," I tease, my voice thick as I finger the long curls in the back that have escaped the scissors, and I try not to cry.

"Don't care," he mutters between kisses that trail down my neck.

And even though it will likely mean my love will get on the bus with a mullet, I toss the scissors on the floor and stop thinking about the fruit we ate yesterday and what tomorrow will bring.

I focus on today.

ACKNOWLEDGMENTS

Acknowledgments are always hard to write, but because this was my first book, it's especially challenging. So many people supported me through this process, and I couldn't have done it without them. So apologies if this is long, but I'm overwhelmed with gratitude.

First, none of this would be possible without Rena Bunder Rossner, agent extraordinaire. Thank you for falling in love with this book, for believing in it through turbulent times, and for your unwavering support. I'm grateful beyond measure for your hard work in bringing this book to the world and not letting me give up.

The people at Amberjack have been wonderful partners in this endeavor. Dayna Anderson, Kayla Church, and Jenny Miller have been lovely to work with on the editorial side. And, of course, an enormous thank you to the fabulous Cassandra Farrin, who really brought her talents to make this story into the book it is.

I don't know what I would have done without my critique partners Amy Pine, Megan Erickson and Lia Riley. We bonded over our first books, and your love for this story helped me keep the faith. Our daily conversations go so far beyond our writing, and your friendships are invaluable to me.

Rachel Simon might be the best cheerleader out there for Dov and Lucy. Thank you for reading version after version and having such fantastic comments each time. Marieke Nijkamp, Rachel Lynn Solomon, Katie Bailey, Jen Meils, KK Hendin, Rachel Mesch, Jennifer Zwiebel, Jessica Hirsch, Dahlia Adler, and Olivia Hinebaugh also gave invaluable feedback.

Nina Black had the herculean job of being the first one to read this story (back when it was still about *Chess*). I literally sat beside her, handing her one chapter at a time. Without her praise and gentle constructive comments (like dumping the *Chess* element), this story would have likely just stayed on my computer forever.

Daphne Price, Devorah Katz, and Zehava Cohn have kept me going in this process every day. Whether Devorah was helping with the Israel aspect or the Hebrew (though mistakes are all mine); to Z's massive edits and suggestions; and Daph's cheers and prizes for when I reached writing goals, I couldn't ask for better faraway friends. See, the friends you make at sixteen stay with you . . .

Every writer should also have friends who ask gently how your writing is going, listen to you when you vent or spout nonsense or growl, and still love you. I am blessed with many of those friends. Rachel Sollinger, Deborah Hamilton, Jill Kushnir LeVee, Tamar Shapira, Anat Geva, Chava Alpert, and Inbar Kirson are the ones I count on in my day-to-day life, even if we aren't driving carpool anymore. And Rebecca Ben-Gideon, Kara Rosenwald, JAR, and the rest of the Camp Ramah crew have become an extension of my family. Which is where I also put the iCenter crew, who could never be considered "work friends." They are so much more, and much of this book is influenced by our conversations.

And finally, my family. I owe so much to my mom (who bears no resemblance at all to the mother in this story), Happy and Lou, Ginette, all my sisters- and brothers-in-law, nieces and nephews. And I'm grateful for my dad, who bought me trucks full of books and always encouraged me to dream big. I love you and miss you terribly.

Jonah, Micah, and Toby—thank you for dealing with having a mother who writes (and growls about writing) and all the craziness that goes with it. And of course, an enormous thank you to Josh, who has always been more encouraging than I probably deserved. As the florist wrote on the card you sent: "Thank you for marring me." Love you, hp.

ABOUT THE AUTHOR

Natalie Blitt is the author of young-adult and middle grade novels. She lives in the Chicago area with her husband and three sons, but spends a lot of time daydreaming about going back to Canada where she grew up. You can visit her online at www.natalieblitt.com.